Please to remember the fifth of November:
Gunpowder, treason and plot.
For I see no reason why gunpowder treason
Should ever be forgot.

Gunpowder Plot

Plot

A Daisy Dalrymple Mystery

C A R O L A   D U N N

ROBINSON

Constable & Robinson Ltd
3 The Lanchesters
162 Fulham Palace Road
London W6 9ER
www.constablerobinson.com

First published in the US by St Martin's Press, 2006

First published in the UK by Robinson,
an imprint of Constable & Robinson Ltd, 2011

A copy of the British Library Cataloguing in
Publication Data is available from the British Library

ISBN: 978-1-84901-710-7

Typeset by TW Typesetting, Plymouth, Devon

Printed and bound in the UK

1 3 5 7 9 10 8 6 4 2

ACKNOWLEDGEMENTS

My thanks to Belinda Dettman, Elizabeth Rolls and Anne Gracie, Strine experts; Paul Mulcahey, firearms expert; Jane Rosen of the Imperial War Museum; Stuart Hadaway of the Royal Air Force Museum; Howard Poskitt, vintage car expert; Dr Trevor Jordan of the Queensland University of Technology; Jacqueline Cox of the Cambridge University Archives; Rosemary Horton of Trinity College, Perth; Stuart Ivinson of the Royal Armouries Museum; and, as always, Nancy Mayer, for her help with English legal history.

CHAPTER 1

'I'm going to learn to drive,' Daisy decided as the Triumph two-seater slowed on entering the village of Didmarsh-under-Edge.

'I quite enjoy it,' said Gwen. 'Except for cranking the engine when it's cold.'

Though the November air was chilly, the sun shone on pale gold Cotswold stone, and michaelmas daisies still bloomed in cottage gardens. Here and there, the last bronze and yellow leaves clung to the twigs of tall beeches and elms. 'It would be spiffing to be able to hop in the car on a beautiful day like this and buzz out of London into the country for a few hours. I could go and visit Belinda, my stepdaughter, at school. Imagine not having to worry about train timetables and being picked up at the station and all that rot.'

'I don't mind picking you up at the station,' Gwen assured her, her thin face earnest. Turning into a narrow, steeply rising lane between the churchyard and the Didmarsh Post Office and General Store, she raised her voice to be heard over the roar of the motor. 'Would your husband let you drive?'

'Alec? Good gracious, he doesn't tell me what to do! Just because he's a policeman, it doesn't mean he tries to lay down the law. At least . . .'

Daisy paused. She had been going to make an exception for the times when she found herself involved in one of Alec's cases, when he most definitely, if unsuccessfully, did attempt to control her actions. But those times were best not talked of, though Gwen had probably heard rumours through the Old Girls' network.

'I wouldn't have married him if he'd shown signs of wanting to dictate what I can or can't do,' she amended. 'This is 1924, after all, not the Victorian Dark Ages. By the way, I hope you haven't told all your family that Alec's a policeman. Lots of people get a funny look in their eyes when they find out I'm a policeman's wife.'

'No, you asked me not to and I haven't. But I wasn't thinking so much about that; more about . . .' Gwen took her eyes from the road to cast a quick glance at Daisy's bulging midsection.

'The baby?' Daisy patted the bulge, which her coat so nicely concealed when she was standing but seemed to emphasize when she was seated. 'I suppose I'd better not take driving lessons until after it's born. Soon I won't be able to fit behind a steering wheel. Another three months! I never dreamt nine months could seem so long. But that has nothing to do with Alec.'

'Daisy!'

Daisy laughed. 'Sorry, I mean my being pregnant doesn't have anything to do with Alec being, or not being, dictatorial. If you see what I mean.'

'I do. I'm just so used to my father always getting his way

– not just with Mother, with all of us – that I can't quite fathom how a modern marriage works. Here we are.'

The lane continued slanting upward across the steep slope, the Cotswold escarpment, between hedges wreathed with old-man's beard and berried briony. Soon the hedges gave way to drystone walls. After a quarter mile or so, always climbing, Daisy saw on their left stone gateposts bracketing a gap in the wall. Gwen neatly negotiated the sharp turn into the drive between open wrought iron gates. In curlicued script picked out in gold, the left-hand gate bore the legend 𝔈𝔡𝔤𝔢, the right-hand 𝔐𝔞𝔫𝔬𝔯. The small gatehouse looked deserted.

'No gatekeeper since the war,' Gwen observed. 'Biddle, our gardener, lives there now. He's not there during the day, of course, and Mrs Biddle "obliges" in the house, so we leave the gates open for convenience.'

'Hardly anyone has gatekeepers these days.'

A row of yews sheltered the cottage to the north. As the Triumph drew level with the bushy ever-greens, a series of ear-shattering explosions rang out. Daisy's heart skipped a beat before she realized the car was backfiring.

Or was it? Gwen stamped on the brake, staring back at the trees. Following her gaze, Daisy saw movement amid the dark green foliage, and then her ears rang with a second set of bangs and pops. This time, guessing the cause, she spotted flashes on the road behind the car.

'Squibs.'

'Those little devils!' Gwen jumped out of the car and tore in among the trees.

She emerged triumphant a few moments later, each hand grasping the collar of a small, wiry and decidedly grubby boy.

She marched them over to the car. 'Apologize to Mrs Fletcher at once,' she snapped, 'or I'll tell your grandfather and he'll give you a proper whopping.'

'Mummy won't let him,' the younger whined. He was eight or nine, the elder perhaps ten.

'Your mother won't hear about it till it's over. Addie's brats,' she said to Daisy. 'I expect you remember my sister Adelaide from school?'

'Vaguely. She's a couple of years older, isn't she?'

'Yes, she'll be thirty in January.' She shook the boys. 'Hurry up and apologize, or it'll be too late.'

'Sorry,' the elder muttered sullenly, echoed by his brother.

Gwen gave them another shake. 'You can do better than that.'

'We're very sorry, Mrs Fletcher, but it was only squibs. They're not dangerous or anything.'

'They jolly well are when you throw them at a car,' their aunt pointed out. 'I could have been startled enough to run it off the road. Get into the dickey, both of you, and be careful of Mrs Fletcher's luggage. Adrian will have to sit on your lap, Reggie.'

'We don't want to go to the house,' Reggie said mutinously.

Adrian panicked. 'We said sorry, Aunt Gwen. You can't tell Grandfather now!'

'I ought to. But I won't if you both empty your pockets and give me every squib you possess.'

'But we bought them with our own money!' Reggie protested. 'What if we promise not to throw them at cars?'

'Every one,' Gwen said, uncompromising.

Well acquainted with the contents of her eldest nephew's pockets, Daisy was not surprised at the odds and ends laid out on the running board. Besides a dozen squibs, and a roll of caps, which Gwen also confiscated, the collection included three fluffy toffees, a matchbox containing two dead beetles, quantities of string, a stub of pencil, several small, smoothly rounded stones and a catapult. Gwen hesitated over this last.

'Didn't Aunt Babs take this away from you?'

'She just gave it back. We promised not to shoot at the farm animals or the greenhouses or anything. She kept it for a *whole week*, and it's a 'specially good one!'

'Oh, all right. Take your stuff and get in.'

'Why?'

'Because I say so. Because you're going to tell your mother exactly what you did. Not that she'll do anything about it,' Gwen muttered, resuming her place behind the steering wheel, her comment supported by the boys' insouciance as they climbed into the dickey. 'I have a feeling I'm going to regret giving in over that catapult.'

'But they're easy to make,' Daisy pointed out. 'They could easily replace it.'

'Too true.'

'Boys will be boys,' Daisy murmured, though she had always hated the second part of her nanny's favourite saying: 'but girls must be young ladies.'

The drive led back across the hillside, for the most part on the level. As they passed some farm buildings on the lower slope, Gwen waved to a woman in trousers talking to a man perched high on the back of a massive cart horse.

'My sister Barbara. She's the eldest of us.'

'Aunt Gwen?' came Adrian's quavery voice from behind. 'You won't tell Aunt Babs, will you? About the squibs?'

'Why shouldn't I?'

'Because she said if we do anything else bad this week, she'll duck us in the horse trough and she doesn't care if we catch our death of cold.'

'It would jolly well serve you right.'

'It would be murder,' Reggie said self-righteously.

'Well, we don't want murder in the family, so I won't tell her, as long as you behave yourselves till bedtime. Sorry, Daisy, when I invited you, I'd forgotten it was the boys' half-term holiday. And there are other ructions in the family at present, I'm afraid.'

'Never mind, I'll just ignore all that and concentrate on my article. It's jolly decent of your people to let me come. My American editor is really keen. They don't know about the Gunpowder Plot over there, so he thinks it's frightfully exotic. It came just before the *Mayflower* and the Pilgrims and all that, which is when their history begins.'

Gwen laughed. 'If I recall correctly, we started at school with Caesar's invasion of Britain in something B.C.'

'But after that, there wasn't much besides Alfred and the cakes until 1066. I hope you'll be able to tell me the history of your Guy Fawkes celebration. It'd be nice to have some background as well as a description of tomorrow's fête.'

'Father will be only too glad to expound.'

'Good.' Daisy's insatiable curiosity got the better of her. 'And if you want to let off steam about the ructions, I'll lend a sympathetic ear . . . or not, as the case may be.'

'It might help to have an outside opinion,' Gwen said thoughtfully. 'Besides, after all, your father was a viscount and Father's only a baronet.'

'I shouldn't dream of interfering! On that basis or any other.'

'What's a viscount?' Adrian enquired.

Gwen and Daisy looked at each other in dismay. They had forgotten the little pitchers with big ears in the dickey.

'A lord, you dunce,' said Reggie, his manner insufferably superior.

'I'm not a dunce!' Adrian was at a disadvantage, seated as he was on his brother's knees, but he made a spirited attempt to bring his fists to bear.

'Horse trough!' Gwen warned.

The rest of the journey was accomplished in peace.

Daisy had visited Edge Manor several times during her school days. She and Gwen had never been particularly intimate friends, but her own childhood home, Fairacres, was less than twenty miles away across country. She knew Gwen's family had owned the land hereabouts since the Wars of the Roses. The Tyndalls had accommodated themselves over the centuries to the whims of history, having managed to remain inconspicuous but always on the right side at the decisive moment, like the Vicar of Bray.

Edge Manor, built and periodically rebuilt with local limestone, had likewise accommodated itself over the centuries to the whims of its owners and the exigencies of its situation halfway up a steep hillside. The south front, before which the Triumph drew up, was taller and narrower than most small country houses. To the right of the cobbled forecourt stretched a row of garages, once carriage houses, more usually tucked away somewhere out of view of residents and visitors.

Beyond the façade, the building stretched northward with,

as Daisy recalled, a great many inconvenient flights of two or three or half a dozen steps here and there to adjust to the terrain. But to compensate, the long west side provided a spectacular view of the terraced gardens and the village and across the Vale of Evesham, where most of the Tyndall acres lay.

'Leave your camera and typewriter in the car, Daisy,' said Gwen. 'Someone will fetch them. You boys can carry the rest in.'

She ushered Daisy into the house, followed by her subdued nephews struggling with the luggage. The wide entrance hall, two storeys high, was floored with polished oak. Apart from a couple of antique chests, it was furnished as a sitting room, with sofas and chairs grouped on a large rug around a blaze in the fireplace opposite the front door. The late-afternoon sun poured in through tall south and west windows, each graced with a vase of golden beech leaves, crimson-berried hawthorn and pink and orange spindle.

This inviting scene was marred by the two angry men in the middle of the room.

One was an imposing figure, whose voluminous plus fours and shooting jacket with baggy pockets made him appear even larger than his already-impressive size. Daisy recognized Sir Harold Tyndall. His girth had grown and his hairline had receded since last she saw him, but his reddish moustache bristled as fiercely as ever. A tall, bull-necked bear of a man, to mix a few metaphors, he was roaring like a lion: 'What the devil made you suppose the bounder would be welcome at Edge Manor?'

'Miller is not a bounder, sir!' The boyish young man confronting him, bursting with indignation, was an inch or two taller and equally large-boned. However, his frame had not yet filled out and he was loose-limbed, lanky, in his light blue blazer with a Cambridge college crest on the pocket and wide-legged Oxford bags. 'He's a—'

'Pshaw! He's aiding and abetting this nonsense of yours, and he's got his eye on your sister, or I'm a Dutchman.'

'Gwen?' The youth must be Jack Tyndall, Daisy realized. She saw that Gwen was very pink-cheeked, whether embarrassed by an unwarranted assertion or dismayed by its accuracy. Jack, obviously astonished, continued, 'I don't think—'

'That's the trouble, my boy, you don't think! Tyndalls have run this estate for centuries, passed directly from father to son, and my son is not going to break that trust for some footling, short-lived fad.'

'Aeronautics is not a—'

'Father, Jack,' Gwen interrupted, 'here's Mrs Fletcher.'

The combatants swung round. Sir Harold advanced to shake hands.

'Ah yes, Dalrymple's daughter. We're delighted to have you come and write about our festivities, Mrs Fletcher. The Tyndalls have held a Guy Fawkes fête nearly every year since 1606, even during the Commonwealth. Oddly enough, Bonfire Night was the only traditional festivity allowed by the Puritans, though it celebrates the foiling of a plot against the monarchy.'

'Cromwell should have been grateful to the plotters for their attempt to blow up James the First, which might have saved the Puritans the trouble of beheading Charles the First,' said Jack. 'How do you do, Mrs Fletcher.'

'You remember my brother, Daisy? He must have been twelve or thirteen when you last met.'

'A horrible, cheeky pest of a schoolboy.' Jack had a charming grin.

'Not half as pestilent as—'

Daisy nudged Gwen to remind her she had promised not to tell her father of his grandsons' misdeeds. The boys themselves had vanished.

Jack pulled an expressive grimace. 'What have they done now?' he asked.

But Sir Harold had not noticed the byplay, intent as he was on urging Daisy over to the windows so that he could point out the site of the fireworks display and the beginnings of the bonfire. 'You see, down there on the meadow below the terraces? My gardeners and tenants have been piling up brush for weeks.'

As her host maundered on, telling how the fireworks had begun as a demonstration of loyalty to the first Stuart king and continued as a much anticipated local event, Daisy grew increasingly desperate. The baby had decided to bash her in the bladder, over and over again, as if bouncing a ball off a wall. She might be a modern, emancipated, working woman, but explaining her situation to the baronet was more than she could face.

To her relief, Lady Tyndall came to the rescue. A faded, delicate, anxious-looking woman, she inserted herself between her husband and her guest and said almost pleadingly, 'Harold, I'm sure Mrs Fletcher will be interested in your stories later, but first she wants to wash off the grime of the journey and put her feet up for a while before tea.'

Though Sir Harold looked offended, he made no objection. 'I'll see you at teatime, Mrs Fletcher,' he said, and stamped off.

'The downstairs cloakroom is over there, as I expect you remember,' said Lady Tyndall, pointing. Daisy fled.

When she emerged, feeling much better, Gwen was waiting for her.

'Mother said she took one look at you and knew what you needed. I saw you were desperate, but I thought it was just my father. He often makes me feel that way. I didn't dare interrupt when he was on his hobbyhorse. Sorry I didn't realize what was wrong, but I've never been pregnant.'

'The little brute was kicking me like mad, in a sensitive spot. It's a very strange sensation. You've no idea.'

'I can't imagine! Come on up to your room. Your stuff's been taken up. I had Jack fetch the typewriter and camera because I knew you were concerned about them. You're all right on the stairs, aren't you?'

'Perfectly all right.'

'I must say you look positively fit as a fiddle. Addie used to fuss like anything when she was pregnant, and Mother cosseted her.'

At an easy pace, Gwen led the way up the superbly carved Jacobean oak staircase. Following, Daisy asked, 'Has Adelaide come back to live at Edge Manor? Her husband was killed in the war, wasn't he?'

'No and yes. She married a neighbour and lives with her mother-in-law just down the lane, between here and the village. Stephen was killed in 1915, when she was pregnant with Adrian.'

'Widowed at twenty, with two young sons!'

'I know it's hard, but Addie really manages to make the worst of things. She never stops moaning and groaning, and she spoils the children abominably when she's not complaining about their mischief. I'm afraid Mrs Yarborough encourages her to spend most of her time here in the bosom of her family.'

For all her brave words, Daisy was tired from the train journey and glad to reach the top of the stairs. 'At least the boys are old enough to go away to prep school, aren't they?' she asked as they crossed the landing, a gallery open to the hall below.

'Yes, but she won't send them. They go to a day school in Evesham, where the discipline appears to be nonexistent. And she intends them to go on to Prince Harold's Grammar in Evesham, so there's no relief in sight. She claims she can't afford a Public School.'

'Wouldn't Sir Harold . . . ?'

'He might, if he could be persuaded that it's his own idea. The trouble is, Reggie and Adrian are scared to death of him, so they behave themselves when he's around. One really can't go talebearing, and they're beginning to realize it, so threats don't work very well any longer. I'm not sure he'd really cane them anyway. He was so proud of Addie when she produced two boys so quickly, he's inclined to think they can do no wrong.'

'Pity!'

They had turned up another three steps into a passage and passed several doors. Now Gwen announced, 'Here's your room. Mind the steps down. Two of them.'

The warning came just in time as Gwen opened the door on a dazzling flood of golden evening light.

Descending the steps with care, Daisy had an impression of comfortable blue furnishings, but her attention was on the view across the Vale to the Malvern Hills, so near her own childhood home. 'Oh, lovely! I do envy you your view. There are advantages to living in St John's Wood, so close to central London, but views aren't one of them.'

'Mother told me to give you the best spare room, not stuck away up on the second floor with the rest of us like when you were a mere school friend. It doesn't run to its own bathroom, though, I'm afraid. You'll share with the parents, but there's plenty of hot water. That's their rooms we passed on this side, bathroom, et cetera, opposite, and Father's den at the end.'

'Are you still up at the top?'

'Yes, Babs and Jack and I, and Jack's friend who's visiting.' A faint pink rose in Gwen's cheeks as she mentioned her brother's friend. Miller, Daisy recalled, the bounder who was encouraging Jack in his aeronautical nonsense and might or might not have his eye on Gwen. 'I expect you remember what a strange layout this house has.'

'Vaguely.' Daisy took off her hat and coat and went over to the washstand, waving Gwen to a chair.

'We live on the west side and the servants get the east side, facing the hill. Difficult as it is to get servants since the war, I keep expecting those who remain to rebel one of these days and demand a decent share of light and air. On the other hand— I don't expect you remember our butler, Jennings?'

'I have a vague impression of an ancient personage in rusty black.'

'He's even more ancient now, but he refuses to retire to a nice comfy cottage, and to give up that coat. He can't manage the stairs anymore and he only appears at dinner. Most of his time seems to be spent doing the silver, but he still rules the staff with a rod of iron.'

'Another reason for them to quit en masse, I'd think, besides the dark rooms.'

'At least they have electricity now. When Father put in the generator, he had the servants' side electrified as well as the rest.'

'Anything that makes things easier for the servants must make things easier for your mother. I thought she looked . . . not very well.'

'She's been "not very well" as long as I can remember. I suppose we never thought twice about it when we were children, but looking back, I can see she was always fragile. But she hasn't had to run the house since the end of the war. As soon as Babs and I were demobbed from the Land Army, I took over.'

'Babs still works on the land, though?'

'She found she really enjoyed farming, and she needed something to keep her occupied. We both lost fiancés in the war, you know. Three unlucky sisters – it sounds like one of the grimmer fairy stories, doesn't it?' Gwen fell silent, a faraway look in her eyes.

Daisy nearly told her that she, too, had lost her fiancé. But Michael had been a conscientious objector, a Quaker pacifist who had been blown up driving a Friends' Ambulance. Though he had been at the front, he had not fought, and the prejudice against 'conchies' remained strong. Besides, though her first love would always have a place in her heart, she had found a second, whereas the Tyndall sisters had not.

Or was there something going on between Gwen and the unknown Miller? Before Daisy could come up with a delicate way to probe, Gwen sighed and went on.

'But your brother was killed, wasn't he? We're lucky that

Jack's the baby of the family by several years and was too young to join up. It would have killed Mother to lose him. I just wish he hadn't invited . . . But I mustn't trouble you with our squabbles.' She stood up, with an effortful smile. 'The Guy Fawkes fête always makes Father feel frightfully Lord-of-the-Manorish and he's thrilled that you've come to write about it, so he jolly well ought to be in a good temper. I'll leave you in peace now. I've got to go and try to persuade Addie to punish those blasted boys. Tea in half an hour in the drawing room, if you feel up to coming down.'

'I'm eating for two, remember. I'll be there,' Daisy promised, hoping the bounder Miller, sower of dissension, would be present. She was dying to meet him.

CHAPTER 2

When Daisy left her room and turned towards the stairs, Lady Tyndall was coming out of a room ahead of her, the last on the right. She saw Daisy and waited for her.

'I hope you've managed to rest a bit after that dreadful journey.'

'Oh yes, thank you. I put my feet up for a while.'

'That is my sitting room.' She gestured back at the door she had just closed. 'You are very welcome to make use of it, to relax in, or for your writing.'

'That's very kind of you, Lady Tyndall. My bedroom seems to have everything I need.' Even a second bed, which she wished Alec was occupying.

'I know Gwen had a desk moved in for you. I wasn't sure if it was adequate for a professional journalist.'

'Perfectly. I'm looking forward to writing about your celebration. I hope my dashing away like that didn't upset Sir Harold so much that he won't be willing to tell me the rest of the history.'

'Harold isn't used to being thwarted.' Lady Tyndall gave her a tired smile. 'Usually, I don't find it worth the effort to cross him, but I could see you were in dire need of rescue.'

'I was,' Daisy said gratefully. 'It's one of those flies in the ointment they don't warn you about. In general, I'm very well.'

'I'm glad. I was unlucky; my pregnancies were very difficult. But you look blooming.'

'I'm healthy as a horse, and with an appetite to match, I'm afraid.'

'Don't worry, there will be plenty to eat at tea. Pam is always hungry, and Jack – if he's too thin, it's not because he doesn't eat enough. He's just a boy still, in many ways. But he's too old to accept his father's laying down the law, if Harold would only realize it.' Lady Tyndall had been speaking half to herself. As she and Daisy reached the foot of the stairs and started across the hall, she gave herself a little shake and said, 'I expect Gwen told you we have another guest.'

'Yes, a Mr Miller?'

'He's a friend of Jack's . . . rather unsuitable, I'm sorry to say. Not quite what you might call "out of the top drawer". I hope you won't mind meeting him.'

'Of course not, Lady Tyndall. I'm a journalist, after all. I write about all sorts of things and talk to all sorts of people. My articles about stately homes were the thin end of the wedge in a way, something I could do that most journalists can't.'

'I've read some of them. Most impressive.' She ushered Daisy into the drawing room.

Everyone in the room was at the windows, absorbed by the sunset, a spectacular fiery blaze set off by expanses of cool green and lemon yellow. They turned as Lady Tyndall shut the door against draughts from the hall.

'"Red sky at night, shepherd's delight,"' Jack Tyndall quoted. 'It looks as if we're going to have good weather for the fireworks. I'm glad you didn't come all this way, Mrs Fletcher, just to attend a washout.'

'So am I,' Daisy assured him.

'May I introduce a friend of mine? Martin Miller – he's an aeronautical engineer.' This last was pronounced in a defiant tone.

The man who stepped forward was not in the least what Daisy had anticipated. The 'bounder', far from being dressed in flashy bad taste, wore a perfectly acceptable dark suit, well cut, if not of Savile Row tailoring. He was older than one might have expected of a friend of the youthful Tyndall heir, with the beginnings of crow's feet at the corners of his eyes and dark cropped hair greying at the temples. At least forty, she judged; perhaps that was why his influence over Jack was feared, though he seemed rather on the serious side, more likely to be a good influence than bad.

As for his possible influence on Gwen, he wasn't particularly good-looking, but there was nothing to object to in his appearance. And Gwen was a spinster of twenty-seven in a world where a large proportion of men of 'suitable' age and class had perished in the war.

'How do you do, Mr Miller.' Daisy offered her hand and he shook it, his clasp firm, warm, and dry – no handshake like a filleted fish to make Sir Harold take against him. 'Were you building aeroplanes during the war? My husband was in the Royal Flying Corps, a spotter pilot. Perhaps you had a hand in producing the "crates" he flew?'

He smiled, but his eyes were wary. 'I did, though not so much actual production. My company was mostly working on design.' The final *g* of *working* was voiced, faintly but distinctly grating on the ear and placing his origins firmly in the Midlands and the lower middle class.

Not that Daisy cared, but Sir Harold was bound to take a dim view.

'What are you doing now?' she asked. 'I mean, now that we don't need fighters any longer. I presume you're a believer in the future of air passenger travel?'

Jack intervened eagerly. 'We still need war planes! Germany can't be trusted. And now Winston Churchill – he was Minister for Air after the war, remember? It took a while but he ended up convinced of the necessity of air power. Now they say he's going to join the Conservative cabinet, and he's bound to push for rearmament.'

'Ridiculous waste of money!' Sir Harold had come in unnoticed. 'The Bosch knows when he's beaten. As for air travel, no one in his senses would risk his life in the air only to save a little time.'

'With all due respect, sir,' said Miller, 'a number of airlines have been operating here and in Europe for several years. Now that the government has formed Imperial Airways and started to subsidize—'

'Ridiculous waste of money!'

Daisy was torn between interest and trying to think of a polite way to escape.

'That's a matter of opinion, Father. The fact is, people are going to go on designing and building aeroplanes, and I want to be one of them.'

'And my company needs bright young engineers like Jack.'

'Over my dead body! What this country needs is land-owners who take care of their land. Where should we be without farmers to feed us, eh? Jack's place is right here, running the place like twenty generations of his forefathers.'

'But I'm not in the least interested in farming, sir,' Jack protested. 'Babs knows all there is to know, and what's more, she likes doing it.'

'Babs is a girl.' The baronet glared at his eldest daughter, who had just come in, switching on the electric lights at the door. 'No, by George, Babs is a woman, and if she doesn't stop messing about on the estate and hurry up and find herself a husband, she'll be past praying for.'

Babs shot her father a look of venomous dislike. Though she had changed from trousers into a tweed skirt and long hand-knitted cardigan, it was obvious that she didn't expend much effort on her appearance. She had made no attempt to disguise with powder and lipstick the effects of her outdoor activities on her complexion. Her straight dark-brown hair was bobbed very short. She wore flat shoes, and her only jewellery was a Victorian ring, a diamond and ruby half-hoop, on her ring finger.

An heirloom engagement ring, Daisy assumed, destined never to be joined on the work-roughened hand by the intended wedding ring. Gwen's ring finger was bare, she thought; could it be a sign that Gwen had new hopes? And if so, was Martin Miller their focus?

With an abrupt nod to Daisy, Babs went over to her mother and Gwen. Both were still standing at one of the windows, looking out, but Daisy guessed from their taut stance that both had been listening to the altercation behind them.

They turned to greet Babs. The family resemblance between the three women was obvious. All were slight and fine-boned, perfect for the current low waisted, straight-up-and-down fashion. In Lady Tyndall's case, this was emphasized by the frailty of ill health, as Daisy had already noted. In contrast, the way Babs moved suggested a wiry strength still brimming with restless energy after a day out and about on the estate. As for Gwen, Daisy remembered the delicate prettiness of her girlhood and wondered which was most responsible for its fading: the passage of time, the loss of her fiancé, or the anxieties of life with her irascible father.

Gwen was still pretty when she smiled, but now, distressed, she looked quite plain. Seeing Daisy stuck amid the squabbling men, she said something to Babs, who shrugged. After a moment's hesitation, Gwen visibly braced herself and moved forward to extricate her friend.

By this time, the antagonists were repeating themselves. Daisy decided she wasn't going to learn anything new. She was about to slink away to forestall the rescue effort, when a couple of maids came in with the tea things.

The argument stopped short. One maid started to set out cups and saucers and plates of bread and butter, cakes and biscuits on the tea table, near the fireplace. The other girl went to draw the cream-and-gold curtains, hiding the last embers of the sunset. The room was transformed from a scene of battle to the cosy haven proper for afternoon tea. Lady Tyndall went to sit behind the table, ready to pour.

Under cover of the bustle, Gwen apologized. 'I'm so sorry, Daisy. I didn't realize you'd got caught up in the conflict.'

'Merely as an observer. They forgot I was there. I dare say I could have sneaked away without their noticing.'

'Jack used to be good at coping with Father, but since he came down from Cambridge, he's become so stubborn . . .'

'I imagine he's growing up. He knows what he wants to do with his life – which, I must say, sounds to me perfectly reasonable – and he has Mr Miller to back him. Miller seems to be a staunch, sensible sort of a chap.'

'You like him?' Gwen asked eagerly.

'I like what I've seen of him. I haven't seen nearly enough of him to form an opinion. Have you known him long?'

'I met him last spring. One of Jack's lecturers worked with him during the war and invites him to Cambridge every Lenten term to speak to the mechanical-engineering under-grads about the aircraft industry.'

'Don't tell me you attended a lecture on mechanical engineering!'

'Heavens no! Come and sit down near the fire. It's a beastly cold night. I'll fetch you a cup of tea and tell you how it happened.'

But as Gwen turned away, her father approached with a cup and saucer and a plate heaped with food, which he presented to Daisy.

'Need to keep your strength up, eh?' he said genially, sitting down beside her. 'If you ask me, half my wife's trouble was that she didn't eat enough when she was expecting the girls. I kept hoping for a son, but she kept dropping females.'

A number of sharpish retorts raced through Daisy's mind, but she reminded herself that Sir Harold was her host. 'You got a son in the end,' she pointed out, and seeing a scathing comment about Jack on the tip of his tongue, she hurriedly added, 'Not to mention two grandsons. Aren't you going to have a cup of tea?'

'Never touch the stuff. "Cat lap", my grandfather used to call it.' He raised his voice. 'Dodie, where are the boys? Weren't they up here today?'

Lady Tyndall looked helplessly at Gwen, who said, 'Addie took them home, Father. I think she decided they needed an early night. They were getting a bit . . . overexcited about the fireworks tomorrow.'

Not to mention the fireworks today, Daisy thought. 'You were going to tell me the history of your Bonfire Night celebration, Sir Harold,' she reminded him.

That kept him happily occupied while she devoured the plateful of delicacies and sipped at the distasteful tea, which was far too sweet. Lady Tyndall wouldn't have sugared it without asking, so perhaps Sir Harold was trying to feed her up. Kindly meant, no doubt.

While listening to and taking mental notes on his lecture, she watched the others. Jack and Babs had their heads together, both with disgruntled expressions but eating with unimpaired appetites. Gwen and Miller sat on either side of Lady Tyndall. All three looked unhappy and their conversation appeared to be desultory.

Gwen glanced over and happened to catch Daisy's eye just as she took a sip of the syrupy tea. Perhaps Daisy's nose wrinkled involuntarily. At any rate, Gwen said something to her mother, and a moment later Martin Miller came over.

'Beg pardon for interrupting,' he said, 'but Miss Gwen wondered if you'd like a fresh cup of tea, Mrs Fletcher? Yours must be getting cold.'

'Yes, please. A spot of milk, no sugar, thanks.'

He grinned at her, his sober face lightening. Daisy wondered if Gwen had tried to stop her father oversweetening the first cup. 'Right you are. Can I fetch you anything, sir?'

'No, thank you,' Sir Harold said ungraciously. As Miller left, the baronet went on, quite loud enough for him to hear, 'Running errands for Gwen! He needn't think she'll get a penny from me if she takes him. Dashed counter jumper!'

'Whatever Mr Miller's origins,' Daisy ventured, 'engineering is an altogether respectable and necessary profession.'

'So is street sweeper. That doesn't mean I'll accept one as my son-in-law. Did Gwen invite you here to try to talk me round? Because, I warn you, you might as well try to drink the Severn dry.'

'Certainly not. She invited me because she thought, quite rightly, that I'd be interested in writing about your Guy Fawkes fête. I am a journalist, after all. A profession of doubtful respectability and questionable necessity.'

Sir Harold waved his hand dismissively. 'An odd hobby for a young lady of your birth, to be sure, but there can hardly be any question of your respectability.'

Daisy fumed. Not that she wished her respectability to be questioned – though she did wonder what Sir Harold would think if he knew her husband was a policeman – but writing was her profession, not a hobby, and she had made a living at it before she married. She fumed silently, however. Having come all this way, she was jolly well going to get her article. She was too *professional* to spoil it by quarrelling with her infuriating host.

'You were telling me about when Prince Albert died,' she reminded him.

'Yes, that was in 1861, in December. The following November, the Queen was still in mourning, so my grandfather was of two minds about holding the fête.' He blathered on about his grandfather's quandary.

Miller brought Daisy's fresh cup of tea and deposited it on the table at her elbow. She thanked him with a smile. Sir Harold talked on, ignoring him as though he were a servant. The younger man's answering smile died and his lips tightened.

If it was just a question of Miller's courting Gwen, Daisy rather doubted Sir Harold cared enough to be so rude to a guest. Should his daughter dare defy him, he would just wash his hands of her and write her out of his will. What really rankled with the baronet was what he saw as the engineer's subversion of his son and heir's duty to the land and the traditions of his ancestors.

Miller obviously supported Jack's enthusiasm for aeronautics, but Daisy had so far seen no sign that it had originated with him or would fade should he vanish from the face of the earth. Perhaps the uncertainty was all that had prevented Sir Harold from kicking Miller out of his house.

Nor was Daisy convinced of any serious romantic tie between Miller and Gwen. A few hints, yes, but nothing Alec would consider to be evidence. With luck, Gwen would decide to confide in her.

Sir Harold had run down at last, Daisy realized. She had missed the whole story between 1862 and the present, including the Great War, but she could always ask for a repeat later, with the excuse that she didn't have her notebook on hand. He hadn't noticed her inattention. His large face smug, he was watching Jack and Babs, who were still talking earnestly together.

'Babs will change his mind for him,' he said with

confidence, good humour restored. 'She knows the worth of the land. All young men with any spirit rebel against their parents for a while. I don't say I didn't myself! Jack'll soon see this tomfoolery of his in the proper perspective. By George, I'm thirsty after rattling away for so long. I hope I haven't bored you, Mrs Fletcher. I believe I'll drink a cup of tea after all. Shall I have Dodie refill your cup?'

'Yes, please. No sugar,' Daisy said firmly.

Two and a half cups of tea made Daisy head for the downstairs cloakroom as soon as the tea party broke up. By the eighth month, she thought, she wasn't going to dare to move more than a hundred yards from a lav. When she came out into the hall, no one was about. She decided to go up to her room and type up notes of what she could recall of Sir Harold's discourse.

She was halfway up the stairs when Lady Tyndall and Jack came out of the drawing room. They didn't notice her.

'Dearest,' Lady Tyndall was saying, 'it's not that I mind your being an engineer, if that will make you happy.' She turned and took his hands. 'You know I only want you to be happy.'

'I know, Mother.'

'But I will hate your living so far away. I thought once you were finished with school and university, you'd come home for good.'

'Coventry's not far. Not much more than thirty miles. I'll be able to buzz over at weekends.'

'If your father will have you in the house. Oh Jack, I've never known him so angry!'

'I'm still his only son. But if he does disown me, I can earn my living doing what I love instead of dying of boredom. You've no idea how I loathe the idea of spending my life worrying about pruning and late frosts and blossom rot and peach-leaf curl, if that's what it's called. If the worst comes to the worst, you can always come and visit me in Coventry. I say, doesn't it strike you as rather funny?' Jack said gaily. 'Instead of being sent to Coventry as a punishment, I'm being threatened with disinheritance if I go there.'

Lady Tyndall burst into tears. 'Jack, you're such a child still,' she sobbed. 'How can you know how you want to spend the rest of your life?'

He hugged her. 'Wait till I show you round the factory, Mother. You'll see why I want to be part of it all. Maybe I'll even be able to take you up in a plane!'

Daisy, though greatly tempted to linger and listen, had continued to tiptoe up the stairs and across the landing. She turned up the three steps into the passage and heard no more.

CHAPTER 3

After half an hour's work, Daisy had enough historical background for her article, barring a sentence or two about the form of the celebration, if any, during the Great War. Though she hadn't really listened, thinking back she heard an echo in her mind of Sir Harold saying they had dressed the guy as Kaiser Bill. She hoped so. It would be a nice touch.

The article had to start with an explanation of the Gunpowder Plot for her American readers. No, first she'd quote 'Please to remember . . .' and then go into the explanation.

The baby started doing acrobatics. Daisy put her hand on her abdomen and felt its head, then an elbow or knee. Girl or boy? she mused. She didn't really mind, and Alec claimed he didn't, either. Belinda, her stepdaughter, wanted a little sister. Daisy missed Bel, who had chosen to go to boarding school with her friends instead of staying at home and attending a day school in London.

Daisy loved Belinda dearly, but she could understand now that it might be even more difficult to let go of one's own child, a child once carried in one's own body. Lady Tyndall, after suffering the separation of school and university, had

had every reason to expect Jack to come back to Edge Manor and stay. His home and the home of his ancestors awaited him. Yet he chose to follow his own dream, even if it meant renouncing his inheritance.

Could Sir Harold legally disinherit him? Since he had threatened to do so, presumably the land was not tied up in trusts or entails or whatever it was that had caused Daisy's family estate to revert to a distant cousin when her father and brother both died. Though the baronetcy would no doubt go automatically to Jack, he would be Sir John Tyndall of nowhere in particular. But who would end up with those rich orchards and market gardens?

Not Babs, the logical person, if Sir Harold's tirade meant anything. Adelaide's older boy, perhaps? Reggie was at least a direct male descendant, though through the distaff side. Might the baronet require him to change his name to Tyndall and conveniently ignore the intervening female generation?

A knock on the door interrupted Daisy's reflections. 'Come in!'

Gwen stuck her head around the door. 'Oh, sorry, you're working. I don't want to interrupt.'

'No, I've finished what I was doing.' Daisy moved over to the two easy chairs by the fireplace. 'Come and sit down.'

In the hearth, surrounded by blue-and-white Dutch tiles, a wood fire had burned down to glowing embers. Gwen took a log from the basket on one side and placed it on top, sending a shower of sparks up the chimney. 'One thing about owning orchards, we always have wood to burn.' Still looking into the fire, red-faced, she added, 'I have to apologize. I'd never have suggested your coming down here now if I'd known my father was going to kick up such a dust.'

'That's all right. He's not kicking it at me.'

'Of course not. He's really pleased that you're writing about Guy Fawkes. The thing is, he's always so cock-a-hoop over Bonfire Night that I assumed he'd let all this other business lie while you're here. If I'd known Jack was going to invite Martin – Mr Miller – I'd have told him to wait till next week. But he had the same idea, that Father would be easier to deal with now.'

'It doesn't seem to have worked.'

'On the contrary. It's reminded him that the annual celebration is another thing that's been passed down from father to son for centuries. I walked out in the middle of yet another row about it. Father's obsessed with not breaking the chain. He doesn't realize how much the world has changed, that these days young men won't allow themselves to be chained to family tradition.'

'And young women won't allow their parents to dictate whom they may marry?' Daisy said on a questioning note.

Blushing, Gwen leant down to poke the fire. 'It's not a question of marriage. He hasn't said anything.'

'But you like him.'

'I like him a lot. Babs thinks I'm being unfaithful to Larry's memory. She was madly in love with Frank and I don't think she'll ever get over his death. I was very fond of Larry, but I want a home of my own, children . . .' She sighed.

'You were telling me how you met Mr Miller.'

'Oh, yes. I told you he gave a lecture at Cambridge to the engineering students. He invited any who were interested in going into the aeronautical industry to visit the factory during the Easter vac, and go up in an aeroplane.'

'An irresistible invitation!'

'Actually, very few accepted, but Jack went, on his way home. He stayed so late, Martin put him up for the night. Then next morning, his car wouldn't start. It turned out to need a part that couldn't be got till Monday – this was Saturday – and Jack had invited a friend here for the weekend. Martin would have flown him home if there were anywhere suitable to land. As it was, he drove him home, so of course Mother invited him to stay, and as Jack had to entertain his friend, I ended up entertaining Martin.'

'I see.'

'Of course Mother never dreamt I might fall for him. He's quite a bit older, and ... and of a different social class. But he's every inch a gentleman,' Gwen said fiercely, 'in the true sense of the word. And he's frightfully clever, doing very well in his job. He can easily support a family.'

So it wasn't 'a question of marriage', Daisy thought, amused. 'What does your mother think now of the ... um ... attraction between you?' she asked. 'Obviously your father is very much against it.'

'Poor Mother's torn between disapproving of Martin's background, worrying about Father's disapproval, and wanting desperately to get a spinster daughter married at last. That generation's shibboleths – well, you know. What did Lady Dalrymple think of your marrying a policeman?'

'She was absolutely appalled. I sort of led her to believe Alec was a bobby, a uniformed constable.'

'Oh, Daisy, you didn't!' Gwen laughed.

'So when she discovered he was no less than a Detective Chief Inspector at Scotland Yard, it came as quite a relief. Besides, she'd actually given up on me long before, when I chose to work for a living instead of joining her at the Dower

House. Gosh, when I think what life would have been like if I'd given in! Either we'd have squabbled constantly or I'd have become a doormat.'

'I can't imagine that.'

'No, more likely I'd have turned into a sour old cat. Just think, I'd never have met Alec. Lucy and I survived on eggs, sardines and cheese for a couple of years, but we had a lot of fun.'

'Have you seen much of Lucy since she married Lord Gerald?'

'We've dined with them a couple of times, and we've been to the theatre. It's difficult to arrange evening engagements – Alec works such unpredictable hours. I lunch with Lucy in town now and then. She's still photographing away, but now that she doesn't have to worry about making a living, she can choose her subjects. I think she's very happy. It's not always easy to tell with Lucy.'

'I must admit, she used to rather terrify me at school, the way she mocked everything.'

'Including herself. That's Lucy.'

They went on to talk about other school friends until it was time to dress for dinner.

When Daisy went down to the drawing room, only Jack and Miller were there, standing beside a tray of drinks. She heard Miller say, 'To tell the truth, I'd rather have a beer, but I hope I know better by now than to ask for one.'

'Not at all, my dear chap. I'll ring for Jennings . . .'

'Good Lord, no! I'd hate to be responsible for the old fellow taking a step more than he need.'

In time, one might cease to notice the intrusive g, Daisy supposed.

Jack laughed. 'Right-o, have a gin and It.'

'No, thanks. Give me a sherry, a very small one.'

'Here, but you needn't drink it. We'll stroll down to the Three Ravens after dinner for a pint or two.'

'As a matter of fact, I was thinking of hopping it after dinner. I'm only making things worse, for both you and Miss Gwen.'

'Miller, you can't leave now!' Swinging round to confront his friend, Jack caught sight of Daisy, who had hesitated on the threshold. 'Hullo, Mrs Fletcher, what can I offer you? A cocktail? Don't tell me you despise them, like my father and this old fuddy-duddy here.'

'As a matter of fact, it's sherry I dislike.'

'So do I. What's it to be?' He turned back to eye the drinks tray with dissatisfaction. 'Not that there's a great deal of choice. Gin and It?'

'Could you manage just a drop of It, with soda? Oh, you have Dubonnet. That would be nice, a small one.'

'Coming up, one Dubonnet. By the way, I expect you heard us planning an excursion to the local pub after dinner. Would you care to pop down with us? It's quite a nice inn actually, though most frightfully rural and full of yokels. But Babs is going down to meet a couple of our tenant farmers, and if you come, I'm sure Gwen will, too.'

'I'd like to.' Daisy remembered the hill. 'There's a footpath to the village, isn't there? We wouldn't have to walk right round by the road. I'm sure I could make it down, but oh dear, I'm not sure about walking back up all those steps.'

Jack blushed, his glance flashing involuntarily to her

middle. 'Oh, of course, sorry! But that's all right; I'll run you down and back in the old bus.' He looked at Miller, who gave a resigned shrug. 'Good, we'll all go down, then. Oh Lord, here's Addie. I hope she doesn't decide to come with us.'

Adelaide, like her sisters, took after their mother, but she was plump – a condition with which Daisy entirely sympathized – and her mouth was set in a permanent pout of discontent. Her income might not run to a public school for her sons, but it apparently covered the latest in London fashion, if not Paris. Her pale green silk crepe frock was embroidered with gold and crystal beads from the scalloped hem at knee level to the spaghetti straps. The back was cut even lower than the front neckline, which barely came within hailing distance of Addie's neck. Daisy felt cold just looking at her, in spite of her own long sleeves and high neck.

'It's freezing in here,' she said petulantly.

'I'll lend you a cardigan,' said Babs, following her from the front hall.

'One of yours? No thanks! I wouldn't be seen dead in any of your clothes. I'll have a gin and ginger, Jack, and for pity's sake, don't overdo the ginger. Oh, hullo, Daisy. Mother Yarborough, my revered mama-in-law, was going to some dreary dinner party, so I thought I might as well come up and see you. I hate dining alone.'

'You're dining here, Addie?' Gwen entered from the corridor. 'Did you tell Jennings?'

'No, but I gave my coat to that stupid maid you just hired. She'll tell him.'

'Why should she? I doubt it would cross Dilys's mind that you'd turn up for dinner so late without warning. Why on earth didn't you ring up on the phone? There won't be a place set for you.'

'For heaven's sake, just ring for Jennings and tell him I'm here.'

Gwen looked ready to explode. Jack said quickly, 'I'll go and tell him, Gwen. You know we only ring for Jennings in dire emergencies, Addie.' His laughing, half-guilty look at Miller acknowledged that he'd been on the point of committing that sin a few minutes ago. He chucked his cigarette in the fireplace and went out to the corridor.

'Jennings would be useless in a dire emergency,' Addie pointed out. 'It takes him hours to get from his pantry to the dining room. I can't imagine why you don't pension him off.'

'I've told you – he doesn't want to go and Father won't insist. If you want to argue with either or both, go ahead. Martin, would you mind pouring me a small sherry?'

'Coming up. Here's your gin-gin, Mrs Yarborough.'

Adelaide accepted her drink with an ungracious nod. Apparently, she disapproved of Martin Miller. She took a sip and pulled a face. 'Ugh, I *told* Jack not to drown the gin!'

Jack returned just in time to hear her. An incipient squabble was interrupted by the arrival of Sir Harold and Lady Tyndall. A few minutes later, the connecting door to the dining room opened and the butler appeared. A bent, wizened figure in faded black, Jennings kept one hand on the door-jamb for support as he announced in a voice like a badly oiled hinge, 'Dinner is served, m'lady.'

It was kind of Sir Harold to keep the old man on, Daisy thought. Though, on the other hand, he might be difficult to replace. These days, one didn't have a string of footmen eager to move up to the top of the servants' hierarchy. Doing without a butler would be a lowering of standards Sir Harold was unwilling to face, even if the one he had wasn't much use.

Throughout dinner, Jennings stood by the side-board, discreetly leaning against it, and in the creaky voice he seemed unable to lower to a butlerian undertone, he directed the two parlour maids who served the meal. The maids, one very young, one elderly, withdrew after serving each course, but Jennings remained propped in his place. Whether it was his inhibiting presence or a truce for the sake of digestion, dinner passed without any overt quarrelling, to Daisy's relief. However, the polite conversation was decidedly strained.

Lady Tyndall led the ladies from the dining room, leaving the gentlemen – or two gentlemen and a 'not quite' guest – to the port and brandy and cigars.

'They won't be long,' Gwen whispered to Daisy. 'Jack's not keen on port, Martin loathes it, and Father hates sharing it with people who don't appreciate it. I should think we'll be able to get away in a quarter of an hour or so.'

'I'll fetch my coat. What about your parents – do they know we're going?'

'Gracious no! To a pub? They'd have forty fits. All right for the men, of course, but no lady would be seen in a public bar. The Three Ravens is perfectly respectable, though. I've been several times with Jack, and Babs goes down quite often to talk to the farm people about modern agricultural methods Father won't consider, won't even discuss. If it was good enough for his forefathers . . .' She grimaced.

'Then how will we explain leaving the house?'

'Jack's going to tell them he's taking us for a spin. It's a clear night and the moon's coming up.'

Clear and cold: frost already sparkled on the grass when

Jack and Daisy set off in the Triumph. He'd offered to take everyone in the family Crossley, but the other three elected to walk down the footpath to the village. Adelaide showed no disposition to want to join them. She was busy describing some frightfully clever exploit of her boys to their admiring grandparents.

Though the moonlight was beautiful, the chilly air nipping at Daisy's ears almost made her wish she had asked Jack to put up the hood. She pulled her hat down and tucked in the motoring rug he had thoughtfully provided.

Her mind full of questions, she racked her brains for something to say which would appear neither nosy nor critical of his family or friend. She was about to enquire what part, if any, he was going to play in the fireworks display tomorrow, when he said abruptly, 'I say, do you mind if I ask you something, Mrs Fletcher?'

'Ask away. I won't promise to answer.'

'No, of course not, if she told you in confidence . . . The thing is, it's what my father said, about Gwen and Miller. You heard, didn't you? I just . . . I can't imagine . . . I mean, he's quite old!'

'Gwen's my age. We're no longer spring chickens, alas. I dare say you still think of her as your big sister. Well, in a way she still is, but you're an adult yourself now.'

'She's always been my favourite sister. She's nearest to me in age, though she's six years older. I'm twenty-one, so she's . . .'

'Don't say it!' Daisy laughed. 'We ladies of a certain age prefer not to examine that particular number.'

'So I suppose Miller isn't really too old for her, is he? Only, I haven't seen any sign that they . . . care for each other particularly. Not that I'd mind if she married him. He's a jolly good fellow, absolutely brilliant, and what does it matter if he's not a gentleman? I mean, all that tommyrot is frightfully old-fashioned, don't you think?'

'Rather. My husband's father was a bank manager.'

'No, really? And your father was a viscount. It just goes to show!'

'But you can't expect your parents to see it that way. Parents do tend to be antediluvian.'

'I suppose so,' Jack said disconsolately. 'It's just that Father thinking there's something between them, even if there's not, gives him one more reason to object to Miller. It's all my fault.'

'What, exactly?'

'If I'd only broken it to him gradually! You see, he sent me to Cambridge to make the right sort of friends, punt on the Cam and row in the Mays, and generally kick up a lark. I should have told him when I first got interested in engineering.'

'Why didn't you?'

'I funked it. I knew he'd be angry. I mean, he's always been jolly good to me, and let me do pretty much what I wanted, but I'd never before wanted most frightfully to do something I knew he'd strongly disapprove of. I suppose I thought, too, that perhaps I'd find I wasn't so keen after all, and then he need never know I was buckling down to my books instead of boating on the river and developing a taste for fine old port.'

'When did you decide engineering was *it* for you?'

'I was pretty sure last summer, summer 1923, that is, and quite sure by the end of the Michaelmas term. I couldn't decide which branch I wanted to go into – hadn't even considered aeronautical – till Miller came to talk to us. Then he showed me around the factory.'

'Gwen said Mr Miller came here last spring. Is that when you told your father? He's surely had time to get over the shock!'

'No, I asked Miller not to say any more than that he'd taken me up in a plane. I was afraid Father might refuse to let me go back for the Easter term, my last term. There was nothing definite at that point anyway. They couldn't give me a job till they saw how I did in the Tripos. They only take the top people, you know. There's no room for mistakes with an aeroplane.'

'Gosh no!'

'Well, I didn't do too badly,' Jack said modestly as they passed the gatehouse, now with lights in the upstairs windows. He swung the little car around the sharp bend into the lane with a verve that made Daisy clutch her seat. 'They offered me a job. Since I wasn't desperate to start earning a living, Miller suggested I should take the summer off before I started, and read all the latest stuff on aeronautics.'

'Summer's long past,' Daisy pointed out.

They entered the village. Jack turned right into the main street and came to a halt in front of a many-gabled building of the inevitable Cotswold stone. The moon, a lantern and the Triumph's headlamps illuminated the inn sign: three ravens perching on the body of a fallen knight in armour.

'What a grim sign!'

'"And I'll pick out his bonny blue e'en,"' Jack quoted, grinning.

'"Many a one for him makes moan . . ."' She didn't attempt a Scots accent. '"But none shall ken where he is gone. O'er his white bones when they are bare, the wind shall blow for evermair." But that's the "Twa Corbies" – *two* ravens. "The Three Ravens" is "God send every gentleman such hounds, such hawks, and such a leman." The hounds and hawks and his lady keep the ravens away.'

'I bow to your superior knowledge.'

'Well, they didn't teach us any science at school, and not much arithmetic, but we did learn our literature.'

'Don't tell Dawson, the landlord. He's dashed proud of that sign. I'll tell you what: if you don't mind sitting here for a minute, I'll pop in and see if the others are here yet. You won't want to be the only lady present.'

Daisy wasn't so sure of that. In spite of coat, hat, gloves, scarf and a motoring rug, she was cold. But no doubt all sorts of rumours and speculation would go around the village if she walked in, pregnant, alone with Jack. She said, 'Yes, do,' and tucked the rug tighter around her legs.

They had arrived just too soon for her to find out when and how Jack had broken the news of his grand ambition to his parents. On the other hand, she hadn't been forced to deny or acknowledge any attraction between Gwen and Miller. In any case, she knew only one side of that aspect of the story.

Before Jack returned, she heard the other three approaching. Miller and Babs were discussing farm machinery. Glancing back, Daisy thought she saw Gwen holding hands with Miller, but away from the inn's lantern the deceptive moonlight made it hard to be sure. Jack came out just then and hailed the walkers, and when they reached the car, Gwen and Miller were a good yard apart.

Three boys came up to them, pulling a handcart containing a bundle of old clothes vaguely human in shape.

'Penny for the guy!' they chanted. 'Penny for the guy!'

Jack and Miller delved into their pockets for change and dropped a few coins into the out-stretched cap. The boys, apparently impervious to cold, settled on the pavement near the door of the pub, waiting for customers to come out.

'Don't you lay a finger on the car, or I'll skin you alive,' Jack threatened.

Notably, the three glanced at Babs before swearing and crossing their hearts and hoping to die if the car came to any harm at their hands.

'Is that your guy?' Daisy asked Jack as they went in.

'No, they just throw something together as an excuse to beg for money to buy a few fireworks of their own. Ours is a work of art. I should know, I made it this year. Come to think of it, it's rather a gruesome custom, isn't it, Mrs Fletcher?' Jack teased. 'As gruesome as the inn sign. Burning an effigy, I mean. And Guy Fawkes wasn't burnt at the stake anyway, he was hanged.'

CHAPTER 4

The pub was snug, with a roaring fire in the hearth and crimson-cushioned oak settles black with age, as were the ceiling beams and the bar itself, at one end of the long room. The brass handles of the beer pumps gleamed through a haze of pipe smoke.

A dozen men and three dogs turned to stare at the newcomers in their evening frocks and dinner jackets. Daisy wondered if the Ravens really was the sort of pub where the presence of a strange female was acceptable. It was all very well for the Misses Tyndall, daughters of the lord of the manor, to waltz in as if they belonged. In fact, the building might well belong to their father, along with the rest of the village.

The men at the bar looked like local farmworkers and tradesmen, except for one stout fellow in a flashy checked suit, a commercial traveller perhaps. The checks reminded Daisy of Alec's detective sergeant, Tom Tring, who was wont to say villains were so stunned by his suits that they didn't notice who was wearing them until too late, when he collared them. Maybe the traveller's clothes had the same effect on his customers – they didn't notice what they were buying until they'd signed for it.

In the moment taken by this reflection, most of the men had turned back to their beer and chat, and the dogs to their patient waiting for their masters.

A couple of prosperous-looking farmers in leggings, sitting in a corner, stood up and nodded to Babs as she went to join them.

'Evening, Miss Tyndall,' called out the one with a round red face fringed with white.

'Evening, Miss Tyndall.' The second raised a hand in greeting. 'Evening, Miss Gwen.'

'What will you have, chaps?' Jack asked them jovially. 'Just let me get the ladies settled. Come here by the fire, Mrs Fletcher. You look half-frozen. What will you have?'

'I'll stick to ginger beer, thanks.' She sat down, and Gwen took the place beside her.

'Half of cider, Gwen? Right-oh. The usual for you, Miller?' Jack went to the bar.

As Miller joined Gwen and Daisy, she saw a middle-aged couple at a table at the far end of the room from the bar. They appeared to be finishing a meal, so perhaps they were staying at the inn. The woman had silver hair piled on top of her head in a loose, untidy bun. Her face was much more youthful – she was in her early forties perhaps, plump and good-humoured. She was beaming across the table at her companion, who had his back to Daisy.

He shook his head. Even from behind, Daisy sensed doubt and worry in the gesture. The woman said something vehement, pleading, and he got up slowly and reluctantly. A short, stocky man, he wore a new-looking blue suit. His face was very brown, except for the upper part of his forehead. He was definitely not happy as he walked towards the bar.

Miller interrupted her thoughts. 'We'd like your opinion, Mrs Fletcher. I've invited Gwen to go up for a sight-seeing flight, and she can't make up her mind. Would you – not at present, I imagine, but in the normal way – would you ever consider going up in an aeroplane?'

'Actually, I already have. A year ago, Alec and I flew right across North America, from New York to Oregon, on the West Coast.'

'Daisy, you didn't!' Gwen gasped. 'Was it fun?'

Remembering that cold, cramped, noisy, endless flight and the hair-raising bits when they zigzagged between the snowy peaks of the Rocky Mountains, Daisy said, 'I wouldn't exactly call it fun, not overall. But the first bit was, and that's all you'd be doing. I wouldn't mind flying to Paris in an air-liner, for instance.'

They peppered her with questions, Gwen about her adventures in America, Miller about the type of aeroplane, flying conditions, American airfields and similar matters. Daisy was laughingly confessing her entire ignorance of the capacity of the fuel tanks when Jack brought their drinks.

'Half of ginger beer, Mrs Fletcher. Half of cider, Gwen. Pint of the best bitter, Miller.'

'Thanks.'

'I say, Mrs Fletcher, would it be frightfully rude of me to go and have a few words with those people over there? They're from Australia. I was talking to the chappie, Gooch, at the bar, and he said his wife's originally from this part of the world. She's heard of our Bonfire Night do but never attended and wanted to know if we'd mind their coming along with the village people. I just want to go and assure Mrs Gooch that will be quite all right.'

'Why don't you ask them to join us?' Daisy suggested. 'We – you, rather – could pull up a couple more chairs.'

'They're not what he calls "flash", which I take to mean gentry,' Jack warned.

'Jack, how can you say such a thing?' Gwen demanded.

Her brother glanced at Miller and flushed. 'Sorry, old chap. The thing is, I forget.'

'I'll take that as a compliment,' Miller said dryly.

'Ask them over,' Daisy urged. 'I've never met any Australians, and all is grist to my journalistic mill, you know. Presumably they're not from the absolute dregs of society or they couldn't have afforded the passage to England. They look perfectly respectable.'

So Miller brought two more chairs to the table while Jack fetched the Gooches. Mrs Gooch was sensibly dressed in a grey woollen frock – merino, thought Daisy, with vague memories of geography lessons – but adorned with a big chunky gold brooch set with a huge blue-green opal. She appeared to be in quite a flutter, somewhere between nervous and jubilant, more so than the situation warranted.

Jack introduced the couple and seated Mrs Gooch with all the courtesy of a well-brought-up young man. He sat down beside her and asked whereabouts in the district she came from.

'Evesham,' she said. 'You've lived all your life here, haven't you, just up the hill? Did you go away to school?' Her voice, tentative at first, mixed the soft, familiar cadence of Worcestershire and the sharper tones of Australian English.

Mr Gooch spoke broad Australian. He was sitting opposite

Daisy, so she found herself involved in the conversation between him and Miller. The Gooches now lived in Perth, in Western Australia, he told them. He had gone west from Victoria in 1892 when the gold was found at Coolgardie, and set up in business in the outback supplying miners with everything they needed.

'Started out with billies and boots and beer. A lot of them wanted to pay with gold, so I told 'em good-oh and got into the gold business.'

'"Billies"?' Daisy asked.

'What you might call a kettle, ma'am, or a teapot, but it's just a big tin can. Out in the bush, you boil water over a fire and drop in a handful of tea leaves, to wash down the damper and 'roo steak. And I sold 'em the flour for the damper and the knives to cut the steaks.'

'How on earth did you come to meet Mrs Gooch, out in the wilds?' Miller wanted to know. It seemed as unlikely as his own meeting with Gwen.

'Ellie came out west the year after they put the water pipeline in, in 1904, with a bit of a stake, looking to buy into a business. She wasn't hardly more than a girl, but she's a bonzer businesswoman, my Ellie,' Gooch said with pride and a fond glance at his wife. 'She reckoned there was more opportunity in the west and she turned up just when I was looking for a bit of capital to expand. But Coolgardie ain't bush, or the wilds, as you said. She's a beaut town and only around three hundred and fifty miles from Perth.'

'Three hundred and fifty miles!' Miller echoed. 'They're both in Western Australia?'

'That's nothing. From Coolgardie east to the South Orstrilia border is another five hundred miles or so, and north to south, she's about twice the width. Course, half is desert, but that still leaves a lot of outback to get around in.'

'It sounds as if you're ripe for air travel.'

'Too right. Fellow started a regular service up in the Kimberley in 1921 and extended it to Perth just this year.'

The men started discussing the future of aviation in Western Australia. Turning to the other end of the table, Daisy saw that Gwen was listening to Miller with a look of fond pride, very like Gooch's for his wife. Jack and Mrs Gooch were getting on like a house on fire. It sounded as if Jack was telling her the story of his life. Daisy thought hers must be much more interesting, but she was listening with apparent fascination to his tales of university life.

Babs, her business completed, came over and was introduced. As soon as she found the Gooches were not involved in farming, she lost interest. 'Time we were heading home,' she proposed.

'Not yet,' Jack objected, pulling up another chair. 'Have a seat, Babs.'

'I'd rather—'

'I'll run you all home later, so you don't have to walk up the hill. We can all squeeze into the old bus.'

'I really don't—'

'No need to squeeze,' said Mrs Gooch. 'We've got a hire car, a big Vauxhall. Jimmy'll take you, won't you, Jimmy?'

'Or'right, Ellie.' Gooch sounded resigned. 'Let's have another round, my shout. What's yours, Miss Tyndall?'

Babs gave in and settled for a bottle of pale ale. Daisy refused another drink, as she hadn't finished her first. She was making it last, having no desire to have to go in search of what was almost certainly an outside lav, frequented by pub patrons, in the dark.

Polite if indifferent, Babs asked what the Gooches had seen on their visit to England. Since landing at Southampton, they had spent a fortnight in London. In the ensuing discussion of the sights of London, Mr Gooch stoutly upheld the superiority of Perth on every count save that of antiquity.

'Which I don't call such an advantage,' he pointed out, 'when it means you got a whole lot of crook buildings, dirty, cramped cubbyholes that ought to be pulled down.'

The landlord called for last orders. As they finished their drinks and got up to leave, Mrs Gooch said eagerly, 'Is it really all right for me and Jimmy to go to the fireworks?'

'Of course,' Gwen assured her. 'People come from the farms roundabout, as well as the villagers.'

'I'll tell you what, though,' Jack said. 'Why don't you both come up to the house? Even with the bonfire, you'll freeze down in the meadow, coming from a warm part of the world such as Mr Gooch assures us Perth is. A couple more won't throw off your housekeeping, will it, Gwen? It's a buffet supper.'

Gwen and Babs exchanged a glance of dismay, but Gwen said, 'Of course not. There's always plenty.'

'Well, it's mighty kind of you,' said Mr Gooch, 'but we wouldn't want to intrude amongst the flash society folks, would we, Ellie?'

'Oh, Jimmy, do let's go!' Mrs Gooch's lips quivered. 'Just for once. What harm can there be?'

The Tyndalls were far too well brought up to rescind an invitation once given.

'You needn't worry about evening dress,' said Gwen. 'People wear their warmest because we watch from the terrace.'

Under their reassurances, Mr Gooch capitulated. 'Good-oh,' he said. 'Or'right, I'm off to bring the car round to the door for them that's in need of a lift. Won't take two ticks. Starts like a dream, that car.' He went out.

It was decided that the ladies would take advantage of the comfort of the Vauxhall while Jack drove Miller in the Triumph. They all took their leave of Mrs Gooch, Jack with especial warmth, as if to banish any suspicion that the Gooches might not be entirely welcome at Edge Manor. She went upstairs, smiling.

Daisy, Miller and the Tyndalls stepped out into the street. 'Jack, how could you!' Babs exclaimed. 'Father will be furious. If you want his blessing to go off and build aeroplanes, inviting a couple he'll strongly object to isn't the way to go about it. And tomorrow, of all times, when the cream of two counties will be there to meet them!'

As the Vauxhall touring car pulled up before them, Jack said with youthful exuberance, 'Don't worry, Babs, we won't tell the parents they're coming, and we'll keep them apart. Wait and see, it'll be all right on the night.'

Having been advised that Lady Tyndall always had breakfast in bed, Daisy decided to follow suit the next morning. When she got up, the sun shone in a pale blue sky without a hint of a cloud. From her bedroom window, she saw three men and two small boys down on the lowest terrace of the gardens.

Several more figures moved about in the meadow beyond, where the bonfire had visibly grown. From their motions, she guessed they were pitchforking faggots on top of the heap.

She put her notebook and a couple of pencils in her handbag and went downstairs. In the hall, servants scurried about, dusting and sweeping in last-minute preparations for the party.

'Do you know where Miss Gwendolyn is?' Daisy asked a housemaid wielding a feather duster.

'In the kitchen, I think, ma'am. Down the passage there, ma'am.' She pointed to a door to the right of the fireplace. 'Just across from the dining room.'

An unusually sensible arrangement, Daisy thought, recollecting mansions where the kitchens were separated from the dining room by miles of draughty corridors. Edge Manor, long and narrow, was bisected by a single passageway, its only natural light a large fan-light above the door.

Stepping through, Daisy recognized from a previous visit the dingy watercolours of local landscapes, painted by some long-ago lady of the family. The passage was used mostly by servants and seldom by guests.

To her left were the doors to the drawing room and dining room, and at the end, if she remembered correctly, one to the combined smoking/billiard/gun room, whence a staircase led to Sir Harold's den. To her right, a row of baize doors gave access to the usual offices: the butler's pantry (where Jennings must be polishing his silver – or snoozing), the housekeeper's room, the servants' hall, kitchens, sculleries, larders, broom cupboards, back stairs and cellar stairs, and so on.

In fact, she was faced with a positive plethora of baize doors, none exactly opposite the dining room door. She was trying to decide between the two nearest when Gwen came out of one, looking harried.

'Oh, Daisy, were you looking for me? I'm so sorry! I'm

being a rotten hostess this morning. The thing is, the aspic didn't set and the mayonnaise curdled and Cook panicked. She just needed soothing. Everything's under control now. Mother's doing the flowers.'

'Judging by the displays I've seen, she does a wonderful job. Is there anything I can do to help?'

'Good gracious no. You're a guest. But I can tell you, if Father did the catering instead of setting up the fireworks, he wouldn't be so keen on his Bonfire Night party! It's not just the buffet supper here: we provide sausages and potatoes for the village people to cook in the bonfire embers, and ginger-bread and drinks and so on.'

'You mustn't feel you need to entertain me. I'm not a guest today, I'm a journalist. I'll just poke around and try not to get in anyone's way.'

'Bless you, Daisy!'

'It won't upset Sir Harold if I go down to watch him setting up, will it?'

'I dare say he'll be delighted. Jack and Martin are down there, too.'

'I think I saw your nephews.'

'I expect so. I hope Father isn't letting them mess around with the fireworks . . . and that he's not snubbing Martin too badly. Yes, Jenny, what is it?'

Leaving Gwen to deal with whatever was making the young maid twist the corner of her apron in nervous fingers, Daisy slipped away. She went on into the billiard room, which had a door to the outside and was less likely than the dining and drawing rooms to be overrun by hordes of servants with brooms and dusters.

The room smelled faintly of tobacco smoke. Though

smoking rooms weren't necessary these days, now that everyone smoked all over the place, Jack and Sir Harold probably lit up while playing billiards.

At least, she hoped they didn't indulge while handling the firearms racked on the walls alongside the billiard cues. A landowner's daughter, she recognized a couple of rook rifles and half a dozen double-barrelled shotguns of different bores. Less conventional was a glass-fronted case of pistols. There were antique duelling and horse pistols, family heirlooms from the days of highwaymen and duels, but also modern, efficient looking automatics like the one her brother had worn as an army officer. Apparently, the family's fascination with fireworks extended to firearms.

The scarred, stained table would be for cleaning and oiling the guns and filling cartridges and such chores. The nearby cabinet must hold ammunition, Daisy assumed. It was as a policeman's wife, not a landowner's daughter, that she noted with disapproval the key left in the lock.

CHAPTER 5

From the billiard room, French doors led out onto the paved terrace. Before she opened one, Daisy buttoned up the jacket of her warm tweed costume and put on the gloves she had brought in a pocket. Nonetheless, she recoiled as the icy air reached for her. The sunshine was misleading.

A couple of shabby, nondescript mackintoshes hung on hooks near the door. Deciding they were the sort that don't belong to anyone in particular, she donned one. She eyed the adjacent tweed caps and mufflers, rejected the former and chose one of the latter, striped in navy and white. With that over her head and wound around her neck, she ventured out.

The flags of the terrace were still frosted. The sun wouldn't reach this west side of the house for some time. Daisy trod with care as she crossed to the steps. Pausing at the top, she realized what a splendid view the guests on the terrace would have of the firework display.

What did they do the years when it rained? She must remember to ask.

Holding the stone rail, she descended to the second terrace, laid out in flower beds with lots of roses. At this time of year the bushes were bare and straggly, though here and there a bloom flaunted, defying the frosts. The third terrace had a gazebo at the north end and a lily pond at the south.

The next terrace was the last, where Sir Harold, Jack and Miller were erecting a complicated metal framework and a sort of wooden gibbet, 'for the Catherine wheels,' as Sir Harold later explained. Reggie and Adrian were taking rockets from a big wooden crate and carefully inserting the sticks into bottles. No messing about under Grandfather's stern eye.

Actually, the baronet was in a cracking good temper and greeted Daisy effusively. 'What ho, Mrs Fletcher!' he shouted as she came down the last steps. 'We're going to have a ripsnorter of a set piece tonight. "Ripsnorter" – that the right term, Jack?'

'That's it, sir. Morning, Mrs Fletcher. As you see, we big boys get to play with big Meccano.'

The struts they were bolting together did look rather like giant pieces of Meccano. Miller stopped tightening a nut to wave to Daisy with an adjustable spanner. 'Good morning, Mrs Fletcher.' Even he looked cheerful.

'Useful fellow,' Sir Harold confided in a low voice, 'when it comes to this sort of thing. Once I'd explained the effect I'm going for, he got the layout worked out in half the time it usually takes me. Quarter!' he added with a burst of generosity. 'And drew up a neat little plan, too. This here, that there, we'll be done in no time.'

'It looks very complicated. I can't wait to see the result this evening.'

'Want me to explain it to you?'

'No, never mind, thanks. I don't want to get too technical

for my readers. Besides, I'm really more interested in the party and the guy, and all the history. I'm afraid the fireworks are somewhat of a sideline as far as the article is concerned. According to my editor, they rather go in for big fireworks displays in America, especially on their Independence Day in July.'

'July! Hmph, silly time to have fireworks, if you ask me. What about the children, eh?' He cast a fond glance at his grandsons, who promptly stopped squabbling about which bottle to use for a particularly large rocket. 'It doesn't get dark till ten o'clock at night.'

'I expect they're allowed to stay up late. It's a holiday, unlike Guy Fawkes.'

'My great-grandfather tried to have the fifth of November proclaimed a holiday. I didn't tell you this bit, did I?'

'No,' said Daisy, busy scribbling in her idiosyncratic version of Pitman's shorthand. 'What happened?'

'Sir John, that was. Jack's named after him. He actually went up to Parliament and proposed a bill, or whatever it is they do. Not a very political family, I'm afraid, but that was before Reform, so he had no trouble getting elected. Getting his bill passed was another matter. No one else was interested. I suppose . . .' Sir Harold huffed and puffed a bit. 'I suppose it just goes to show the Americans were happier to be rid of King George than the English were *not* to be rid of King James, what?' He chortled, very pleased with himself. 'I say, Jack, Miller, listen to this!'

While he repeated his joke, Daisy wrote it down. It ought to appeal to her American readers, though Jack's and Miller's laughter was at best polite.

'You're putting that in your article, eh, Mrs Fletcher?' Sir Harold was delighted. 'Respectable hobby for a lady, writing.

You might have a go at talking my Barbara into trying her hand at it, instead of sticking her nose into men's business.'

Daisy had no intention of sticking her nose into Babs's business. 'I'd like to take a look at the bonfire,' she said, 'and the guy.'

'The guy's up at the house. We'll set it out on the front porch for people to see as they arrive; then Biddle will bring it down to the fire. He's in charge of setting off the fireworks. I'd like to do it myself, but can't desert my guests, what? Here he comes now. Hi, where have you been?' he shouted to the grizzled man coming down the steps. 'You're late!'

'Sorry, sir,' Biddle said soothingly. 'Her la'ship needed more greenery for her vases. Here I be now, sure enough.'

'So I see, you fool. Jack, give Mrs Fletcher a hand down the steps. She wants to see the bonfire.'

The lowest terrace was separated from the meadow by a ha-ha. Unlike the broad, shallow flights between terraces, the steps down the ha-ha wall were much narrower and quite steep, with the wall itself on one side and no railing on the other. The drop from the top was only ten or twelve feet. Normally, Daisy would have taken the steps in her stride, but unbalanced as she felt these days, she was glad to have Jack going down in front of her, half sideways, his hand steadying her.

'Thanks!'

'My pleasure. Any questions about the bonfire?'

'I'll ask these chaps, thanks.'

'Right-oh. I'll go back to playing with the Meccano, then.' He grinned. 'When you're ready to come up, call out and I'll come down to push from behind.'

'You still are a horrible, cheeky schoolboy, I see,' she retorted with a smile.

The bonfire was a good fifteen feet tall by now. The farmhands were climbing ladders to add fuel to the top. Daisy spent twenty minutes talking to them, learning how they used a framework of timbers and netting to pile the stack of wood and brush high so that it didn't fall over.

Ready to return to the house, she eyed the hill with misgivings. It was all very well coming down, but as she had said last night, going up was a different kettle of fish. She was about to hail Jack to request his aid on the ha-ha steps, when a 'Hulloo' came from behind her, from the direction of the village. Miller appeared on the footpath through the belt of trees.

'I've brought my car down to give you a lift, Mrs Fletcher. It didn't seem like such a good idea you climbing all those steps.'

'That's awfully kind of you, Mr Miller. I was just thinking I didn't much fancy the climb.'

Miller's car was a Jowett. 'Not the most elegant of vehicles,' he said, apologizing, 'but the engine is unusually reliable, and when you build aeroplanes, reliability is what you tend to look for in an engine. Mrs Fletcher, may I ask you something?'

Daisy turned on him her 'misleadingly guileless blue eyes', as Alec persisted in describing them. 'Ask away,' she said hopefully, as she had said to Jack last night. 'I won't promise to answer until I've heard the question.'

'It's no good asking any of the family, because they've got their own axes to grind, one way or another. You're looking in from the outside, yet you grew up with all this tradition stuff, father to son in an unending line century after century.'

'Well, the Dalrymples didn't quite manage that, but I know what you mean.'

'Do you think it's wrong of me to encourage young Tyndall to break with tradition?'

'Oh dear, I'm not really the best person to ask. I'm not exactly a traditionalist myself. If you'd heard what my mother said when I decided to work for a living . . .'

'Your writing isn't a hobby?'

'Certainly not!'

'Sorry! Sir Harold seems to think—'

'It's not worth the trouble of correcting him. Not that I *need* to write for money now, but it paid the bills before I married. And that's another thing: Mother was just as upset by my choice of husband. Alec isn't at all "suitable".'

'You mean you . . . No, I'd better not ask.' After a glance at her, Miller drove on in a thoughtful silence. A slight smile played about his lips.

While Daisy hadn't exactly intended to encourage him to pursue Gwen, she was not at all sorry if that was the result. She liked him and didn't believe he was only after Gwen's money – not that she'd have any if Sir Harold carried out his threat.

When they reached the house, Miller handed Daisy out and she thanked him for fetching her from the bottom of the hill.

'Not at all,' he said. 'Thank *you*. You've given me considerable food for thought.'

'If you really feel obliged to me, may I ask a favour? I was going to ask Jack or Gwen to drive me down to the meadow this evening, just for a quarter of an hour or so, to take a peek at that side of the festivities. But I expect they'll have their hands full helping to entertain the invited guests and—'

'Not to mention trying to keep the Gooches away from their parents!'

'That, too.'

'I'll be happy to run you down, Mrs Fletcher. I'll make sure the car isn't boxed in by guests' motors, and you just tip me the wink when you're ready to go.'

Daisy had enough information now to plan her article, so she spent the rest of the morning at her typewriter. At lunch, Sir Harold was still in an excellent humour. He told Daisy about some Guy Fawkes disasters of the past, like the time an insecurely fastened Catherine wheel had flown from its place and rolled along a row of rockets, prematurely igniting the lot.

After lunch, she again asked Gwen if she could lend a hand with anything.

'You already have.' Gwen exchanged a meaningful glance with Miller, making Daisy hope her unspoken but clearly implied encouragement of the engineer would not lead to disaster. 'This afternoon it's mostly organizing the moving of furniture.'

'I'm not volunteering for that! Neither the organizing nor the moving.'

'Certainly not,' said Lady Tyndall, giving Daisy her faint, exhausted smile. 'Why don't you take a nap after the morning's exertions? That's what I'm going to do.'

'Yes, do, Daisy,' said Gwen, seconding her mother. 'Then you'll be full of beans for the evening's exertions.'

'Gwen, dear, where on earth did you come by such a dreadful expression!' Lady Tyndall gave Miller a look cold enough to turn the lily pond into solid ice.

'At school, Mother. See you later, Daisy.'

Daisy and Lady Tyndall went slowly upstairs together. 'I don't know,' Lady Tyndall said wretchedly. 'I really don't know. Gwen is twenty-seven, and if he's the only chance she's going to have to marry . . . But he's encouraging Jack to go off to Coventry – to be an engineer, of all things! – and I was so looking forward to having him home for good at last. What do you think of Mr Miller?'

'I like him,' said Daisy, and refused to be drawn further.

The guy propped up by the front door to greet the Tyndalls' guests wore a long frilly nightgown and a lace nightcap, from which the mask of a wolf peered out.

'Gwen found the clothes when she turned out some old trunks in the loft,' Jack explained to Daisy. 'The wolf in "Little Red Riding Hood" used to terrify me when I was little, so I thought I'd take my revenge. There's no law says the guy has to be a person.'

'No, and after all, the whole thing is really for the children.'

He grinned. 'Don't let Father hear you pronounce such blasphemy!'

'I shan't. Your wolf looks quite sinister in the dusk with just the oil lanterns lighting it.'

'Electric light would spoil the effect. Here comes someone. Let's go in, or we'll end up exchanging greetings on the doorstep and freezing, and spoiling Jennings's fun the one time of year he actually opens the door.'

Headlamps approached along the drive. Jack and Daisy slipped into the house. A screen had been set up before the door in an attempt to keep some of the cold air out as guests entered. Jennings waited there, a small, bent figure in his best, slightly less rusty black.

The invitations had stated 'Dress for warmth', and Daisy

had done so, wearing a long-sleeved wool frock, lisle stockings and walking shoes for her projected visit to the meadow. She had brought her coat downstairs. The Tyndalls were equally sensibly dressed, except Adelaide. She was once again backless and sleeveless, elegant but not at all practical. Her boys were there, too, in shorts with jerseys under their school blazers. Several other guests would be bringing children, so lemonade and cocoa were provided along with the cocktails, sherry and whisky at a long table to one side of the hall.

The hall had been rearranged, with small tables and groups of chairs throughout, ready for the buffet supper. A blaze in the fireplace looked cheerful, even if it did little to warm the air in the distant corners.

Jennings appeared around the screen and announced in his creaky voice, 'Mr and Mrs Dryden-Jones.'

It was the only announcement Daisy heard, as his voice became totally inaudible once people started talking. She and Miller kept out of the way as the Tyndalls moved forward to welcome a swelling stream of guests. The constant opening and closing of the door chilled the air, and though the gentlemen doffed their hats of course, most people unbuttoned their coats but kept them on.

Gwen brought over Colonel Sir Nigel Wookleigh, Chief Constable of Worcestershire. He was a very tall, very thin man, whose narrow face, fringed with old-fashioned white whiskers, made Daisy think of an Afghan hound. Not only had Sir Nigel known Daisy's father and been colonel of her brother's regiment, he had been extremely forbearing when Daisy dragged Alec willy-nilly and very unofficially into a kidnapping in his county. She was happy to see him but hoped he wouldn't mention Alec's profession.

She averted the possibility by telling him at once that she was at Edge Manor to write an article. They talked about her writing for a minute or two. Then Jack, looking mischievous, appeared with a pretty young woman in tow who was at least two months more pregnant than Daisy.

He introduced her as Mrs Snelgrove, saying, 'I think you ladies will find you have a great deal in common.'

'Naughty boy!' said Mrs Snelgrove coyly. Daisy was sure she would have tapped his arm with her fan were fans not long out of fashion.

Miller and Sir Nigel had identical expressions of alarm at the prospect of being caught up in a conversation about babies. Taking pity on them, Daisy suggested to Mrs Snelgrove that they should sit down. They found chairs near enough so that Daisy could hear the two men amicably discussing the future of aviation, Sir Nigel apparently undismayed by Miller's lowly antecedents.

All Mrs Snelgrove wanted to talk about was whether the bangs of the fireworks would be bad for her baby-to-be. Since Daisy had no idea, this was not a fruitful topic. She was delighted when Mr Snelgrove arrived with a drink for his wife and she was able to escape.

The room was filling up. Daisy decided it was time she went down to the meadow. As she looked around for Miller, who had moved off, she saw the Gooches enter. She was too far away to hear what was said, but she saw Jack hurry over to smooth their entrance. He escorted them into the room, and she saw that Mr Gooch looked worried, Mrs Gooch determined. And she saw Sir Harold and Lady Tyndall turn to stare after them, both with identical expressions of horror.

CHAPTER 6

Down in the meadow, lit by lanterns, villagers and farm folk warmed their hands on mugs of cocoa and hot mulled cider. They willingly chatted to Daisy about their part in the festivities. They told her about the grand celebrations in 1887 and 1897 for the old queen's Jubilee and Diamond Jubilee. Children ran around playing, or stood with sparklers, drawing glittering shapes in the air. Older boys thrust potatoes into the bottom of the great pile of wood and brush, to be retrieved later from the embers.

Daisy watched the arrival of the guy, carried down the terrace steps by Biddle and the garden boy. Red Riding Hood's wolf was considered a very good joke by most, though some of the older women were shocked by the brazen appearance of a nightgown in public. It was being hoisted to the top of the bonfire as Daisy and Miller left.

Back at the house, people were buttoning their coats and winding around their necks woolly mufflers from the colourful pile supplied by the Tyndalls. In chattering groups, they drifted through the drawing room and out of the French doors onto the top terrace. Daisy saw Mr Gooch alone and looking lost, so she joined him and they went out together. It wasn't entirely altruistic: she had an idea for an article on the Australian visitor's view of Britain.

'I suppose it's hot in Perth right now,' she said as they emerged with a shiver into the frosty air.

'Too right. November's late spring, so it'll be eighty or better in the shade right now. Coolgardie's a bit hotter, and dry, my word! The miners used camels instead of packhorses. I remember the days before the pipeline, when you paid a shilling for a gallon of water.'

'Is that why you moved to Perth?'

'No, the easy gold ran out and the big mining companies moved in. No room left for an independent agent, but luckily I'd made my pile by then. Ellie wanted our kids to go to school in the city. Lots of outback kids go to boarding schools, but she didn't want to be parted from them. They're boarding this term, while we're away, though.'

'How many children have you?'

'Three boys. I miss 'em,' Gooch said simply.

'I hope you're enjoying your holiday here anyway. I'm afraid it's not the best time of year to visit England.'

'Last week was a fair cow. Hardly stopped raining and cold with it, and a wind like to cut you to the bone. This ain't so bad, now.'

The lights in the house behind them went out. In the sudden darkness, a million stars spangled the sky.

'Gosh!' said Daisy. 'What with rain and clouds and fog, you hardly ever see so many stars.'

'Ah, you want to go out in the bush with your swag and—'

A huge bang and a series of pops signalled the beginning of the show. Blue, green and red lights shot up from the bottom terrace. Then a couple of rockets soared up to burst in a shower of gold and silver globes, which parachuted slowly down. People crowded towards the balustrade. 'Women and children first!' someone said jovially. In the shuffle, Daisy lost Mr Gooch.

By the eerie glow of half a dozen blue fountains, she found herself near the top of the steps, beside Babs, who was hanging on to the collars of her nephews.

'I don't see why we can't go down to the next terrace,' Reggie whined, to the accompaniment of various explosions from below. 'Mummy would let us.'

'Your grandfather wouldn't. Oh, hullo, Daisy.'

'Why can't we have sparklers?' Adrian had his brother's whine pat. 'The village brats have sparklers.'

'Don't call the village children brats,' Babs said sharply.

'Mummy does. Why can't we have sparklers, too?'

'There's no room up here. Someone would get hurt.'

'Then let us go down to the next terrace!' said Reggie self-righteously, with logic on his side.

'If you behave yourselves now, I'll find you some sparklers for later, when people go in.'

The boys' response was lost in a fusillade as glowing balls floating down from rockets sent out exploding sparks. Babs let go of them and they slipped away through the crowd.

'I'd better provide some sparklers.' She sighed, taking an electric torch from her pocket. 'I suppose the rest of the children will want them, too. Thank heaven they go up to their nannies in the schoolroom for their supper. Are you all right, Daisy? Need to sit down?'

'No, I'm enjoying the show, thanks.'

The balustrade was lined with children now, oohing and

aahing, while adult guests moved about, talking when they could make themselves heard. The constant, ever-changing glare of rockets and Catherine wheels, Roman candles and Greek fire seldom left them in darkness for more than a moment. Clouds of smoke drifted up from the bottom terrace into the sky and the smell of gun-powder began to pervade the air.

Alternating green and red flares made people's faces ghastly as a woman came up to Daisy and introduced herself as Mrs Yarborough, Adelaide's mother-in-law. Gwen had just told her about Reggie and Adrian throwing squibs at the car and she wanted to apologize for her grandsons' misbehaviour.

'I'm afraid they run wild.' She sounded harassed. 'Adelaide can't control them and won't let anyone else try to discipline them. My poor son must be turning in his grave.'

Daisy's commiserating murmurs were drowned by a flurry of extra-noisy explosions from below, including whistles and squeals as well as the commoner bangs, cracks and pops. Mrs Yarborough drifted away. As the show continued, Daisy exchanged admiring remarks with the succession of strangers who paused momentarily nearby.

Her toes were beginning to freeze when Jack came and stood beside her. 'Doing all right, Mrs Fletcher?'

'It's spectacular. You and your father and Mr Miller have done a wonderful job. I can't wait to see the set piece.'

'Just coming up. The next item is— Hold on! What's that fool Biddle up to? That's only half the rockets. I'd better go and see what's happening.' He took a torch from his pocket and bounded down the steps.

Daisy hoped the torch, combined with the gold sunburst and showers of silver, blue and green sparks from the remaining rockets, would provide enough light to prevent his breaking a leg. She lost track of him as a brilliant rainbow followed the sun and showers. It faded in turn, leaving one small golden glow, which gradually grew tall and put forth branches. Green leaves appeared, followed by white blossom, then red fruit. As the tree faded, there was a round of applause.

Down in the meadow, flames flickered around the base of the bonfire. Up on the terrace, everyone headed for the house.

Babs and Gwen stood at the French doors, handing out sparklers to children and directing adults to the dining room, where the buffet supper was laid out. Daisy debated staying outside to watch the children, but her toes were frozen and she was famished. She stayed just long enough to see the bonfire blaze up below.

Inside, maids were relieving people of their wraps. Daisy joined Miller and Mr Gooch at the rear of the chattering crowd of fifty or sixty guests moving slowly into the dining room. Gooch asked the engineer about the motive power of rockets, but he hardly listened to Miller's explanation. He seemed uneasy and kept looking about – for his wife, Daisy presumed.

People started coming out of the dining room with piled plates. Most of them headed straight through the drawing room to the entrance hall, now warmer, with luck, as the front door had been closed for some time. The maids circulated with trays of drinks.

Daisy and her escorts reached the dining room at last. Gwen and Addie were there, making sure everyone got what they wanted, aided, or perhaps hindered, by the tottery butler. Addie made a bee-line for Daisy.

'Do you know where Jack is, Daisy? And hasn't Babs sent the children up to the nursery yet?'

Gwen came over. 'It's your children she's entertaining. Stop fussing!'

'I don't live here.' Addie pouted, and it was all too obvious where her boys had learnt their whine. 'I'm a guest. I shouldn't have to help like this.'

'For pity's sake, you're family!'

'I saw the children coming in,' Daisy reported, 'so Babs will be here in a minute, I'm sure. Is there anything I can do?'

'Certainly not!' said Gwen. 'You really are a guest, and we're nearly finished anyway. Here, take a plate. What would you like—'

Jack burst into the room. 'Addie, your little beasts pinched a dozen rockets! I've had enough. They're going to get a leathering they'll remember for a long time.'

'You always blame Reggie and Adrian for everything! They've been with me every moment.'

'Oh no they haven't,' announced Babs, coming in.

Daisy, Miller and Gooch edged away from what was rapidly deteriorating into a full-fledged family row. The half a dozen other guests still in the room finished filling their plates and departed in haste.

Miller and Gooch looked as if they wanted to flee, but Daisy was far too hungry, and they were too polite to desert her. Gwen came over to them.

'I'm so sorry.' She was very upset. 'Please help yourselves and I'll go and tell them to pipe down.'

Miller reached for her hand. 'Keep out of it,' he advised. 'You'll only make it worse, and if Sir Harold hears them, you'd be in for it with the rest. Come and have something to eat with us.'

'He's right, Gwen,' said Daisy. 'Let them fight it out. These vol-au-vents look delicious. What's in them?'

They turned to the table. Daisy, at least, managed to concentrate on choosing among the many dishes, ignoring Jack's and Addie's raised voices punctuated by Babs's acerbic comments. When those voices suddenly fell silent, however, she turned with the others.

Lady Tyndall had come in. White-faced, exhausted, she laid her hand on Jack's arm and said in a failing voice, 'One of our guests told me you're having words. My dears, this is no time to quarrel.'

'Sorry, Mother,' said Babs. 'I'll go and make sure everyone has what they need.' She seized a plate, piled it indiscriminately with food, and disappeared into the drawing room.

'Next year, Babs is jolly well going to have to play hostess in chief,' Gwen muttered. 'Mother's not strong enough.'

'Mother, you look ill,' Jack said. 'Come and sit down.' Leaning on his arm, she let him support her to a chair by the wall. She sat down and her colour improved a little.

Adelaide followed them, complaining. 'Jack accused Reggie and Adrian of stealing fireworks. They're all always accusing my boys of things they haven't done.'

Jack opened his mouth to retort, then closed it, biting his lip.

Lady Tyndall shook her head sadly. 'No, Addie, I'm afraid in every case I'm conversant with, the boys have been the culprits.'

'You always take Jack's side. It's not fair! I'm going to tell Father. He'll make you stop maligning them.'

'I'll tell him myself,' said Jack, striding to the door to the drawing room. 'It's past time he stopped believing the brats are angels.'

Adelaide ran after him. Lady Tyndall leaned her head back against the wall, eyes closed.

'Excuse me,' Gwen said to Daisy, Miller and Gooch. 'I must go to her. Please help yourselves; we can't have guests going hungry. I'm so sorry, Mr Gooch, that you've landed in the middle of a family squabble.' She went to sit beside her mother, holding her hand and talking to her in a low voice.

Miller looked helplessly at Daisy. 'I'm out of my depth,' he confessed. 'What's the proper thing to do?'

'Pretend we haven't noticed anything amiss. Take a plateful as quickly as possible and leave. Otherwise, Gwen will be worrying about us on top of the rest. Mr Gooch, try some of this galantine. Partridge or pheasant, at a guess.'

Gooch eyed the aspic-coated game with suspicion. 'Where I come from, we don't muck about with our tucker.'

'Cold roast beef, sir?' Miller suggested. 'Rolls and butter?'

'Good-oh. Ta, mate. I hope my wife got hers.'

'I'm sure Gwen or Babs found Mrs Gooch something she'll enjoy,' said Daisy. She and Miller searched the table for plain food for the Australian. 'Here's some beetroot salad. Is that too – er – mucked about for you?'

'No, thanks. I'm not that hungry. I reckon I'd better go and look for the missus. She must be wondering where I got to.'

He went through to the drawing room, passing Jack in the doorway. Jack came in, frowning. 'I can't find Father.'

'Perhaps he's in the billiard room,' said Gwen. 'He was talking to someone earlier about the duelling pistols. They might have popped in there to take a look while waiting for the crowd at the table to clear.'

'Why would he have closed the door?' Jack crossed the room and opened the connecting door. 'No lights. No one here.'

'Could he have gone up to his study?'

'I suppose so. I'm not going to track him to his lair. I'll tell him about the rockets later.'

'Oh, do go up, Jack. He must not realize how time is passing. Mother can't possibly do any more, and at least one of the parents ought to be visible after inviting half the county. Two counties.'

'Right-oh.' Jack flicked the electric light switch on and disappeared.

'Is this where we hop it?' Miller asked Daisy *sotto voce*.

'Just a minute. Gwen, if you feel you ought to be out there with your guests, I'll be happy to sit with your mother, or help her upstairs to her room. Would you like to go and lie down, Lady Tyndall?'

A faint movement of her head could have been a nod or a shake. Her eyes were still closed.

'I can easily carry your mother upstairs, Gwen,' Miller offered.

'I don't know,' Gwen said doubtfully. 'Do you think she ought to see a doctor? Dr Prentice is here.'

Lady Tyndall roused herself to shaky speech. 'No, no doctor. If Mr Miller will kindly give me his arm, we shall go up the backstairs and disturb nobody.'

With Gwen on one side and Miller on the other, she rose to her feet. Miller supported her through the door to the passage.

As Gwen shut the door behind them, Jack appeared in the doorway to the billiard room. His face was as white as his mother's. He stood with one hand on each doorpost, staring blindly at his sister and Daisy. His mouth moved, but for a moment no sound emerged.

'Jack! What's wrong?'

'It's . . . it's Father.' He sounded as shocked and confused as he looked. 'He's shot Mrs Gooch. And himself.'

CHAPTER 7

Miller walked in on the stunned silence. 'We met Lady Tyndall's personal maid on the stairs,' he said. 'One of the parlour maids had told her Lady Tyndall wasn't well and she— What's going on?'

Daisy recovered her wits. 'Gwen, go and fetch Colonel Wookleigh,' she commanded. 'No, ask him to come here at once, and then send Dr Whatsisname – Prentice? Don't explain; just tell them they're urgently needed. You can collapse when you've done that.' As Gwen went out, walking like an automaton, Daisy turned to Jack. 'Come and sit down before *you* collapse.'

Jack dropped onto a chair and buried his face in shaking hands.

'What's going on?' Miller repeated, totally bewildered.

Beginning to feel somewhat shaky herself, Daisy said, 'Jack found Sir Harold and Mrs Gooch. Apparently, Sir Harold shot Mrs Gooch and then himself.'

'Mrs *Gooch*? But why the blazes? Here, you'd better come and sit down, Mrs Fletcher. Jack, are they both dead?'

'I . . . I think so. Father . . .' He shuddered, eyes closed. 'Father is.'

'We've got to stop anyone going in there. In the study? That's up the stairs from the billiard room?'

'That's right,' said Daisy, who had followed his advice to sit down. 'But there's another door upstairs, at the end of the passage.'

'You'll see anyone coming through here. I'd better go and check upstairs, lock the door if possible.'

'I'll go,' said Jack. He stood up, his colour slightly improved. 'I'm all right.'

Daisy was about to warn him not to touch the doorknob or key with his bare fingers, when she had second thoughts. The only reason for such a precaution was the possibility that Sir Harold had not, in fact, killed himself but had been murdered. Both Jack and Miller had clashed with the baronet.

But Mrs Gooch? Why should either shoot Mrs Gooch?

Come to that, why should Sir Harold shoot Mrs Gooch?

'I think you'd better wait for Sir Nigel.'

'Colonel Wookleigh?' Miller asked with a frown.

'He's Chief Constable. He can take charge. Here he is now.'

The tall, thin colonel entered with a short, chubby man, whom Daisy presumed to be the doctor. His frizzy gingerish hair stood out in a Struwwelpeter-like aureole that made his head as round as his body. Close behind came another man, considerably younger, and Gwen, who still looked stunned, as if her brother's report hadn't yet sunk in properly.

'What's up, Tyndall?' Wookleigh asked sharply.

Miller stepped forward to explain, but Jack said, 'I'm all right, I tell you. It's my father, sir. He . . . Up in the study . . . It looks as if he's shot one of our guests, and himself.'

'Dead?' demanded the younger man, pushing forward.

'I think so, Doctor.'

'Think so! Don't stand around thinking. Show me the way!'

Jack paled. 'Miller?' he said appealing to his friend.

'This way, Doctor.' The engineer led the way towards the billiard room.

'Don't touch or move anything you don't absolutely have to!' Daisy called after them.

'That's right, by Jove!' Wookleigh exclaimed. 'Don't disturb the evidence, unless to save a life. You're absolutely right, Mrs Fletcher. I may not have police training, but I've learnt that much, only it skipped my mind in the press of the moment. I'd better go with them, hadn't I, Mrs Fletcher?'

'I say, old chap,' bleated Struwwelpeter, 'not your county, you know. Chief Constable of Worcestershire, and Edge Manor is in Gloucestershire. My county, old chap, don't you know.'

'My dear fellow, you're Lord Lieutenant, a purely ceremonial post, nothing to do with the police. At least I have some experience with police investigations.'

'Not your county,' the other persisted. 'Got a perfectly good Chief Constable of our own. What's his name, now? Helot, Hazlitt, Harrington—'

'Herriott. We'll ring him up, of course, but in the meantime, someone needs to keep an eye on things, eh, Mrs Fletcher? From a police perspective.'

'No offence to the lady, but what the deuce d'ye mean by consulting her, Wookleigh? The name's Dryden-Jones, madam.' He bowed slightly. 'No offence, I say, but you're not one of these newfangled policewomen, are you? Course not. See you're a lady with both eyes closed. No more police experience than I have!'

'On the contrary, my dear fellow. Mrs Fletcher's husband is a detective, a Chief Inspector of Scotland Yard, no less. I dare say she knows more about police investigations than the two of us put together.'

'I know a bit,' Daisy interjected before Dryden-Jones had recovered from his surprise. 'And I do agree, Sir Nigel, that you'd better go up and keep an eye on things.'

'I'm on my way,' said Wookleigh triumphantly, and his long legs carried him rapidly to the billiard room's door, where he stopped and turned. 'It is your county, Dryden-Jones,' he admitted with an air of making a great concession. 'I'll tell you what. Why don't you go and ring up Herriott and tell him to ask the Yard to send Detective Chief Inspector Fletcher down to take charge? Dashed good fellow, Fletcher. He knows how to keep his mouth shut.'

Dryden-Jones glanced at Jack and Gwen. Close together, they were clasping each other's hands and talking quietly. Tears poured down Gwen's face. Jack led her to a chair and made her sit.

Turning to Daisy, Dryden-Jones said rather sourly, 'You seem to be our expert, Mrs Fletcher. Should I advise Herriott to call in your husband?'

'It's up to the Chief Constable, of course, but if he wants Scotland Yard involved, Alec may be available. He's just winding up a case in Birmingham and he was going to pick me up tomorrow to go home, but he might be able to get here tonight.' *Please, please let him get here tonight*, she thought. She badly wanted the comfort of his presence. 'The sooner investigators are on the scene, the better.'

Jack came over. He was still pale, but he had pulled himself together in the best tradition of the stiff upper lip. 'Mrs

Fletcher, Gwen tells me your husband is a detective, and since we're going to have to have the police in the house, she'd rather he came than anyone else.'

'It's not up to me, Jack.'

'I'll see to it,' said Dryden-Jones gruffly. 'Needn't say I'm devilish sorry, Tyndall. I'll need a telephone.'

'In Father's— Oh Lord! You'd better use the one in the butler's pantry, sir. It's more private than the one in the hall. I'll show you.'

They both went out into the passage. Daisy sat down beside Gwen. She was searching for words when the door to the drawing room opened again and Gooch came in, still carrying his plate, looking disconsolate. Daisy's heart sank.

'I can't find Ellie anywhere. Have you seen—' Realizing Gwen was weeping into a hankie, he came to a halt. 'What's up? Here, Mrs Fletcher, what's the matter?'

Daisy did not want to be the one to tell him. Reluctantly, she started to stand up, but Gwen stopped her.

'No, it's my responsibility.' She swallowed a sob. 'But how?'

'An accident,' Daisy whispered. 'Tell him there's been an accident and the doctor is with her.'

Gooch took a step towards them. 'Ellie?' he asked pleadingly.

Gwen went to him. 'I'm sorry, I have bad news, Mr Gooch. Dr Prentice is with your wife now.'

'She's crook? Been took ill?'

'There's been an' – she stumbled over the word – 'an accident.'

But could it have been an accident? Daisy wondered. Suppose Sir Harold had been showing one of his antique pistols to Mrs Gooch and it had fired accidentally. Having killed her through sheer carelessness, he might have thought to atone by blowing out his own brains.

Daisy felt sick. Till now, she'd managed to hold at bay the image suggested by Jack's announcement. Now she fought to dismiss it from her mind, to distract herself with speculation. Why should Sir Harold take Mrs Gooch up to his study to show her a pistol, instead of staying downstairs in the billiard room? Why, horrified as he had looked when she and her husband arrived, should he have gone to any trouble for her in the first place?

Was she blackmailing him? But she had seemed such a pleasant person!

Jack returned. Seeing Gooch, he turned bright red. He rushed up to the Australian. 'Sir, I wouldn't have had this happen for the world! I liked Mrs Gooch so much. If only I hadn't invited—'

'Liked!' Gooch's face turned a horrid clay colour. 'She's not—'

'The doctor's with her,' Gwen reminded him apprehensively.

'Where is she? I gotta see her!'

Miller came back just in time to hear the Australian's desperate plea. His grim expression offered no hope that Jack had misinterpreted the gravity of the situation. Gwen, Jack and Gooch all turned to him.

'I'm afraid it won't be possible for you to see your wife, sir,' he said. 'This is a police matter and nothing can be done until they arrive.'

'Ellie's dead.' Gooch's shoulders slumped as the certainty sank in. 'If only I'd put me foot down . . . !'

'Tyndall!' The Lord Lieutenant bustled in from the

passage. 'I have Herriott on the line. Chief Constable, don't you know. Dashed officious fellow – wants to speak to someone who's actually seen the scene, so to speak.'

Jack blenched. 'Must I?'

Dryden-Jones gave him a look of surprised disgust, as if describing over the telephone the gruesome scene of his father's death ought to be taken in his stride. Daisy sympathized. It wasn't as if Jack had been through the bloody hell of the trenches and become inured to slaughter – though for some men those memories made things harder.

Again Miller came to his rescue. 'I've seen. I'll go.'

'Who the deuce are you?' Dryden-Jones barked.

'Martin Miller,' Gwen told him. 'A friend of the family. Martin, this is Mr Dryden-Jones, Lord Lieutenant of Gloucestershire.'

'I'll speak to Mr Herriott, sir.' Miller went out before Dryden-Jones could start an argument. Dryden-Jones followed him, tut-tutting.

Gwen and Jack returned their attention to Gooch. His colour was slightly improved, but his face revealed his hopeless misery. He stood with his arms hanging, as if he didn't know what to do with them.

'How'm I going to tell the boys?'

He didn't know yet that Sir Harold was also dead, Daisy realized. She couldn't leave it to Gwen and Jack to break that bit of news to him. But they were going to have to rally round. Babs undoubtedly needed their help with the guests, who mustn't be allowed to leave without giving details of their whereabouts for the next couple of days. Gooch needed somewhere private to sit down, and he probably could do with a drink before he spoke to the doctor.

Someone had to start getting things organized. Miller appeared to be willing and competent, but he was otherwise occupied just now and presumably inexperienced in police investigations.

Daisy was unwilling, and Alec would doubtless question her competence, but she was on the spot and more experienced than even Wookleigh might guess. Wearily, she gathered her remaining energy and stood up.

Detective Sergeant Tring, enormous in his bottle green and maroon check suit, hoisted his pint in the direction of Detective Constable Piper. Light gleamed equally on the glistening tankard and the shiny dome of his bald head. 'Well done, laddie!'

'Cor, Sarge, you feeling all right?'

'Never better.' He wiped froth from his luxuriant moustache. 'It's back to the Smoke and the old woman's steak and kidney pud tomorrow.'

'I mean,' Piper said, appealing to Alec, 'how often d'you hear him giving me any credit, Chief?'

'Rarely.' Alec smiled and sipped the whisky he'd treated himself to after the conclusion of a difficult and exhausting case.

'Don't want him getting too big for his boots, do we, Chief?'

'Heaven forbid. But there's credit enough for both of you in this one.'

Ernie Piper's eye for detail had discerned a pattern in the string of pawnshop robberies, and Tom, much speedier on his feet than his bulk suggested, had bagged the villain on the brink of escape. The Birmingham Chief Superintendent was duly grateful. Favours were owed, to be called in at need.

And tomorrow Alec would see Daisy. He hadn't been keen on her going off on one of her writing outings in her condition, but he knew better than to say so. The timing had worked out very neatly. Tom and Ernie would hop on the London express in the morning, and he'd drive his Austin Chummy via Didmarsh-under-Edge to pick her up on the way home. The weather forecast looked set fair for at least another day, promising a pleasant journey.

In the meantime, he was enjoying his whisky and the easygoing teasing between his men.

'Telephone for Mr Fletcher!' The Buttons hurried straight across the hotel lounge towards their table. He had somehow penetrated their incognito, and the name of Scotland Yard was a potent one to a fourteen-year-old. 'Trunk call for Mr Fletcher!' Arriving, slightly out of breath, he added in a conspiratorial whisper, 'It's from Lunnon, sir. The Yard, I bet!'

Piper groaned. 'Where to now? Timbuktoo?'

At the words 'trunk call', Alec's first thought was that something had gone wrong with the pregnancy. Relieved that the call came from London, not Didmarsh, he overtipped the boy a florin and went to the telephone cubby in the lobby.

'Fletcher here.'

'London, I have your party,' said the girl. 'Go ahead, please.'

'Fletcher, you there?' Superintendent Crane's ire sizzled down the wire in spite of a bad connection. 'How the deuce does she do it? That's what I want to know! You'd better get over there right away.'

'I beg your pardon, sir?'

'Your wife, man, your wife! Murder-suicide at Edge Manor, where I gather Mrs Fletcher is a guest. The Lord Lieutenant of Gloucestershire personally instructed Herriott, the CC, to ask the AC for you. Also present is the CC of Worcestershire, who was acquainted with Mrs Fletcher's late father.'

'Sir Nigel Wookleigh?' That gentleman's friendship with the late Lord Dalrymple had been responsible for saving Alec's bacon. Wookleigh had been remarkably forgiving last year when Alec, dragged in by Daisy, had operated in a flagrantly unofficial manner in his jurisdiction.

'That's the chap,' the Super confirmed. 'You know him, don't you? But you're out of luck – it's not his county. You'll be dealing with Herriott, and he can't give you much help till tomorrow. Some gang blew up a vault in a Customs warehouse at the Gloucester docks under cover of the fireworks and he's got all available men onto that. Did you know Gloucester is a port?'

'No, sir.'

'Nor did I. The village bobby is on his way to Edge Manor, but knowing village bobbies, you and your chaps can probably get there almost as quickly.'

'About an hour, sir. I have my car here. We're on our way.'

'Good. I needn't tell you the Assistant Commissioner is breathing fire. How does she do it, Fletcher?'

'If I knew, sir, I might have some hope of stopping it. I don't exactly like having my wife mixed up in murder cases.'

'No.' Crane sounded somewhat mollified. 'I don't suppose you do. Off you go then; Good luck, and my best regards to Mrs Fletcher.'

'Thank you, sir.'

How *did* Daisy do it? Alec mused on the perennial problem as he hurried back to the lounge. It wasn't as if she was the kind of siren who swanned through life leaving flaming passions in her wake. The crimes that beset her way had nothing to do with her, but her personal combination of sympathy and curiosity invariably led her into the heart of the matter. She simply couldn't help meddling – or 'assisting', as she preferred to call it.

The truly extraordinary part was the way people rushed to tell her things they would never reveal to the police. Those deceptively guileless blue eyes of hers. . .

Alec couldn't wait to see them again.

CHAPTER 8

Shortly before ten o'clock, Alec and his men arrived at Edge Manor. The door was opened by a uniformed constable. A screen hid the high-ceilinged room beyond.

'Detective Chief Inspector Fletcher,' Alec announced himself.

The young man came to attention with a smart salute. 'Blount, sir. Cor, I'm that glad you're here, sir,' he added in accents of profound relief.

'What's up?'

Blount lowered his voice. 'Well, sir, aside of two dead bodies, we've got a Lord Lieutenant and a Chief Constable which can't agree on nothing, a visiting engineer, and Mrs Fletcher, sir, which is the only one seems to know what needs to be done.'

'Good for Mrs Fletcher!' said Piper, not quite *sotto voce*, his boundless faith in Daisy once more renewed.

'Then there's the Squire's family, him being one of the deceased, which is gathered upstairs.'

'They'll have to wait until I've talked to my wife and the CC. This is DS Tring. Take him to the scene and stay to give him a hand photographing and fingerprinting, as he directs.'

Blount paled and gulped but said manfully, 'Yes, sir. This way, Sergeant.' He took the camera, tripod and magnesium lamp Piper handed him. Tom Tring was carrying the precious Murder Bag he took everywhere. One could never be sure what equipment provincial police forces would be able to provide.

As they headed for the stairs, Alec moved around the screen, knowing Ernie Piper was at his heels with his notebook and his ever-ready supply of well-sharpened pencils. A group of people, seated in easy chairs by the fireplace on the far side of the large hall, were all gazing his way with varying degrees of anxiety. They rose as he appeared.

'Alec, at last!' Daisy came to meet him, looking decidedly wan. She held both hands out and he clasped them, wishing etiquette did not proscribe taking her in his arms in front of other people.

'Come and sit down, love. You look worn to the bone.'

'You look rather toil-worn yourself, darling. No rest for the wicked! Hullo, Mr Piper.'

'Evening, Mrs Fletcher.'

'Sir Nigel, you remember my husband?' Daisy introduced Alec to the other two men, Dryden-Jones and Miller, and how-d'you-do's were exchanged. They all sat down by the fire, Daisy and Alec together on a sofa, the others in chairs facing them, with Ernie Piper slightly behind the rest. They would speak more freely if not reminded that their words were being recorded.

'Sir Nigel,' Alec began, 'would you mind telling me what's happened? Assume I know nothing at all, which is pretty much the truth.'

'Harumph!' Dryden-Jones cleared his throat testily, his reddish mop of hair bristling like an irritated hedgehog. 'Not Wookleigh's county, don'cha know.'

'By all means go ahead, my dear fellow.' Wookleigh's tone was cordial, but the gleam in his eye was malicious. 'I should think you'd better start with the appearance of the bodies and why it led you to believe a crime had been committed.'

The Lord Lieutenant's cheeks puffed and turned purple. 'Most improper subject in the presence of a lady!' Tugging on the Albert chain stretched across his round belly, he produced a gold hunter watch from his fob, snapped it open and checked the time. 'Dash it, look at the time. The wife will be wondering where I've got to. Besides, the chauffeur came back to wait for me after he took her home, and it doesn't do to keep servants waiting these days. Don't need to tell you, Chief Inspector, I'm ready to answer any questions you may want to put to me, but I trust tomorrow will do.'

'Certainly, sir.' With equal courtesy and curiosity, Alec stood up as Dryden-Jones took his leave, then turned with raised eyebrows to the Chief Constable. 'What was that about, sir?'

If Wookleigh were not such a distinguished gentleman, his expression might have been described as a smirk. 'As a matter of fact, Dryden-Jones didn't actually see anything. To give him his due, he followed my instructions impeccably in ringing up Herriott and insisting that he send for you, Fletcher. He's right about one thing, though. I shan't describe the scene in Mrs Fletcher's presence.'

'Nor I,' Miller agreed.

'No, it can wait,' Alec said, wondering where the devil Miller came in. Had he discovered the bodies? What had

Blount meant by 'visiting engineer'? Had he come to repair the electric plant? 'My sergeant has gone to take a look.'

'As for the rest, Mrs Fletcher ran the show and she can best tell you the story – if you're not too tired, young lady.' Wookleigh's glance at Daisy was full of concern.

Ran the show? Alec's glance at Daisy was full of suspicion. What had she been up to?

'All I did,' she said defensively, 'was try to make sure that nothing was disturbed in the study, that we had all the guests names and addresses before they left, and that Mr Gooch wouldn't leave the country before he'd been questioned.'

'I have his passport.' Sir Nigel, with the air of a conjurer, produced the document from his inside breast pocket and handed it over.

'Australian! Mr and Mrs James William Gooch. Just visiting?'

'The fellow's staying at the Three Ravens in the village. I didn't feel justified in keeping him here in the house where his wife was murdered. Not my county, you know,' he apologized. 'At least, Edge Manor isn't, but Didmarsh-under-Edge is. Come to think of it, the village bobby's outside his district.'

'I shouldn't worry about that, sir, now that we're here. But all I know is what my superintendent told me, that we'd been asked to investigate a murder-suicide. Someone had better begin at the beginning, if you please.'

Wookleigh looked to Daisy, but Miller spoke first: 'I've been thinking about just that, Chief Inspector.' The touch of Midlands accent made Alec wonder all the more what he was doing there. 'It seems to me it all began when we met the Gooches at the Ravens. Wouldn't you agree, Mrs Fletcher?'

'Ye-es.' Daisy nodded. 'Yes, you're right. There was something rather odd . . . But for now, we'd better just stick to telling Alec what happened this evening. Everyone was out on the terrace, darling, watching the fireworks. The moon hadn't come up yet and it was black as pitch.'

'Tyndall always has the house lights put out for the show,' Wookleigh put in. 'I believe the family all carry electric torches for emergencies.'

'No one would have noticed Sir Harold and Mrs Gooch leaving. When the fireworks went off, at least the brightest ones, you could just about see who was standing next to you, but other people were just bluish faces, or greenish, or whatever, depending on the colour of the lights.'

Wookleigh nodded. 'And they were quite noisy. Not like the front line in the middle of a bombardment, of course. All the same, with all the explosions, no one would have noticed a howitzer going off in the house, let alone a couple of pistol shots.'

'At the end of the show, everyone came in from the terrace,' Daisy continued. 'Jack Tyndall—'

'Jack?'

'The only son of the house. John, strictly speaking,' she told Piper for the record, then turned back to Alec. 'He got into a row with his sister Adelaide and she went flouncing off to find her father to support her, with Jack in hot pursuit. Or vice versa? I'm not sure. We were in the dining room, but most guests had already helped themselves and gone to sit in the drawing room or here in the hall. Jack came back and said they couldn't find Sir Harold. Someone – Gwen, was it? – suggested that he might be in the billiard room.'

'It was Gwen.' Following Daisy's example, Miller turned

his head momentarily to address DC Piper. 'Miss Gwendolyn Tyndall. She had heard Sir Harold talking to someone earlier about his antique duelling pistols. She thought he might have gone to show them off. Jack went to look for him.'

'The billiard room is a gun room, too,' Daisy explained. 'Sir Harold's study is above it, with a connecting stair. Up there is where . . . where it happened. Jack came back looking like a ghost and said his father had shot Mrs Gooch and himself.'

Daisy was beginning to look somewhat ghostlike herself. Alec took her hand. 'You didn't go to see!'

'No.' Her other hand went to her abdomen, where his baby was growing, and he suspected that but for her pregnancy she might have gone up to the study. He was profoundly grateful that she hadn't. 'I sent Gwen to find Sir Nigel and a doctor, who were among the guests. She was in a state of shock, but not as bad as Jack. He actually saw . . .' She turned to Miller. 'You weren't there.'

'I came in just then, but I didn't know what was going on. I'd helped Lady Tyndall upstairs, remember? Handed her over to her maid. She wasn't at all well.'

'That's right. She's something of an invalid, darling, and though Gwen did most of the work, entertaining the hordes was too much for her. There must have been fifty or sixty people here, not counting the children.'

Alec swallowed a groan. Fifty or sixty people to be tracked down and questioned about where they'd been, what they'd done, whom they'd seen and talked to, and when. He'd have to rely on the county forces for most of it. A sudden shocking thought struck him. 'Great Scott, not your mother, Daisy?'

'No, thank heaven! It wasn't really her sort of party.'

'Thank heaven!' Sir Nigel echoed. 'Lady Dalrymple and murder – it doesn't bear thinking of!'

Daisy and Alec exchanged a reminiscent glance. Carrying on a murder investigation with the dowager viscountess in the house was an experience they never wanted to repeat.

'So Miss Gwendolyn fetched you, sir?' Alec asked Sir Nigel.

'Yes. She kept her head, said nothing about shooting, just that I was urgently needed. Unfortunately, I was chatting with Dryden-Jones at the time. He stuck to me like a burr and argued with every decision. Never been in the army, you know.'

Alec wished he had taken the time to change into his Royal Flying Corps tie, which generally went down well with upper-class gentlemen sporting their own regimental or public school colours. Still, Wookleigh knew his credentials, and Miller did not appear to be an upper-class gentleman. Who was the man and what was he doing here?

'Gwen brought Dr Prentice, too,' Daisy continued, 'the local GP. He rushed off to see if he could do anything for Mrs Gooch. Mr Miller showed him the way.'

'Mrs Fletcher pointed out that nothing must be moved or touched unnecessarily,' said Sir Nigel. 'Dashed clever to remember such a thing at such a time. So I went along as well, as soon as I'd detached Dryden-Jones from my coattails. You'll want to have a word with Prentice, of course, but Miller and I can tell you what he said and what we saw.'

Daisy's hand twitched in Alec's clasp. 'Later,' he said firmly. 'Daisy, is there anything else you really need to tell me now, anything Sir Nigel doesn't know that can't wait until the morning?'

She frowned. 'No, I suppose not. You're going to question the family tonight?'

'Yes, I must talk to them.' He knew she wanted to tell him all about the Tyndalls. Her judgements of people she knew were often useful, if sometimes misleading. She had a way of taking one or more suspects under her wing and failing to notice anything to their detriment. Tomorrow was soon enough to hear her views, though, and the wild theories which would undoubtedly accompany them.

Presumably she had an opinion about Miller, too. And the Gooches? Their appearance in the drama seemed even more mysterious than Miller's. He was on the point of asking her, when she succumbed to an enormous yawn.

'I beg your pardon!' she said, blushing.

Alec managed to suppress a strong desire to kiss her. He escorted her to the stairs and bade her a fond but discreet good night.

When he returned to the fireplace, Miller was holding out a packet of cigarettes, Player's Navy Cut, to Sir Nigel.

'Thanks, my dear fellow, but I never touch 'em. May I offer you one of these?' He produced and opened a silver cigar case. 'Dash it, only one left.'

'All yours, sir. I prefer my own. Chief Inspector?'

Alec was already feeling in his pocket for his pipe and tobacco pouch. 'No, thanks. I'm a pipe man.'

After a moment's hesitation, Miller offered the packet to Piper, who looked to Alec for permission before taking one. They were a cut above his usual Woodbines.

The others had all lit up while Alec was still tamping the tobacco in his pipe. In spite of their long day, Ernie was bright-eyed and alert, his pencil hovering at the ready over his notebook. Wookleigh's soldierly pose had relaxed; he sat, as it were, at ease, not forgetting that he was a Chief Constable, nor that a murder had taken place, but remembering that he was not in his own county.

More interestingly, Miller had also relaxed. The death of his host did not appear to cause him any distress. An engineer, as firmly middle-class as was Alec himself, he was an anomalous figure in this house where an anomalous event had occurred. To a detective, anomalies are meat and drink.

However, Alec had no reason to suppose Miller's visit had anything to do with Sir Harold having shot the Australian woman. Since the murderer was as dead as his victim, his motive was of little interest to anyone except their families. The local police ought to have handled it, and would have, no doubt, but for Daisy's presence and the rivalry between Wookleigh and Dryden-Jones.

Still, since Scotland Yard was on the scene, Scotland Yard had better show its paces.

The pipe caught at last. Alec puffed a couple of times, then said, 'Sir Nigel, what do you know of the Gooches?'

'Absolutely nothing whatsoever, my dear fellow. Never heard of them, never seen them before, never exchanged a word with either of them.'

'Mr Miller, you mentioned meeting Mr and Mrs Gooch at the Ravens. That's the pub in the village?'

'Yes, the Three Ravens. We all went down for a drink – good heavens, it was just last night. It seems like a century ago.'

'Dash it,' said Wookleigh, 'I could do with a whisky, but I suppose in the circumstances, helping ourselves would hardly be cricket.'

'"All"?' Alec queried. 'My wife and you, Mr Miller, I gather, and who else?'

'Jack, Miss Tyndall, Miss Gwendolyn. Jack drove Mrs Fletcher. The rest of us walked.'

'Sir Harold didn't go with you?'

'Lord no! We were . . .' He clammed up, then went on, 'No. Nor Lady Tyndall, nor Mrs Yarborough.'

'Mrs Yarborough?'

'The middle sister, Adelaide. She's a widow and she doesn't live at Edge Manor, but she spends a lot of time here.'

'Oh, yes, Daisy mentioned her having a dust-up with her brother which led to the discovery of the bodies.'

'I simply cannot understand why Sir Harold took Mrs Gooch up to his study!' Miller exclaimed.

'Come, come!' said Wookleigh. 'No need to beat about the bush now Mrs Fletcher has gone up. I saw Mrs Gooch, though I didn't speak to her – a nice-looking woman, must have been a stunner in her youth, and I understand she came from Evesham originally. I imagine she was Tyndall's mistress, come back to blackmail him.'

CHAPTER 9

On her way to her bedroom, Daisy passed the door of Lady Tyndall's sitting room. Or rather, she nearly passed it, but a moment's hesitation was her undoing. She paused long enough to hear low voices.

She hadn't expressed her condolences properly, she remembered, having been too busy organizing things. It would be bad manners to trot off to bed as if nothing had happened. She knocked.

After a moment's silence, Babs opened the door, her face impassive. 'Oh, it's you. We were expecting the interrogators. It's Daisy, Mother.'

'I just wanted to—'

'Come in, Daisy.' Lady Tyndall's voice was less feeble than Daisy had expected. Her eyes were reddened, as if she had wept, but putting her feet up for a while seemed to have restored her somewhat, in spite of the shocking news of her husband's death. She reclined on a chintz chaise longue, a shawl around her shoulders and another across her legs.

The room was comfortable, though slightly shabby. Jack sat on the rose-patterned carpet beside his mother, holding one of her hands in both of his. As Daisy stepped in, he started to unfold his long length.

'Don't get up,' said Daisy. 'I don't want to intrude. I just wanted to say how frightfully sorry I am. You must be wishing me at Jericho. I'll move down to the Ravens in the morning – Alec's taken rooms there.'

'Oh no!' Gwen started up from a low cabriole chair. 'You mustn't leave. I don't know what we'd have done without you this evening.'

Daisy glanced at Lady Tyndall, who nodded. 'Yes, do stay, Daisy.'

'You must,' Jack said impulsively. 'We were just saying how glad we are that your husband is in charge, and if you go, we might just as well have a stranger nosing about.'

'Jack!' his mother chided.

He coloured. 'Sorry, that didn't come out quite the way I meant it. But you will stay, won't you, Mrs Fletcher?'

Babs said nothing. Her face remained uncommunicative.

'Do,' Gwen urged. 'I've already told the maids to make up the other bed in your room for your husband. And they've prepared a couple of the unused servants' rooms for his men. I hope that will be all right?'

'It's very kind of you. I'm sure we'll all be more comfortable here.'

'I'll be glad to have the police in the house.' Lady Tyndall shivered and pulled the shawl more closely about her shoulders. 'Surely while they're here, no ghosts will walk.'

'Nonsense, Mother,' said Babs in her abrupt way. 'I don't pretend to guess what drove Father to do it, what skeletons from the past Mr Fletcher is going to dig up, but you can be sure they won't be parading about the house dressed in sheets.'

'I wouldn't put it past Addie's boys, though,' remarked Jack, turning from the fireplace, where he'd just added a log to the flames.

'If they dare!' Babs exclaimed.

'Addie's not going to tell them what happened,' said Gwen, 'so there's no reason it should occur to them.'

'They're bound to find out,' Jack said. 'They can jolly well haunt their own house, though.'

Gwen's brow wrinkled. 'Why should they find out? We only told people there had been an accident.'

'Someone's bound to talk,' Babs said grimly. 'Since they don't know the facts, rumours will be flying by morning.'

'Oh God!' With a groan, Jack hid his face in his hands. 'If only I'd never thought of going to the Ravens. If only I'd never spoken to Gooch. I liked his wife so much, and it's all my fault she's dead.'

'Nonsense!' Gwen's voice was unusually harsh. 'It's no one's fault but Father's. Goodness only knows what she can have said to set off his temper, but you know very well it never takes— took much. All of us suffered from it enough.'

Daisy saw that Lady Tyndall was once again looking quite ill. 'I'm off to bed,' she said. 'I can't tell you how sorry I am. I know Alec will make things as easy as he can. Good night.'

As if there was the slightest chance that any of them would have a good night.

'I'll see you to your room,' said Gwen, and they went out together. Closing the door, she went on. 'Daisy, Martin hasn't been talking about leaving, has he? Not that I'd blame him for putting as much distance between himself and us as possible.'

'I haven't heard him say anything, but I haven't really talked to him. Doesn't he have to go back to work?'

'Yes, he was going to go back to Coventry tomorrow, whether or not he'd talked Father into . . .' Her voice faltered. 'Whether or not he'd persuaded Father to let Jack take the job. I just wish he'd stay.'

'I expect he will if he can.'

'Won't the police want him here?'

'I can't see why they should. What happened can't have anything to do with him, and he doesn't know any more about the Gooches than the rest of us do.'

'No, of course not.'

'If he manages to stay, it'll be for your sake.' Daisy tried to be soothing, if less than entirely truthful. Alec could hardly fail to find out that Miller, as much as Jack, Gwen herself and Babs, had reason to want Sir Harold out of the way.

Mrs Gooch's death was the sticking point. However determined to dispose of the baronet, surely none of them would have murdered an innocent bystander?

Daisy squeezed Gwen's hand. 'Babs is right: it must be rooted in the past.'

'A blackmailing mistress! That would explain the whole thing,' Alec said with relief. Perhaps he and Daisy would be able to go home together tomorrow after all.

Miller frowned. 'I'm not so sure.'

Alec resigned himself. 'You met the Gooches, talked to them. Explain.'

'For one thing, they were well-off. Gooch told us how he'd made his money in the gold fields. Even if he was exaggerating, why come all the way to England on the off chance of being able to wring a few pounds out of an old lover? For all they knew, Sir Harold might have been dead, or penniless. Or widowed, so that he didn't care much if anyone knew he'd strayed as a young man.'

'But he wasn't,' trumpeted Sir Nigel. 'That is, not dead, not destitute, and Lady Tyndall is still with us, I'm happy to say. Mind you, I don't see why he should care so much – wild oats and all that – but obviously he did, since he killed her and himself.'

'No, those points are valid,' Alec said. 'You have an analytical mind, Mr Miller.'

'I'm an engineer.'

'However, it's possible someone here let them know Sir Harold's present situation. It's even more possible they were in hot water in Australia and had to leave. I may have to get in touch with the police down there. I don't suppose you know which part of Australia they came from? They have gold fields all over the place, I believe.'

'He talked about Western Australia. Coolgardie and Perth.'

'Thank you. You said, "For one thing." What else?'

'Mrs Gooch simply wasn't the type. Blackmail is a really foul crime. She may have had her fling in her youth, for all I know, but she was just a very pleasant middle-aged woman. She and Jack got on like a house on fire. Gooch was— is a nice chap, too. Otherwise Jack wouldn't have invited them to the fireworks.'

'Aha!' said Wookleigh triumphantly. 'That's the mark of the confidence trickster, isn't it, Fletcher? Nice chap, pleasant manners, worms his way in, and before you know it, you're in his clutches.'

Alec had to agree. 'True, although I'd hesitate to say that one should therefore mistrust any nice chap with pleasant manners! Who was first to mention the Guy Fawkes party? Had the Gooches heard about it?'

'Yes. As a matter of fact, Mrs Gooch knew about it from her youth. Jack ran into Gooch at the bar and Gooch mentioned that they hoped to join the villagers in the meadow to watch the fireworks from below. He asked Jack if there would be any objection. Jack brought our drinks and said he was going over to the Gooches' table to assure her that they were welcome to watch from the meadow.' Miller paused. 'Actually, it was Mrs Fletcher who suggested inviting them both to our table.'

Alec clenched his teeth, managing not to grind them. He could hardly hold Daisy's undiscriminating friendliness responsible for the tragedy. 'I hope she didn't also suggest inviting them up to the house?'

'No, that was entirely Jack's notion, and Gooch wasn't keen. But Mrs Gooch was thrilled and he gave in.'

'Typical pattern.' Wookleigh stubbed out his cigar and preened his whiskers. 'He disarms suspicion by making an objection, easily brushed aside.'

'It's possible, sir. Or perhaps he had no idea what his wife planned. Or—' Alec stopped as police boots sounded on the stairs.

They all looked, to see Constable Blount hurrying down. Alec went to meet him.

'Sir!' His voice was low but urgent. 'Sergeant Tring says it can't possibly be suicide! Somebody else shot the both of 'em.'

CHAPTER 10

Glad to leave the gruesome scene of the crime, Alec switched off the lights and descended the stairs from the late baronet's study to the room below.

Tom Tring had already dusted the polished oak banisters for fingerprints. He had found only a few blurred smudges, probably made by gloves. Anyone coming in from outside on that cold night would have worn gloves. The billiard/gun room and the study were not much warmer than outdoors, as they had not been prepared to welcome guests, so no fires had been lit. The female victim still had her gloves on. Sir Harold had taken his off. They lay on the bloody desk, beside the blood-splashed telephone, to the left of his slumped body.

The pistol was a Webley & Scott .32 automatic pistol, like those the Metropolitan Police had used since the Siege of Sidney Street in 1911. It lay to the baronet's right, near his bare right hand. Tom had photographed it in place and replaced it in its original position after checking it for dabs.

The lack of both fingerprints and blood spatters on the gun was sufficient to cast doubt on the suicide theory. The fountain pen clenched in Sir Harold's right hand was conclusive proof that he had not shot himself.

No message from the dead offered a clue. The sheet of paper beneath his head was soaked with blood, but he had died before he started writing.

Following Alec down the stairs, Tom pointed. 'French windows to the terrace not locked, Chief. Key left in the lock. Likewise the gun cabinet, over there. No dabs on the key or the cabinet, just smudges.'

Behind him, Piper said in disgust, 'Everyone in gloves. Pity it wasn't a nice warm evening.'

Alec stopped in front of the glass-fronted cabinet. 'Great Scott, he had half a dozen of the damn things!'

'Seems a bit excessive, don't it, Chief? You can't exackly call 'em sporting guns.'

'On the contrary. Besides being police weapons, many officers carried them in the war as a second sidearm. He might have used one or two for target shooting, I suppose, but six . . .'

'All oiled not too long ago, and polished. One other loaded, besides the murder weapon.'

'Blount?'

'Edge Manor isn't properly in my district, sir,' said the local bobby nervously.

'I'm not holding you responsible, just asking if you know anything about this.'

'Only what I've heard in the village, sir, and I didn't come but a couple o' years back. Master Jack was too young to be called up and Squire never was a military man, but he was very keen on the Volunteer Force, besides they did do a bit of target shooting, like you said. And like you'd expect of country gentlemen, they'd go out after rabbits, pigeons, partridge, pheasant and such, and vermin. What I've heard is they're both good shots, and Miss Tyndall, too.'

'Miss Tyndall?' Alec was surprised. In his experience, women and firearms seldom mixed.

'Miss Barbara, the oldest daughter. Very keen on farming, she is, and don't turn a hair at shooting rooks and jackdaws and jays and suchlike that get into the crops.'

'Thank you, I'll bear it in mind. But first I think we'd better concentrate on the Gooches. It seems to me they hold the key to this puzzle. If we knew what brought them to Didmarsh, possibly intending to try to infiltrate Edge Manor, we might have some notion what this is all about.'

'All I know, sir, is they turned up yest'day morning and took a room at the Ravens. Very pleasant couple, Dawson – that's the landlord – told me. No side, though it was obvious they were worth a bob or two. He didn't mention any partickler interest in the Manor nor the fireworks, but then, I didn't ask.'

'No, why should you? You can do that tomorrow. Now, Tom, you'd better find a telephone other than the one up in the study. First make sure someone is sending a police surgeon and a mortuary van. Where would be the closest place with such facilities, Constable? Gloucester?'

'Cheltenham, I should think, sir,' said Blount doubtfully. 'There's a sergeant at Chipping Campden, but it's a small place. I'd ring up Evesham if so be I had the need in my district, which I hope and pray I never may.'

'I'll try Cheltenham, Chief.'

'On second thoughts, if Sir Nigel is still here, see if he's willing to let us use Evesham's facilities, and if he'll square it with the Gloucestershire CC. He's been helpful so far, but there's rivalry in the air, and I don't know if it's with the Gloucestershire force or just with Whatsisname, the Lord Lieutenant.'

'Dryden-Jones,' Piper put in.

'Right, Chief,' said Tom. 'These county-boundary cases are a proper pain.'

'We'll need the Evesham police to make enquiries about Mrs Gooch's past, too.' Alec took the passport from his pocket and opened it. 'Here's her maiden name in their joint passport. Too late for that tonight. Here you are, Tom. Get on to the Yard. I want enquiries telegraphed to the police of Western Australia, Perth and – what was the other town Miller mentioned, Ernie?'

'Coolgardie, Chief.'

'That's it.'

'Got it.' Tom went out, moving more heavily than was his wont. It had been a very long day, as had yesterday.

'Let's go and sit down in the next room,' Alec said to the two young constables. They followed Tom as far as the dining room, now cleared of the remains of the interrupted feast. 'I need all you know about the Tyndalls, Blount, fact and rumour, but make sure you let me know which is which.'

Blount's report, though based more on hearsay than observation, gave Alec some idea of how to approach the family. A picture emerged of Sir Harold as a bully who ruled his family not so much with a rod of iron as with explosions of temper. His family were the only ones to suffer, however. The local gentry regarded him as a cordial gentleman and good neighbour, and he treated his tenants and servants well enough.

Unfortunately, the servants had all been too busy preparing for the Bonfire Night festivities to relay the latest gossip to their relatives in the village, who might have passed it on to Blount. Alec would have to count on Daisy to tell him who had most recently suffered the force of the baronet's displeasure. He wished he hadn't sent her off to bed without asking a few more questions, but he didn't want to disturb her, in her condition.

Nonetheless, he wanted a word with the Tyndalls while they were off balance. The only question was whether he should see them singly or all together, and with or without the mysterious Martin Miller, about whom Blount knew next to nothing.

He led the way through the deserted drawing room. Glasses and plates had been cleared away, but the room was still in some disarray from the influx of diners. The servants must have dealt with the worst of the mess and then gone off duty. They would be a source of information about the family, of course, but Tom was the one to tackle them. Servants felt more comfortable with him, females in particular, despite his undoubted attachment to the equally mountainous Mrs Tring.

In the entrance hall, Miller stood by the fireplace with a pale young woman, her hands clasped in his. Lost in earnest conversation, they didn't hear Alec step from the drawing room carpet onto the oak boards of the hall, but the constables' boots were not to be ignored.

The woman glanced round, hastily withdrawing her hands and stepping back. Miller came forward.

'Chief Inspector!' he said with the heartiness of a not

naturally hearty man caught in an embarrassing situation. 'Sir Nigel went with your sergeant to the telephone, in case his authority was needed. They're in the butler's pantry. Would you like me to show you the way?'

'No, thank you. I'm sure DS Tring and the Chief Constable can manage between them.' Alec looked at the young woman, his eyebrows raised in enquiry.

Miller introduced him with obvious reluctance. 'Detective Chief Inspector Fletcher. Miss Gwendolyn Tyndall. Miss Gwen is dreadfully upset by . . . what's happened. Can't it wait till morning?'

'It's all right, Martin.' Gwen had blotted her eyes with a handkerchief, but they were red-rimmed. 'Daisy warned me that Mr Fletcher would want to see the family tonight. How do you do.' She shook hands with Alec.

So this was Daisy's friend, and she appeared to be involved with Miller. Blount had passed on hints that the engineer might be courting the squire's youngest daughter, but Alec had hoped the rumours were unfounded. He suppressed a sigh, foreseeing complications. 'I'm afraid Daisy's right, Miss Gwendolyn. I should prefer to talk to you all while your memories are fresh.'

'My sister Adelaide went home, but the rest are upstairs in Mother's sitting room. Would you like to come up?'

'Not just yet, thank you. Perhaps we could sit down here while I ask you what you know of the Gooches?'

'Yes, of course, not that there's much to tell. Do have a seat.' She dropped wearily onto the sofa. 'Martin?' Her voice held an appeal.

With a somewhat defiant glance at Alec, Miller sat beside her, leaving a discreet space between them.

In a low voice, Alec said to Blount, 'Go up to the landing. I don't want any of the others interrupting.'

'Sir!' Blount saluted and tramped off.

Alec and Piper sat down, as far apart as the arrangement of chairs allowed. Piper selected a fresh pencil from the collection in his breast pocket and opened his notebook.

'Mr Miller has already informed us of the meeting with Mr and Mrs Gooch at the inn,' said Alec. 'I doubt I can add anything.'

'He's given us the briefest of accounts, and in any case, what you noticed is probably different from what he noticed. Mr Miller, you may stay, but I must ask you not to speak. If you disagree with anything Miss Gwendolyn says, or have anything to add, let me know afterwards. All right, let's start with whose idea it was to go to the Three Ravens.'

'Babs, I suppose, in a way. At least, she had arranged to meet a couple of tenant farmers.'

'Do you know why?'

'To discuss something to do with the orchards. Something about planting pear trees, I think.'

'I meant, why should Miss Tyndall meet these men at a public house rather than having them come here to Edge Manor?'

'She ... They ... I suppose it was more convenient for them.'

Alec let her hesitation and the unlikely explanation pass – for the moment – while noting both as indicating a desire to protect her eldest sister. 'Who suggested the rest of you going with Miss Tyndall?'

'I don't know. Jack and Martin and Daisy had all agreed when I first heard about it.'

Miller looked as if he was about to speak. Alec frowned him down.

'You walked down to the village?'

'Jack drove Daisy, because of . . . because of the walk back up the hill.'

'They must have arrived first, then.'

'Only just. The footpath is much shorter than round by the road. In fact, Jack popped in to see if we had arrived already. He was just coming out when Babs and Martin and I got there.'

'Then you all went in together. What happened next?'

'I don't know. It's hard to remember, when so much has happened since!'

'Was the taproom busy?'

'Fairly. Babs's farmers were already there, and she went straight to their table. I think Jack went over and offered them a drink, then came back to see what we wanted before he went up to the bar. It's not the sort of place that has waiters. We sat by the fire. Daisy was a bit chilled from sitting in the open car. She doesn't seem to have taken any harm from it, though,' Gwen reassured Alec anxiously. 'She was wonderful tonight. I don't know how we'd have managed without her.'

From the corner of his eye, Alec saw Piper's smirk, quickly hidden. To give Daisy her due, she did appear to have made herself useful, to both the family and the police. The trouble would start when his investigation began to step on the toes of people she liked.

'What brought the Gooches to your attention?'

'I didn't notice them at all. I had my back to their table. Mr Gooch must have passed us when he went to the bar, but I didn't *notice* him. Then Jack brought our drinks and said something about meeting an Australian at the bar and wanting to assure the chap's wife that they were welcome to watch the fireworks from the meadow. And how I wish they had gone to the meadow! Then Father wouldn't have met her. None of this would have happened.'

Alec let this pass. The longer the family and Miller and Gooch thought the police believed Sir Harold had shot Mrs Gooch and himself, the better. Only the murderer would be on the defensive.

That was assuming one of them was the murderer. If not, fifty or sixty people spread out across two counties would have to be investigated, quite apart from the possibility that someone not invited had taken advantage of the party to bump off the baronet. The thought was daunting – and still left Mrs Gooch to be explained.

'Did your brother go straight away to speak to the Gooches?'

'Not quite. Daisy wanted to meet them – she thought the opinions of Australian visitors about England might be useful for an article.' Gwen started to look at Miller, then changed her mind and went on, 'So Jack invited them to join us.'

'Had he met them before?'

'No, of course not. They'd only been in England for a week or two, and they arrived in Didmarsh that day, yesterday, I gathered. We none of us knew them from Adam. But Jack got on swimmingly with Mrs Gooch, and Mr Gooch was quite entertaining with his stories of the gold fields and the— what did he call the wilderness, Martin?'

'The outback. We talked about flying also, the prospects for air travel . . . Oh, sorry, you don't want to hear that.'

'I do. I want to hear anything and everything about the Gooches. But not from you at the moment, if you don't mind, Mr Miller. Miss Gwendolyn—'

'Gwen, please. I've known Daisy forever.'

Daisy's involvement in a case tended to lead to Alec's being on Christian-name terms with a suspect or two, which made it difficult to keep a proper distance. He compromised.

'Miss Gwen, did you gather why the Gooches should have chosen to spend part of their holiday in England in this rather out-of-the-way corner of the country?'

'Well, Mrs Gooch did come from Evesham, and I dare say she has— had relatives there she wanted to visit. But now that you mention it, it is a bit odd. I mean, our Guy Fawkes celebration is a big event to us and to the villagers, but even if people in Evesham have heard of it, we don't get crowds turning up in charabancs, or anything like that. I can't imagine why she should have remembered about it for twenty years and wanted to see the fireworks so badly that she'd put off seeing her family.'

'Do you know that she had family in the district?'

'No, I don't recall their mentioning any. But why else should they have come here? Surely not just for the fireworks. Oh, it's all such a muddle!'

Since Gwen apparently had no facts to report, Alec dropped that unproductive line of conjecture. 'You implied that Mrs Gooch went out to Australia twenty years ago. Is that what she or her husband told you?'

'Not exactly. Something he said gave me that impression. Do you remember, Martin?'

Before replying, Miller looked to Alec, who nodded permission to speak. 'Gooch said she arrived in Australia the year after the pipeline went in, in 1904. That's twenty years ago, of course, but it wasn't clear whether 1904 was the year the pipeline was completed or the year he met her.'

'That's right. She had some money – a "stake", he called it – and she was looking for an investment, just when he needed capital for his business.'

'Ah, so it was a marriage of convenience?'

'It may have started that way. Who knows? But they seemed a very affectionate couple. That's what makes it all so much worse! I shall never be able to forget his face when we told him.' Gwen's eyes welled with tears. 'It *must* have been an accident, Father shooting her!'

As Alec felt for a handkerchief, Miller produced one first.

'That's enough for tonight,' he said angrily. 'I'll tell you anything else I can, Fletcher, but Gwen's had enough.'

Alec let her go. He would get more impartial information about the Tyndalls from Daisy, perhaps even from Miller except where Gwen was concerned.

'I'll go up with you to meet the rest of your family,' he said, standing up. 'Mr Miller, perhaps you wouldn't mind staying down here so that I can have a word with you afterwards? It's getting rather late, I know . . .'

'That's all right. It doesn't look as if I'll be dashing back to work tomorrow.'

'Martin, I hope you'll stay, but won't they be annoyed when you don't turn up?'

'I'll ring up in the morning. They won't be pleased, but you needn't worry that I'll lose my job. They can't do without me. Besides, I'll tell them I'm on the brink of hiring Jack.'

A sudden stillness fell between the two. Gwen looked horrified. Miller looked as if he devoutly wished those innocuous words unsaid. Alec hoped one or the other would say something to give him a clue to the significance of the moment, but after a pause laden with silent meaning, all Gwen said, in an unsteady voice, was, 'Good night, then.'

Miller's tone was wooden. 'I'm sorry. Good night.'

Alec and Ernie Piper followed Gwen up the stairs. As they reached the landing, PC Blount came to attention and saluted. Alec sent him downstairs.

Gwen showed them to the door of Lady Tyndall's sitting room. 'You don't mind introducing yourselves, do you? I don't think I can cope . . .'

'That's quite all right. I hope you manage to get some sleep.'

'Thank you.' Gwen became the hostess. 'That's Daisy's and your room, the last door on the left, with the bathroom et cetera opposite. I hope you have everything you need, you and your men. Good night.'

She returned down the three steps to the landing. Alec knocked on Lady Tyndall's door.

CHAPTER 11

'Miss Tyndall?'

'Yes.' The woman who opened the sitting room door regarded Alec with mixed hostility and resignation. Even at this time of night, a restless energy emanated from her, an intensity sharpened by her mannish crop – and her reputation as a good shot. Her face showed no signs of having wept. 'I take it you're Daisy's Chief Inspector.'

Alec heard a muffled snicker behind him. With an effort, he managed not to turn and glare at Piper. 'I'm sorry to intrude at such a time, but I'm afraid I have a few questions to put to you all.'

'Need you pester my mother tonight? She's stayed up to see you, but she's in no condition to answer a lot of questions.'

'I'll disturb Lady Tyndall as little as I possibly can, I promise you.'

'All right, I suppose you'd better come in. Mother, Detective Chief Inspector Fletcher.'

A lanky youth jumped up and came forward eagerly. 'Mr Fletcher! You'll sort it out in no time, I know. I'm Jack

Tyndall, by the way. I can't begin to tell you how terrible I feel about having invited the Gooches to the house, but if I at least knew why—'

'Jack, you can bare your soul later. Let Mother have her say and get to bed.'

'Sorry, Mother!' Jack turned back to the woman lying on the daybed beside the chair he had just left. He stooped to kiss her cheek with obvious affection. 'You go first.'

Lady Tyndall smiled up at him, all his affection returned, and more. 'Thank you, darling. Your turn will come.' The smile disappeared as she held out her hand to Alec. 'How do you do, Mr Fletcher. I wish we might have made your acquaintance under happier circumstances.'

Faced with an unanswerable statement and a hand that looked far too fragile to shake, Alec bowed and took refuge in the well-tried formula: 'I must apologize for troubling you at such a time, Lady Tyndall. I'll make it as short as possible tonight, though there will undoubtedly be more questions tomorrow, when the situation becomes clearer. First of all, I must clarify the position of Mr and Mrs Gooch. Had you ever met either of them?'

She gazed down at her hands, now tightly clasped in her lap, as she replied, her voice low but steady. 'Harold and I greeted them at the door when they arrived, of course. It was a little awkward, as we hadn't invited them and they were obviously – to be honest – not our kind of people, not the sort of people we would ever have known well enough to invite. But Jack explained that they were visiting from Australia, just for a short time, and he'd wanted to offer them a treat. Young people today seem to see things differently from the way I was brought up, don't they?'

It was a rhetorical question, but Alec nodded agreement, deeply grateful that Daisy was one of those who saw things differently. 'Did your son's explanation alter the way you and Sir Harold felt about the Gooches?' he asked.

'As far as I was concerned, Jack was at liberty to invite anyone he chose. I have to admit that his father clearly didn't see it in quite that light, but I couldn't possibly have guessed he was so furious as to ... to vent his anger on the poor woman.' She buried her face in her trembling hands.

'That's enough,' Miss Tyndall said roughly. 'Jack, take Mr Fletcher downstairs, or up to the schoolroom or somewhere. I'll come and find you in a few minutes.'

'Right-oh. Mother . . .' At a loss for words of comfort, Jack touched Lady Tyndall's shoulder, then turned to Alec. He looked like an overgrown schoolboy summoned to his headmaster's office and unsure as to whether or not his offence merited six of the best.

'Upstairs.' Alec preferred to talk to the new baronet without the complicating presence of Miller or the Chief Constable. 'Take your time, Miss Tyndall.'

Already at the door to the bedroom, summoning a maid, she gave Alec an abrupt nod of acknowledgement. In silence, Jack led the way out to the passage, down the three intrusive steps to the landing and up the stairs to the second floor. He opened the nearest door, clicked on the electric light and ushered Alec and Piper through.

'It's a bit ratty,' he said apologetically, 'but it's our own. Except when my sister Addie's hell-born babes are here, and they prefer raising Cain out of doors, thank heaven. This is where we did our lessons until we all went away to school. The children who came for the fireworks tonight had their supper up here, so mind you don't sit in spilled jelly or cake crumbs. The servants won't have had a chance to clean properly.'

The large room was over the entrance hall, to judge by curtained windows to the south and west. It was furnished with a battered, ink-stained table surrounded with battered ladder-back chairs, as well as a massive Victorian sofa and several easy chairs in crimson plush worn thin on seats and arms. Jack went over to the fireplace and poked disconsolately at the moribund embers.

'I feel as if the whole world has gone mad,' he confided. 'Or perhaps just my father? I simply cannot see that inviting the Gooches was such a terrible thing to do, and if it was, why blame her for it? He *must* have run mad!'

'Come and sit down, Mr Tyndall.' Alec took the chair at the head of the table, Piper having tipped it and brushed crumbs off the seat. 'Or should it be Sir John?'

'Not until after the funeral, Mother said. As though I wanted the bloody title! I suppose you're going to ask whether I saw or heard anything. Isn't that the form? Well, I can tell you, even if it hadn't been for the dark and the fireworks exploding, I wouldn't have noticed. I was trying to keep an eye on Reggie and Adrian – Addie's boys. They were obviously ripe for mischief. When aren't they? But they gave me the slip, and I'll swear they pinched the missing rockets.'

'That was the cause of your argument with Mrs Yarborough on returning to the house after the fireworks?'

'With Addie, yes, and that's why I went to look for Father. My God, I wish I hadn't found him!'

'Tell me, please, just exactly how it all happened.'

'Right-oh, I'll try. It was all because of those blasted

nephews of mine. As soon as I discovered some of the rockets were missing, I knew they'd pinched them. They—'

'Just a minute. How did you know the rockets were missing? Were you lighting the fuses?'

'No, I had to stay on the top terrace, doing the polite, asking old ladies if they were warm enough, that sort of thing. We can't just stop inviting people when they get on in years, and there're always a few who don't have the sense— But you don't want to hear about that. Biddle, our gardener, did the setting off, but Father and Miller and I spent most of the day setting them up. Reggie and Adrian hung about – supposed to be making themselves useful. That's when I caught them trying to sneak off with a couple of Roman candles.'

'Which is why you suspected them in the theft of the rockets.'

'Good-enough reason, don't you think? I took the Roman candles off them, but I didn't let Father find out, because he was in a good mood at that point and I didn't want to spoil it. The point is, I knew exactly what was meant to be fired off when. So when the beginning of the grand finale turned out to be less than grand, I dashed down to the bottom terrace to see what was going on. I assumed Biddle had mucked it up and I was afraid he'd bungle the rest.'

'Did anyone see you go?'

Jack grinned. 'Yes, Mrs Fletcher, actually. I was talking to her when things went wrong.' He sobered. 'Not that it seems frightfully important, considering what happened afterwards.'

'Did you speak to the gardener?'

'Yes, he said— I say, is this what you call an alibi? But that means . . .' In some ways still a boy, Sir John Tyndall was nevertheless no fool. Shaken, he stared at Alec. 'Oh Lord, you don't believe my father shot Mrs Gooch and then himself, do you? What happened?'

'We can't be sure. It's still possible Sir Harold shot Mrs Gooch, but we do know that he didn't shoot himself.'

'Then why did you let Mother assume he did?' He jumped up. 'I'm going to tell her!'

'I can't stop you, but please reconsider. Lady Tyndall has had a severe shock. Do you really want to present her with another so soon by telling her Sir Harold was himself murdered?' Alec paused. 'And there's still the question, you know, of why he was in his study with Mrs Gooch.'

Jack slumped back on to his chair. 'Yes. You're right, of course.'

'Let's go back to Tuesday. What made you decide to visit the Three Ravens that evening?'

'It wasn't so much a decision, more of an invitation. You see, Miller doesn't care much for sherry or cocktails, and if I'd got hold of a bottle of beer for him, Father would have taken it as yet another reason to sneer at him. So I suggested going to the Ravens after dinner for a pint. Well, just then Mrs Fletcher came in and heard me, so it seemed only polite to invite her to go with us. Babs was going down anyway, to meet some chaps, and I knew Gwen would go along if Mrs Fletcher cared to come.'

'I understand I have to thank you for giving my wife a lift in your car while the others walked.'

'Oh, it was nothing. She wasn't sure about walking back up the hill because of . . . you know.' Blushing, Jack hurried on. 'We got there just a minute or two before the others.'

'And you went straight into the pub.'

'*I* did. To see if the rest had arrived. Perhaps I shouldn't have left Mrs Fletcher alone outside? I thought she might feel uncomfortable being the only woman inside. The Ravens isn't a haunt of vice or anything, but it's usually just men in the tap. And she agreed. I say, she is a brick, isn't she? There we all were, falling to pieces, and she kept her head and told us all what to do.'

'I'm glad she was able to help.' Alec avoided looking at Piper, sure he was grinning, hoping he had the grace to hide his grin behind his notebook. At least he could be relied upon not to write down the suspect's adulation of Daisy.

'It was just like that poem, the one they make you learn by heart at school. "If", it's called. Kipling, I think. "If you can keep your head when all about you are losing theirs and blaming it on you . . ." Not that we did blame Mrs Fletcher, of course.'

Unlike Superintendent Crane and the AC, Alec thought. 'How long were you inside the pub on that first foray?'

'Just a minute or two. I glanced around to see if the others were there, said hello to the fellows at the bar, and told the chaps waiting for Babs that she was on her way. Let's see . . . Oh, then I asked Dawson, the landlord, if he would build up the fire a bit because of the ladies coming in from the cold. That's about it, as far as I remember.'

'Did you speak to the Gooches?'

'Not then. I can't say I even really noticed them, just saw in a vague sort of way that a couple of strangers were having dinner at the other end of the room. The Ravens doesn't have a separate dining room.'

'You didn't recognize either of them, I take it.'

'No, how should I? It was his first trip to England, and she told me she hadn't been home since she went out in 1903, when I was a mere babe in arms. Even Babs was only ten or eleven. I don't suppose I'd ever have given them a second thought if Mr Gooch hadn't spoken to me when I was at the bar getting drinks.'

'He spoke first? What did he say?'

'Something on the lines of "Am I right in thinking you're a Tyndall of Edge Manor, mate?" I've met Australians, at Cambridge, and I knew at once that was where he was from.'

'Can you describe his manner?'

'"His manner"?' Jack said blankly.

Alec racked his tired brain to come up with adjectives that might describe a con man or a blackmailer making first contact with a prospective victim. 'Hearty, smooth, furtive, confidential, uh . . .'

'Bright and breezy,' Piper put in, 'or reserved, mysterious, ominous, menacing.' He must have been studying a diction-ary, determined to match Tom Tring's unexpectedly erudite vocabulary, Alec guessed, amused.

'Good Lord, no. Nothing like that. He seemed embar-rassed. Nervous and apologetic, and as if he'd rather be somewhere else. He said his wife used to live in Evesham and had heard of our Guy Fawkes fireworks; would we mind if they went to the meadow to watch. That's down below, where the village and farm people go to watch the show and the bonfire.'

'He didn't push for an invitation to the house?'

'On the contrary. He said his wife would be very grateful. They weren't "flash" folk, he said, and they didn't want to push in where they weren't wanted. Of course, after that, I felt I ought personally to assure Mrs Gooch it was perfectly all right.'

Which was exactly the result a confidence trickster would hope for, but it didn't sound like a blackmailer's approach.

Jack, hitherto a model of apparent frankness, appeared to be awaiting the next question with some uneasiness. Alec remembered that both Miller and Gwen had hesitated over this part of the evening's events. But Jack's discomfort could be caused by a gentlemanly reluctance to disclose Daisy's part in furthering the Gooches' acquaintance with the Tyndalls. Alec decided to wait until he had heard Daisy's side of the story before pressing the issue.

'Tell me what was said when you went to the Gooches' table.'

Relieved, Jack said, 'I told Mrs Gooch they were very welcome to watch the fireworks, and she thanked me. I asked if they'd care to come and have a drink with us. She said that was a "bonzer" idea. Then she laughed and added, "as Jimmy would say".'

'She laughed? She wasn't "embarrassed, nervous and apologetic", like her husband?'

'On the contrary, she was happy and excited.' Jack seemed puzzled. 'More as if she were going to Buckingham Palace to hobnob with royalty than across the taproom of a country inn to hobnob with the offspring of a country baronet.'

'And Gooch?'

'Was *not* happy. Thought it wasn't a good idea. Didn't want to intrude. But she persuaded him and they came over. As far as I could see, Mrs Fletcher and Gwen and Miller pretty much put him at his ease. Mrs Gooch was mostly talking to me.'

'What did the two of you talk about?'

'Actually, mostly I was blathering on to her. She said she had three sons at school in Perth and she'd like to take them stories of life at an English school, if I wouldn't mind telling her about my school days. And she asked if I'd been to university, as her eldest is considering attending the college in Perth. And now – Oh God! – she's dead and they'll never see her again!' He dropped his forehead on his folded arms on the table, taking deep breaths as though to fight back tears.

If it was a performance, it was a very convincing performance. All the same, Jack had to top the list of suspects, if only because he stood to inherit from his father the title and presumably the estate.

With a last shuddering gasp, Jack sat up. 'Sorry. I'm all right now. It's just that I liked her awfully. It's too horrible!'

'Murder is always horrible.' Alec was sure he sounded sententious, but it was true nevertheless. 'Are you ready to continue?'

'Yes. What happened next? Babs finished her business and came over, and Dawson called for last orders. I can't remember which happened first, but we all decided to have one last drink. Oh, I know – Babs said it was time to go, and I said no hurry, we could all squeeze into my bus to drive home. It's a two-seater but there's a dickey. My sisters are on the skinny side and Gw— one of them could have sat on Miller's knees. But Mrs Gooch said her husband could run the ladies up in their hire car.'

'Did he object?'

'Not at all. It was jolly decent of them. That was when I had what seemed a brilliant idea at the time,' Jack said bitterly. 'I hadn't had all that much to drink, but Dawson's home-brewed draught is pretty potent stuff, and I suppose I must have been a bit tiddly.'

'You invited the Gooches up to the house for the fireworks party.'

'Precisely. He didn't want to accept, but she begged him and he gave in. And she went upstairs smiling. Smiling!'

CHAPTER 12

Piper sighed. 'D'you reckon it's even worth checking all these people he says he spoke to, Chief? If they remember at all, they won't none of them know exactly what time it was, in the dark and all. Half an hour's long enough for him to have a word or two with a lot of people and still follow his dad upstairs and shoot him.'

'And then go back to the terrace, speak to Daisy, dash down several flights of stairs to check on the missing rockets, dash up again, and quarrel with his sister before ostensibly going in search of his father. A bit tight, but he might have managed it.'

'Or maybe he shot them when he went looking?'

'I doubt it. Wookleigh said the doctor thought they'd been dead twenty minutes to half an hour when he saw them. And several people knew where young Tyndall was going, remember. We'll have to find out how long he was gone.'

'Mrs Fletcher'll know.'

'No doubt,' Alec said dryly. 'I wonder whether shots in the study could be heard in the dining room. We may have to . . . Hello, Miss Tyndall.'

'Jack says you've finished with him.' Babs's manner was as abrupt as her entrance.

Jack had left barely a couple of minutes ago. Alec suspected he had gone straight to Gwen's room and found Babs there already. In a situation like this, it was virtually impossible to keep suspects from talking to one another before they talked to the police. At least telling Babs to take her time had allowed him to interview Jack alone, for all the good it had done him. Unfortunately, Jack would have told his sisters that their father had not shot himself.

'Thank you for coming. Do sit down, won't you? I hope you left Lady Tyndall resting comfortably.'

'Her maid is caring for her. Mendicott has been with Mother for twenty years and knows what's best for her. What do you want to know?'

Alec took her through the visit to the Three Ravens, learning nothing new. She had spent only a few minutes with the Gooches and had paid them little attention after discovering they knew nothing of farming in Western Australia. She thought it stupid of Jack to invite them to the house, knowing he was bound to set their father's back up.

'I understand you're keen on farming, Miss Tyndall. In fact, you went to the pub to meet a couple of farmers on business, correct?'

'What of it?'

'I just wondered,' Alec said mildly, 'why you didn't have them come up to the house.'

'I can't see that it has anything to do with your investigation.' Babs's voice was cold. 'But as it happens, we were discussing planting a new variety of pear trees, and my father was not only uninterested in innovation, he did not care for what he called my "meddling" on the estate. Now he's gone, Jack will let me run things as I think best.'

'So, you see, my question had everything to do with my investigation.'

'My dear Mr Fletcher, I hardly think murdering my father would be an appropriate method of saving myself the inconvenience of his tantrums. I haven't paid them any heed since . . .' A shadow crossed her face. 'For a number of years. In fact, he was not particularly interested in improving the estate; he just disapproved of a mere female taking charge. He'd have liked to hand the whole thing over to Jack.'

'If not the estate, what *was* Sir Harold interested in?'

'Guns and fireworks, and being Squire in a line of squires unbroken for centuries, with all the peasants tugging their forelocks and the County coming to call. I don't say he didn't run the place well enough before the war, but then he lost interest.'

'Guns.' Alec let the word hang heavily between them.

Babs grimaced. 'Hoist with his own petard, I take it. Which . . . ? One of the Webleys, I imagine. He kept a couple loaded.'

'Why?'

'Every now and then, he'd have a sudden urge to go and take a few potshots at a target, and he never did like waiting.'

'And why did he have the Webley & Scott automatic pistols? Half a dozen of them! That's normally a military or police weapon.'

'He was convinced the Jerries were going to invade by sending submarines up the Severn to Gloucester and marching on the Midlands. He joined the Volunteer Force, wangled automatics for all of us, and insisted on teaching us to use them. Odd, isn't it, that he considered his daughters should be able to shoot to kill but he refused to believe that I'm capable of competently managing the estate. But then, consistency – like patience – was never one of his virtues.'

'You're very frank about your differences with your father, Miss Tyndall.'

'Why shouldn't I be?' she asked indifferently. 'I didn't kill him.'

'Have you any suggestions to offer as to who might have?'

'Frankly, I'd say you're looking in the wrong direction. Isn't it more likely that the Australian wanted to get rid of his wife and found the perfect opportunity to make it look as if someone else had shot her?'

'It's possible, certainly. But it wouldn't explain the biggest mystery: why Mrs Gooch was with Sir Harold in his study in the first place. Any ideas on that?'

'No.'

To Alec, the uncompromising monosyllable suggested its opposite, but this was not the time to delve into any theories she might be persuaded to offer. He took her through her version of the evening's events.

She had reluctantly shared the duties of hostess with Gwen and Lady Tyndall. Parties were not much to her taste, but she had spoken to a great many guests, making sure they were well fed and supplied with such warm clothing as they had foolishly failed to bring with them for the fireworks. She hadn't noticed the Gooches' arrival. Later, she had been surprised to notice her father speaking briefly to Mrs Gooch. He would certainly not have said anything inflammatory to a guest, however unwelcome, but she had been too far away to have any idea what he did say. Nor had she noted who was near them at the time, and Sir Harold's back had been to her, so she hadn't observed his expression.

'Though he wouldn't have been outright rude, I doubt it was friendly,' she said. 'He called Mr Miller, who is infinitely more *comme il faut*, a counter jumper.'

Alec wondered briefly what Piper was making of the French phrase – and just where on the *comme-il-faut* scale he himself rated.

Miss Tyndall had not seen her father, Mrs Gooch, or anyone else leave the terrace during the show to enter the house. Having decided that in the dark no one would notice if she took a rest from the duties of hospitality, she made no effort to talk to people.

'I watched the fireworks, a particularly good show this year, thanks, doubtless, to the redoubtable Mr Miller. There was a set of coloured fountains – quite early on. I glanced around to see the effect of blue light on people's faces, and I saw my nephews, looking like two veritable imps of hell, sneaking towards the terrace steps. I collared 'em. Had to bribe them with a promise of sparklers not to go down. They seem not to have kept their side of the bargain, unless they pinched the rockets earlier.'

'Didn't the "collaring" attract any attention?'

'Daisy was standing near the top of the steps. I had a word with her. Then I went to find the sparklers. Jack had left a box of them by the French windows to the drawing room. We always hope the children will forget about them, because it's a beastly nuisance. Someone has to stay outside to supervise them when their parents have gone in for supper, and then shepherd them upstairs for their own supper.'

'Who did that?'

'My job this year. Anyway, I found the damn things and came back out to watch the rest of the show. Then at the end I stood at the French windows with Gwen to hand them out. She went in. I stayed out to make sure the children didn't brand one another, or themselves. Then I brought them in.'

'You shooed them up here, up the main stairs? Did you come into the schoolroom?'

'No, their nannies were waiting to keep order, and by then, they were all eager to get their grubby little paws on the feast.'

'And then you went back, down the main stairs into the entrance hall?'

'That's right. Most people had already collected their plates of food and were settling down. I was hungry, so I just dashed through to the dining room.'

'Where you found . . .'

'Jack and Addie at it hammer and tongs over Reggie and Adrian's misdeeds. Being pretty fed up with the brats, I'm afraid I joined in. Then Mother came in and pointed out that we were behaving as badly as the boys. I went through to the drawing room to do my duty by our guests. After a bit, Jack and Addie came and asked if I'd seen Father, which I hadn't. Jack went off, but I made Addie stay and help me show the flag. She spends so much time here, I don't see why she shouldn't pull her weight as a daughter of the house.'

'Your father taught Mrs – Yarborough, isn't it? – to shoot also?'

'Mrs Stephen Yarborough. Yes, but she was hopeless and dropped it as soon as she married Stephen. I expect you know he was killed in the war?' Her lips pressed together as if in remembered pain.

Her sister's or her own? Alec wondered. It seemed irrelevant to the case, but he made a mental note. 'I gathered she's a widow. I'll have to see her tomorrow, and talk to her sons, too.'

'Good luck! You'll need it.'

'Thank you. If you wouldn't mind telling me what happened this evening, what you did and saw and heard, after your brother left you?'

Babs complied. Jack had returned after a while, with Gwen, both looking frightful. They told her what had happened. Acting on Daisy's advice, they had scattered to explain quietly to the guests that an accident had occurred and the police had been sent for. They had apologized for cutting short the party. As they knew everyone and Gwen had the guest list, they hadn't considered it necessary to take names and addresses.

Having seen off the last inquisitive guest, Babs had gone with Gwen and Jack to break the news to her mother. At that point, Babs clammed up.

After an unpromising start, she had turned out to be a cooperative witness. Alec didn't want to press her, not at this stage. 'Mrs Stephen Yarborough had already left?' he asked.

'Addie? Yes. We have her mama-in-law to thank for that. We didn't tell her what had actually happened – what we thought had happened – but she started to get hysterical anyway. Mrs Yarborough simply swept her and the brats off home, bless the woman. Gwen's going to have to tell Addie the news. I'll be damned if I'm going to.'

'That's something I can do for you,' Alec said, making it sound like a favour, not a normal, if unpleasant, part of his job.

'Will you?'

'I'll have to see Mrs Stephen Yarborough first thing tomorrow anyway.'

'Depends what you call first thing.' Babs gave a sour laugh. 'It's no good going before eleven o'clock. She won't be up.'

Alec let her go. He and Piper headed downstairs.

'Didn't like her pa much, did she, Chief? And she didn't seem to care one way or t'other for Mrs Gooch. Blount said she's a good shot and don't think twice about popping off at birds and such. You reckon she did it?'

'The boy's motive is much stronger. Miss Tyndall may get to control the estate, but he'll own it. At least, I assume so. Tom didn't mention seeing a will in the study. Not that he had a chance to search the desk, what with the body sitting at it. In any case, we'll have to find his lawyer.'

'If the local doctor was here last night, maybe—'

'Hush!'

They had reached the top of the stairs to the hall and Alec heard a murmur of voices below. Looking over the balustrade, he saw Tom Tring talking to Miller. They were both smoking and seemed to be getting on together all right. The engineer so disparagingly described by Sir Harold as a 'counter jumper' might talk more freely to the big detective sergeant than to Alec. If not, all they'd lose would be a little time.

He glanced at the long-case clock standing against the wall. Nearly one o'clock. They weren't going to get much more done tonight anyway. Even Piper was beginning to flag.

The two of them sat down on a well-cushioned Jacobean bench beside the clock. A small table with an ashtray stood at Piper's elbow; he took out his packet of Woodbines and raised questioning eyebrows. Alec nodded. He'd give Tom the time it took Ernie to smoke one cigarette, then they'd go down. Fortunately, since he hadn't yet scraped out the dottle from his last smoke, he had no craving to light his pipe at this chilly hour of the night.

As the clock struck one, Ernie stubbed out his cigarette. They were halfway down the stairs when Tom spotted them and stood up.

'Just having a chat with Mr Miller, sir. He tells me he designs aeroplanes at Armstrong Whitworth in Coventry. You'll excuse me a moment, sir, while I report to the Chief Inspector.' He came to meet Alec and Piper.

'Has he told you what the deuce he's doing here at Edge Manor, Tom?'

'Trying to persuade the old man to let the young chappie go and work with him. Seems young Jack is a very promising engineer. Keen, too. Sir Harold didn't like the idea. It's not like it's Miller's own company, though, that might be going broke and desperate for talent. It don't sound to me like a motive for murder.'

'You never can tell,' Piper observed sagely.

'Too true, laddie. He wasn't shy of talking about it, but there's something he's holding back, Chief.'

'I've a good idea what it may be. Did you get anything else out of him, anything about the family?'

'I've only had a few minutes. Took forever to get a line to London, and you know what the Yard is like this time of night. Then I had a word with the butler while Sir Nigel rang up Evesham about a doctor and a mortuary van, and you know what a country-town copper shop is like this time of night.'

'Don't I just!'

'The CC pushed off after he'd talked to 'em. Nice bloke – offered Blount a lift, so I sent him home, told him to get a good night's sleep because he'll be needed tomorrow. I gave him a note to push through the letterbox at the inn, telling Mr Gooch we'll expect him around nine o'clock to make formal identification of the deceased. That all right, Chief?'

'Excellent.' What a joy to have a sergeant who read his mind! 'Right-oh, I'll have a word with Miller now, and then you can give me the gist of what the butler saw.'

Tom's moustache twitched as he grinned. 'You'd be surprised.'

'I doubt it.'

Alec walked over to the engineer. 'Mr Miller, I appreciate your waiting up for me.'

'You've got your job to do. But so have I. They're expecting me back at work tomorrow.'

'That's in Coventry, correct? Not too far if we need to get hold of you again.'

'No, but . . . The fact is, I'll feel like a rat if I go off and leave them in this bloody awful situation.'

An interesting statement, Alec thought, one tending to confirm the hints he had picked up that Martin Miller's interest in the Tyndalls was not confined to hiring a bright young engineer. 'It would certainly be more convenient for us if your employers could see their way to letting you stay on here for a day or two.'

'That should do the trick. I'll telephone in the morning and tell the boss the situation with regard to young Jack's employment has changed and the police want me to stay on for a bit.'

'Keep it brief. Don't give them any details.'

'I don't know any details. When I showed Sir Nigel and the doctor the way to the study, I glanced in. All I saw was what Jack told us, that Sir Harold had shot Mrs Gooch and himself.' He grimaced. 'I assure you I didn't linger.'

'Appearances can be misleading. It's conceivable, though unlikely, that Sir Harold shot Mrs Gooch. He did not shoot himself.'

For a moment, Miller was very still. He could have been wondering where he'd gone wrong in staging a murder-suicide, but Alec was inclined to think that sharp, logical brain was swiftly assessing the situation.

'You're sure, of course,' he said coolly.

'As sure as you are of your equations. Armstrong Whitworth designed the BE2, didn't they?'

'Yes. I had a hand in that design. Mrs Fletcher told me you flew recce.'

'That's right. When I took off in one of those machines, I trusted that it would fly. You're going to have to trust me now, because I'm not going to explain our reasoning.'

'You want to know if I saw anyone enter the house during the fireworks, I take it. I didn't, not Sir Harold, nor Mrs Gooch, nor anyone else. I was watching the show. I helped set it up, you know, and I was interested to see how it worked out.'

'Are you familiar with firearms, Mr Miller?'

'Not at all. I was exempt. They had plenty of poor sods to be Tommies and never enough aircraft designers. We didn't have time for mucking about with the Volunteer Force, either, I can tell you. That was another strike against me as far as Sir Harold was concerned.'

'You didn't get on with Sir Harold.'

'We rubbed each other the wrong way.' Miller smiled wryly. 'It was no skin off my nose. My notions didn't suit him any better than his suited me. He did his best to make me lose my temper, but you don't persuade a man by quarrelling with him.'

'Very true.'

'In any case, it made no difference to me. Jack's a promising lad and I like him, but he has to make the decision for himself, whether to join the firm or stick with being just another in a long line of squires. Had he chosen the latter, it would have been solely to please his father, I believe. I dare say the police are bound to suspect the heir in this sort of case, but I assure you, Jack doesn't care for the title or the land. His heart is set on building aeroplanes. Besides, he was very taken with Mrs Gooch. He would never have harmed her.'

'Suppose he came upon the scene after Sir Harold had shot the woman, might he not have wreaked vengeance?'

'Hardly! Much as he liked her, he had only just met her. I'll tell you what's much more probable: suppose Sir Harold shot Mrs Gooch and her husband came upon the scene. If you're talking vengeance, he's the one with the motive.'

CHAPTER 13

A thin line of light beneath the bedroom door showed that Daisy had left a light on for him. Alec took off his shoes in the passage and opened the door with infinite care. She needed her sleep.

Despite his effort, a hinge squeaked.

'Darling, at last!' She turned from the writing desk, pencil in hand, bundled up in his dressing gown over her own, with a blue counterpane draped about her lower half. 'I slept for a couple of hours, then woke up and simply couldn't go back to sleep, so I thought I might as well do some work to take my mind off things. Are they – the bodies – still next door?' She hitched a thumb at the wall separating the bedroom from Sir Harold's study.

'I'm afraid so, love. The mortuary van will be here in the morning. Later this morning, I should say. Do you feel like talking? Much as I hate to admit it, I've been saying to myself all evening, I wish I knew Daisy's opinion of these people.'

She wrinkled her nose at him. 'You must be desperate, to admit that.'

'We haven't got far, but far enough to know that Sir Harold didn't kill himself.'

'What! You mean he shot Mrs Gooch and then someone else shot him, or someone else shot both of them?'

'Could be either. We can't be sure. Why don't you give me my dressing gown and hop into bed. Maybe talking will help you sleep.'

'All right, here you are. I'd better just pop to the lav. Being pregnant is getting rather tiresome.'

'Only another three months.'

'That's easy for you to say!' she retorted.

When she returned, they squeezed into her bed together, with all available pillows stuffed behind them. Alec laid his hand on the swell of her belly and felt the baby moving within.

'Lively little chap. Or girl, as the case may be.'

'If it's a boy, he'd better not behave like Adelaide's pair, or I'll disown him! What do you want to know about the Tyndalls? Hasn't Tom found out everything from the servants by now?'

'The maids went to bed before he had a chance, except for Lady Tyndall's personal maid, and she's been occupied with her mistress. The butler seems to be the only manservant who lives in. He was in his pantry, but comatose, according to Tom. He appears to sleep there, in a striped nightshirt and nightcap. Didn't twitch an eyebrow while Tom was telephoning right beside him. Wookleigh's voice roused him, to a degree. However, all Tom got out of him was that Sir Harold didn't like people using the telephone at all hours and they wouldn't half catch it if he came in.'

'Oh dear, Jennings is about ninety and has been with the

family forever. He doesn't want to be pensioned off, and Sir Harold wouldn't force him, which is something to his credit.'

'You sound as if you can't say much to his credit.'

'I suppose he wasn't such a bad old stick, as long as he wasn't crossed. He had a filthy temper, and he had frightfully Victorian notions about the lower orders keeping to their place, just like Mother. But Jack said his father let him do more or less whatever he wanted as he was growing up. He'd just never before particularly wanted to do anything Sir Harold didn't approve of.'

'Such as getting a job as an engineer.'

'Exactly.'

'And introducing a member of the "lower orders" into the household.'

'That was part of the same thing,' Daisy said cautiously.

'Except that your friend Gwen then fell for said member of the lower orders. Don't try to deny it, Daisy. It's pretty obvious.'

'I wasn't going to *deny* it!'

'Just conceal it?'

'There isn't really anything to conceal. They like each other. Given the right circumstances, something might come of it, or it might just fade away.'

'But Sir Harold was the wrong circumstances, I assume.'

'Sort of. He'd certainly never have given his blessing to Gwen marrying a pleb, and it didn't help that Miller was trying to entice Jack into embracing a career wholly unsuitable for the son of a gentleman. But it's not as if Gwen were an heiress. She's not expecting more than a thousand or two, and I gather Miller makes a respectable salary.'

'Did Gwen in general stand up to her father?'

'I don't think I ever heard her argue with him. She's more like her mother, falling in with his wishes for the sake of avoiding rows.'

'What about her sisters?'

'As far as I could see, Babs pretty much went her own way. She was a Land Girl during the war, and when her fiancé was killed, she threw all her energies into agriculture. She didn't look for squabbles, just kept on running the place. In principle, Sir Harold didn't approve of a female in charge, but I suspect he wasn't much interested and was perfectly happy to let her get on with it until Jack came down from Cambridge to take over. Only Jack wasn't interested, either, so Babs kept on keeping on.'

'And Mrs Stephen Yarborough?'

'Adelaide?' Producing an enormous yawn, Daisy rested her head on Alec's shoulder. 'She'd have been out on her ear if the others hadn't conspired to keep her children's misdeeds from Sir Harold. Not because they're fond of the boys, or Addie, for that matter, who's completely self-centred, but because they've grown up in the habit of not upsetting him. Reggie and Adrian counted on it. They were too frightened of Sir Harold to misbehave in his presence.'

'Are the boys really so bad?'

'Truly awful, darling.' Another yawn. 'When I arrived, they . . .' Her voice trailed away. She was fast asleep.

Alec eased her down beneath the covers, kissed her forehead, filched a pillow and retired to his own bed.

He hadn't learnt a great deal, but he felt he had a better understanding of the family. He'd have to take what Daisy said about Gwen with a pinch of salt. Her partiality for her old school friend was obvious, and natural, and it had to be allowed for. But all in all, he had two main suspects: Jack Tyndall and James Gooch.

'Jack Tyndall and Gooch,' Alec said to Tom and Piper early the next morning, after far too few hours of sleep. The sky was light, but the hill still cast its shadow like a pall over the house and gardens and the village below. Standing at the French windows of the billiard room, Alec saw the weather vane on the church spire, projecting above the trees, gilded by the first touch of the rising sun.

'Jack Tyndall,' he repeated, turning to face the room. 'However keen on engineering, he could hardly be indifferent to the prospect of becoming a baronet and a landowner.'

'Wouldn't he get those in the end anyway, Chief?' Tom, sitting at the gun-cleaning table, helped himself to a couple more sausages and spread butter and marmalade thickly on a triangle of toast. The staff of Edge Manor had been generous with breakfast for the detectives. 'I can't see why he'd be in a hurry.'

'The baronetcy is presumably his by law. The estate is probably, but not necessarily, entailed on the eldest direct male heir. If not, Sir Harold was free to will it to whomever he chose. More than likely he had money and investments, too, which Jack risked losing by alienating his father. A will is easily changed.'

'I'll go through the desk as soon as they come and take the bodies,' said Tom., 'His lawyer's name'll be there, if not a copy of the will.'

'I just can't see it,' said Piper. 'A nice, gentlemanly young chap like that might shoot his pa, but I just can't see him doing in Mrs Gooch.'

'In the heat of the moment, laddie, her being a witness. But Gooch looks more likely to me, Chief. For all we know, he'd been planning all along to get rid of his wife and seized the chance to make it look like Sir Harold did it.'

'What about what Mr Miller said, Chief? About maybe Mr Gooch shot Sir Harold because Sir Harold shot Mrs Gooch? Vengeance, he said.'

'I don't know, Ernie. Vengeance is not a common motive for murder in this country. Your average Englishman who arrived on the scene of his wife's murder would knock the assailant down, if possible, and squawk for the coppers. But after all, he's from the wilder parts of Australia, where, for all I know, men are accustomed to take justice into their own hands.'

'Like the Wild West in America.'

'Either way, we're left with the question of why Sir Harold invited Mrs Gooch to his study.'

Piper perked up. 'Hey, Chief, one thing we haven't thought about. Suppose she went up there looking for something to pinch, and he followed her?'

'And invited her to sit down and make herself comf'table?' Tom said sceptically.

Alec glanced at the wall clock. 'Still an hour and a half before we can expect Gooch here. We should have a better idea of the possibilities when we've talked to him.'

'Maybe he'll confess when he sees her,' said Piper.

'It happens. You never know your luck. You going to have him take a look before the questions, Chief?'

'If the the police surgeon arrives in time to tidy things up. Tom, if you've finished guzzling, you'd better go and talk to the servants. With a bit of luck, you may even find the butler awake and *compos mentis* at this hour.'

'Right, Chief.'

'Ernie, you stay here and turn your shorthand into a report I can read. I'm going up to the study to take a look in daylight.'

Reluctantly he climbed the stairs and unlocked the door at the top.

Before leaving the study the night before, they had drawn back the heavy curtains and opened the windows on the north and west sides to let in the icy night air and let out the reek of sudden death. Standing on the threshold, Alec sniffed cautiously. The atmosphere was no longer unbearably fetid.

To his left was the door to the bedroom passage. Beyond the door, against the wall behind which, he sincerely hoped, Daisy was sound asleep, stood Sir Harold's massive walnut kneehole desk. It faced the north windows, and daylight from the west windows would make artificial light unnecessary for writing except on the darkest days. Seated there, the lord of the manor had before him a view of extensive shrubberies and sheep grazing the hillside, while with a turn of the head he could look out over the Vale of Evesham where his richest acres lay. Far in the distance the slate-blue mountains of Wales shaped the horizon.

At present, the sheet wrapped form of the lord of the manor reclined on the Turkish carpet beside his fellow victim. Alec had been reluctant to move the bodies before seeing them *in situ* in daylight, but had they stiffened in place, the mortuary men would have had a devil of a time getting them down the stairs.

Sir Harold had been sprawled across the desk as if falling from a half-standing position. Mrs Gooch had slumped against the arm and back of a Windsor chair set at an angle to the desk, half facing it, at the end farthest from the door. One of the questions Tom intended to ask the servants was whether this was the usual position of the chair. If so, she might have sat down uninvited, but if Sir Harold had moved it into place for his visitor, the meeting must have been comparatively amicable.

What on earth had he been going to write? The blood-soaked paper now stowed away in the Murder Bag was not a printed cheque, but it could have been used for an order to his banker.

To Alec's right lay the brass cartridge cases ejected by the automatic. It looked as if the murderer had entered the study, taken several steps forward, fired twice at one victim, then turned and fired twice at the other. In neither case could the range have been much more than ten feet, though the police surgeon would have to pronounce on that question. For anyone but a complete tyro, it would have been hard to miss.

Gwen brought Daisy her breakfast in bed. She looked exhausted, with dark rings beneath her eyes.

'I hope you slept better than I did,' she said, unloading the teapot, cup and saucer and milk jug onto the bedside table while Daisy sat up.

'Well, I managed to get a lot of work done in the middle of the night.'

'You're going on with the article, then? After . . . everything?'

'Yes, if you don't mind. It's only going to be published in America, and not for months. Of course I shan't mention . . . anything.'

'No, of course, that's all right. I don't suppose Jack will care. I'm sorry you didn't get much sleep. It's important for the baby that you get enough rest, isn't it?'

'Oh, once I'd got my ideas sorted out on paper, I slept quite soundly. I didn't hear Alec get up.'

'I gather he and his men had breakfast an hour and a half ago. Shall I pour?'

'Would you, please?' Daisy took the cover off the plate on the tray Gwen had settled on her knees. 'Mmm, this looks good. I'm famished, as always. At least I have an excuse these days. Do sit down. Would you like a piece of toast?'

'No, thanks.' Gwen perched at the foot of the bed. 'Everything is so awful, I have absolutely no appetite.'

'I must seem heartless, eating.'

'Oh no, it's not your family that's in trouble. At least Martin is staying on. But I can't even be glad about that, because it must mean your husband suspects him.'

'Not necessarily. He's a witness, after all. Here, do eat a bit of toast. You won't feel half so dire with something in your tum.'

Gwen took the buttered toast and nibbled at it without enthusiasm. 'I suppose the police have to suspect everyone. I can't see how it can be anyone but Mr Gooch, though goodness knows why. If only we knew why Father invited Mrs Gooch up to his study! They must have known each other before, don't you think? Before she went to Australia?'

'I can't think of any other way to explain it, though Alec's always ragging me for speculating wildly. What's more, I think that's the only reason the Gooches came to Didmarsh.'

'Because she wanted to see him?'

'Yes. Gooch didn't seem very keen on the whole enterprise.'

'More as if he didn't want to come up to the house at all, and only agreed to please her. But I liked him, didn't you?'

'He seemed a nice chap,' Daisy agreed, only too conscious of Alec's repeated reminders that her liking a person did not mean said person was innocent – which applied to the Tyndalls as well as to Mr Gooch.

After Gooch identified his wife's body, Ernie Piper had to give him a hand down the stairs from the study. He moved like an old man.

Sinking onto the chair Alec placed for him, he muttered, 'We should never've come! What'm I going to tell the boys?' He seemed unaware that he was speaking aloud, repeating, 'What'm I going to tell the boys?' Elbows on the table, he buried his face in his hands.

'Brandy,' Alec told Piper in an undertone, and the DC slipped out through the door to the passage.

From above came bumps and thumps. As soon as Gooch was out of the way, the mortuary men had gone in from the upstairs corridor to remove the bodies. Raising his voice, Alec asked, 'Why *did* you come, sir?'

Gooch lifted his head but he stared blankly ahead, not looking at Alec. 'A holiday, that's bloody all. "Let's go home," she said. "It'll be fun showing you the old country, and boarding for a term won't hurt the boys." Oh my word, how'm I going to tell them their mum's dead?'

'It was Mrs Gooch's idea to come to England?'

''Sright. I'd never have thought of it for meself, being Orstrilian-born and -bred. But we're not short a quid, which is her doing as much as mine, and I thought, if that's what she wants, good-oh. I'd've done anything for Ellie.'

To Alec, the man's shock and grief appeared perfectly genuine. He loved his wife and had come to England to please her. However, husbands who murdered their wives in a fit of passion often bitterly regretted the deed. Sometimes they simply regretted the loss of the woman they loved, sometimes what they perceived as the necessity of killing her.

Piper returned with a bottle and glass. Gooch was more collected now, but Alec poured an inch of brandy and leant across the table to put it beside him. Gooch took a sip, then pushed it away.

'I'm orright. So, what happened up there?'

'That's what we're trying to find out, Mr Gooch. I'm sorry to trouble you with questions at such a time, but that's my job. You say you came to England for a holiday. What brought you to Didmarsh-under-Edge?'

'We was coming this direction anyhow. Ellie's from this part of England. She never kept up with her family in Evesham – her dad was a right wowser – but she wanted to go see if any of 'em's still around. After London, we wanted a coupla days to catch our breath before we went to see would he put down his hymnbook long enough to be glad to see her. She'd heard about the fireworks show here when she was a kid. She thought it'd be fun. Fun!' he said bitterly.

His explanation sounded rehearsed. Nonetheless, it rang true, especially the bit about the father who was a 'wowser' – puritan? The truth, but not the whole truth, Alec decided. This was what Gooch and his wife had decided to tell anyone who enquired.

Gooch's mouth was set in a determined line, the man who

had made his fortune in the rough, tough gold fields coming to the fore. Getting the rest from him would be no picnic.

'Tell me about your meeting with the Tyndalls at the Three Ravens.'

'Nothing to it. I bumped into the lad at the bar. He invited me and the missus to join him and his friends, and we chatted for a while. Turned out three of 'em had walked down, so I gave 'em a lift home. We hired a Vauxhall, me and Ellie, a beaut, comfy and plenty of room, seeing we was touring. Ellie . . .' He picked up the glass at his elbow and gulped down the brandy. 'Strewth, I can't believe she's gone!'

'Who first mentioned the possibility of you and Mrs Gooch coming up to the house for the party?'

'The boy. Young Jack. I didn't like it, and I could see Miss Tyndall and Miss Gwen weren't too happy, but Ellie accepted and it weren't no sense them or me making a fuss.'

'Why didn't you like the idea?'

Gooch's lips pressed together, curbing his instinctive response. After a moment, he said, 'The ladies didn't like it, him inviting strangers with the wrong accents, so it seemed like a crook idea to me. And it was a crook idea. Look what came of it!'

Alec decided to move on. 'All right, tell me about last night. You drove up from the village?'

'I can't talk about last night!' Gooch choked out. 'Not yet!' Abruptly he pushed back his chair, seized his hat, and rushed out by the French doors.

'Reckon it's a good job we've got his passport, Chief,' said Piper.

* * *

When Daisy went downstairs, Gwen was in the hall conferring with the housekeeper. She broke off to say, 'Daisy, I'll be with you in half a tick.'

'That's all right. I want to take another look at the lie of the land now I've seen the whole show.'

'Jack and Martin are down below, dismantling the framework. They both felt in need of something physical to do. Babs went off to the estate office as usual. I think it helps to keep busy. Poor Mother's in no state to come down, though. She's always knocked up after a party, and with everything else as well ... I expect Addie will arrive at any moment. Thank heaven she's a late riser.'

'Don't worry about me. I'm sure you've lots to do in the house.'

'Well, Sergeant Tring's been talking to the maids, which has set us back a bit. Alec's interviewing Mr Gooch in the billiard room.'

'I'll just stay out of your way, Gwen.'

Daisy went out to the terrace and looked down at Jack and Miller on the bottom terrace. They were obviously talking as they worked, but she couldn't hear their voices, let alone what they were saying. She wondered whether they were discussing murder or carefully avoiding the subject.

She might learn something useful if she joined them. However, the steps looked even longer and steeper today than they had yesterday. It was too cold to stand about outside. If she went in, Gwen would feel obligated to entertain her. Besides, gentle exercise was supposed to be good for her. She decided to walk along the drive, which was fairly level.

Turning the corner of the house, she saw the Gooches' dark blue Vauxhall parked in the cobbled forecourt. Beside it was a plain black van. The mortuary people? she wondered with a shudder, and hurried past.

Who had shot Mrs Gooch and Sir Harold? And why?

Alec might know by now, but Daisy decided to put her mind to going through all the obvious suspects one by one.

Husbands and wives were always top of the list. Maybe Mr Gooch had a reason for killing his wife, though they had seemed so fond of each other. Lady Tyndall certainly had suffered years of bullying, which might have driven her to violence, though she had seemed to bear Sir Harold's temper with equanimity. Daisy simply couldn't believe either of them would bump off the other's spouse just to get rid of their own.

As for jealousy as a motive, Daisy dismissed it. Sir Harold might have overlooked Mrs Gooch's common accent had she been twenty years younger, or a fashionable matron with a come-hither look in her eye. She was neither. Even if they had once had an affair, perhaps loved each other, that was at least twenty years in the past. Besides, the baronet had looked appalled when he saw the Gooches, not at all in the mood to indulge in a romantic tryst half an hour later while swarms of guests enjoyed the celebration that was his pride and joy.

What about Sir Harold's children? Daisy remembered Gwen mentioning another row, yesterday afternoon, about Jack's duty to family tradition. She had assumed it was much the same as the squabbles she had heard earlier, but it could have taken a more serious turn. Suppose Sir Harold had threatened to—

'Daisy!' Babs waved from the farmyard on the downward slope. Dressed in breeches and boots, she came striding up the short cart track which merged with the drive, so Daisy stopped to wait for her. 'Do you mind if I walk with you?'

'Not at all.'

Babs moderated her stride to Daisy's more sedate pace. 'I suppose your husband couldn't have made a mistake about what happened?' she said in her abrupt way. 'I mean, is it really impossible that Father shot the woman, whether on purpose or by accident, and then himself?'

'Alec wouldn't say Sir Harold could not have shot himself if he weren't absolutely sure.'

'Pity. It would have been so much tidier. We must all be under suspicion, I suppose.'

'I'm afraid so.'

'Especially since Father was burbling about changing his will. He'd never have done it. Jack is— was his blue-eyed boy, and in any case he was far too attached to the line of succession. Besides, I'm sure he believed this aeronautical business was the whim of a moment, a substitute for youthful wild oats. But I admit it doesn't look good.'

'For Jack, in particular.'

'And for me. Assuming he'd made Reggie his heir – the only alternative I can think of – Addie would have moved back to the Manor like a shot. I can tell you, I couldn't have stood it for long. I'd have had a hard time finding a job. Father wasn't the only one to doubt a woman's ability to run an estate.'

Daisy made sympathetic noises.

'But even if there'd been any likelihood of his going through with it, none of us had the slightest motive for doing in Mrs Gooch. We only met her on Tuesday. It must have been Gooch, don't you— Watch out, there's a car coming.'

The belt of yews by the gatehouse was just ahead. Babs took Daisy's arm and pulled her to the side of the drive as she glanced back and saw Gooch's blue tourer rushing towards them. A hundred yards behind it was the black mortuary van, following at a properly funereal speed.

'The fool's driving much too fast,' Babs snapped. 'There's that sharp turn into the lane. I hope he has good brakes.'

The Vauxhall passed them. At the wheel, Gooch looked distraught, but he began to slow down. And then from the trees a rocket whooshed across in front of the car, trailing blue and green stars and erupting in a fusillade of pops and bangs. The car slewed off the road. With a horrid screech of metal, its left front wing crumpled against the gatepost, it came to rest tilted in the ditch.

Gooch was thrown half out of the driver's side window. When Babs and Daisy reached him, he hung inert, his face a mask of blood.

CHAPTER 14

Black as a carrion crow, the mortuary van drew up beside the wrecked car.

'Blimey,' said the white-coated driver, climbing out. 'What the bloody hell were that? Looked like something out of *The War of the Worlds*!'

'You read too much of that rubbish. It were a flipping Guy Fawkes rocket, idjit,' said his mate, jumping down from the other side. 'You better hop it, ladies, afore the motor goes up in flames. We'll get the poor chap out.'

Distantly, as the world whirled before her eyes, Daisy heard Babs asking the men if they knew what they were doing. Willing herself not to faint – not for nothing had she chosen to work in the military hospital's office during the war rather than volunteering as a nurse with the VAD – she clambered out of the ditch.

Babs scrambled up beside her, looking over her shoulder. 'They claim to be hospital porters and St John's Ambulance men.' She glanced at Daisy. 'Oh Lord, you're pale as whey. Sit down, for heaven's sake, and put your head between your knees.'

'I'm all right,' said Daisy, but she lowered herself to the ground, facing away from the accident. The others didn't need a second emergency on their hands. 'He's not dead, is he?'

'I don't think so. I hope not! If he is, the police may never find out what happened and we'll all be suspected forever. They'll have to bring him back to the house. The nearest nursing home is half an hour's drive – three-quarters going carefully as they'd need to. I wonder if there's a spare stretcher in the van.' She went to the back doors and reached for the handle, then shuddered and let her hand drop. 'I can't!'

Daisy's mind was working again. 'Babs, you'd better get to the house and ring up for a doctor. You'll go quicker than I could.'

'Yes.' She stood for an indecisive moment before saying fiercely, 'So help me, I'll scalp those boys!' and setting off towards the manor at a swinging lope.

Refraining from looking behind her, Daisy levered herself off the cold ground and approached the back of the van. The doors opened easily. Inside were two stretchers covered with white sheets and strapped down. The poles and canvas of a third stretcher lay on the floor between them. She hauled them out.

By that time, the men had carried Gooch up to the drive. Gently, they laid him down on the chalky surface and started to put the stretcher together.

'Bashed his forrid,' one told Daisy, who was taking care not to look at the injured man's face. 'Broke an arm and a leg, and likely there's other injuries we can't see – ribs, I 'spect, for one. But he ain't bust his neck, far as we can tell, and he ain't lost much blood. He may pull through. You never know.'

'Miss Tyndall said to take him to the house. She's gone to telephone for a—'

The sound of a motor-car engine straining up the hill came to their ears. A runabout turned in at the gate and came to a sudden halt. Daisy recognized the youngish man who bounded out, black bag in hand.

'Dr Prentice! But Babs only just—'

'Mrs Fletcher!' He glanced at her abdominal bulge. 'Go and sit in my car, please.' He was already on his knees beside the injured man.

'Miss Tyndall said to take him to the house,' she repeated before, not too reluctantly, she obeyed.

Peering through the dusty windscreen, she watched the doctor examining Gooch. She was far enough away not to see the details. He said something to the van driver, who shook his head. The two men went to the back of the van, and a moment later, one of the murder victims was lifted out and set unceremoniously by the side of the road. The other followed.

Daisy assumed they were making space inside for Gooch, and possibly for Dr Prentice to travel with him. She hoped she was not going to be left to stand watch over the bodies.

Behind her a motor-horn blared. A huge gleaming silver Lanchester had stopped half through the gateway, bumper-to-bumper with the doctor's little car. A uniformed chauffeur climbed out and came round to Daisy's side of the car.

His gaze turning from the crashed Vauxhall to the scene on the drive ahead, he raised his cap and said, 'Mr Dryden-Jones's compliments, madam, and what seems to be the trouble?'

Dryden-Jones? ... Oh, Struwwelpeter, the fiery Lord Lieutenant of Gloucestershire. The last person Alec needed poking his nose into the investigation! Glancing back, she saw his head bobbing about in the back of the Lanchester, ginger hair sticking out on both sides from under his trilby.

'Everything is under control, thank you,' she said, 'but it's going to be some time before the way is cleared. Please convey my thanks to Mr Dryden-Jones – I'm Mrs Fletcher – and tell him I hardly think it will be worth his while to wait.'

'Very good, madam.'

The chauffeur looked as if he doubted his employer would be so easily diverted, but he bowed slightly and turned to go. At that moment came a polite toot from beyond the gates. The rear of the Lanchester must be blocking the narrow lane, Daisy supposed.

Then above the wall rose a tweed motoring cap, followed by a narrow head adorned with white side-whiskers. 'I say, Dryden-Jones, what the deuce do you mean by— By Jove!'

Sir Nigel Wookleigh disappeared momentarily as he stepped down from his motor-car. His hat reappeared, bobbing along, and then the whole of him, striding through the gateway.

'Don't sit there, man, like a stuffed orangutan. Come along and lend a hand! By Jove, Mrs Fletcher! What's to do?'

'Mr Gooch drove off the road, Sir Nigel.' Best not to confuse matters with the rocket for the present, Daisy decided. It would come out soon enough. 'He's ... he's quite badly hurt, I'm afraid. But Dr Prentice turned up and is taking care of him, and there are two ambulance men who were driving the van. You can ask the doctor, but I'd say the best way to help would be to remove Mr— Hello, Mr Dryden-Jones.'

'What's going on, Mrs Fletcher?' The orangutan pointedly ignored Wookleigh.

'I was just telling Sir Nigel – there's been an accident but the doctor has everything well in hand. It would be best if you'd just keep out of the way and let him get on with it.'

But the Chief Constable had gone ahead to speak to Dr Prentice. Dryden-Jones followed with an irritable 'Hi! This is my county!'

Dr Prentice looked up and said angrily, quite loud enough for Daisy to hear, 'What is this circus? Get those cars out of the way! We have to turn the van around.'

Wookleigh seized Dryden-Jones's arm and steered him back towards the gates. 'Yes, yes, my dear fellow,' he was saying as they came level with Daisy, 'no one's disputing that it's your county, but even chief constables and lords lieutenant don't interfere with the medicos. Let's get our motors out of the way. By Jove, now here's a lawyer. Doctor chappie's right, just like Piccadilly Circus. They say you'll meet the whole world if you hang about long enough in Piccadilly Circus. Morning, Lewin.'

'Good morning, Sir Nigel, Mr Dryden-Jones.' A small, nondescript man in a black frock coat, striped trousers, bowler hat and gold-rimmed spectacles joined them. 'I tried and tried to ring up last night,' he said plaintively. 'After due consideration, I thought it my duty. But the number was constantly engaged.'

'I was obliged to spend quite some time on the telephone last evening,' said Dryden-Jones. 'Assisting the police, you know.'

'Then it is still ... er ... a police matter? I am shocked! I was calling upon a client in the neighbourhood, and after due consideration I thought it my duty to come to Edge Manor in case the police required my evidence. We guests were informed of an accident, but the circumstances were odd, very odd. I am Sir Harold's solicitor, you know.'

'Was, my dear chap,' said Sir Nigel. 'Or perhaps I should say "were". You *were* Tyndall's solicitor. He is no longer among us.'

'As I feared! There is mischief afoot. But you err, sir, in saying I am no longer Sir Harold's solicitor. My duty to him as his executor continues. And if a ... er ... crime has been committed, I must see the police at once. What is holding us up? If I cannot reach the house instantly, perhaps I should report to you, sir, as Chief Constable.'

'Not of this county!' Dryden-Jones howled.

Though dying to find out what the lawyer knew, Daisy decided it was time to intervene. 'Dr Prentice asked you to move your vehicles, gentlemen,' she said with a touch of her mother's *grande dame* manner. 'There is a seriously injured man to be considered. Mr Lewin, we didn't meet last night. My name is Fletcher. I'm a guest at Edge Manor and my husband is the police officer in charge here. I believe your motor-car must be blocking Sir Nigel's. If you would be so kind as to back down the hill, then the others can do likewise.'

Lewin and Dryden-Jones looked ready to take offence at being directed by a mere female, but Wookleigh said firmly, 'Quite right, dear lady; come on, chaps,' and herded them away.

The lawyer started to object. Sir Nigel, his voice lowered but quite audible to Daisy, told him, 'The Dowager Lady Dalrymple's daughter, my dear chap.'

There were no further protests. But they left Daisy to the humiliating realization that she was sitting in one of the cars blocking the drive, and she didn't know how to move it.

For heaven's sake, she admonished herself, you've seen it done often enough. That was the hand brake, and that stick was the gear lever, between her seat and the driver's seat. Those three pedals were the clutch, the foot brake and the accelerator. Surely one could discover by trial and error which was which? The big dial on the dash-board showed how fast one was going. Did it work in reverse? Still, she had no intention of going faster than a snail's pace. Oil pressure she could safely ignore for the few yards she needed to drive. At least she hoped so.

There remained the question of starting the machine. Peering at the floor by the pedals, she saw no self-starter button. Blast, she'd have to crank it.

The baby within, whose antics she had been ignoring, turned a somersault. Reprieve! No one could expect a six-months-pregnant mother-to-be to crank an engine. Which, now she came to think of it, was just as well, as she wasn't at all sure how to find reverse gear, and wasn't there something called double declutching? She hadn't the foggiest what that involved.

As if reading her mind, Dr Prentice stood up and called, 'Mrs Fletcher, can you drive?'

'No!'

'All right, come here then. Please.'

The 'please' was definitely a perfunctory after-thought. Daisy reminded herself that he was a doctor dealing with an emergency. As she went to him, one of the van's crew came to move the little car.

Daisy tried not to look at Gooch, but she noted from the corner of her eye that his head was bandaged and one arm splinted. 'What luck that you came along!' she said warmly.

'I want a word with the police, and I thought I'd better look in on Lady Tyndall. Have you any nursing experience?'

'I'm afraid not.' Daisy felt more useless by the minute. She was definitely going to learn to drive, if not to become a nurse. 'Is he going to be all right?'

'It's touch-and-go. I'll have to go with him in the van, and you'll have to stay with the corpses. We can't leave them unattended. The van will return to pick them up as soon as the men have carried this poor fellow into the house. How many months along are you?'

'Six.'

'You can walk up and down, then, so as not to get chilled. But I'll give you a rug from my car anyway.'

'Thank you,' Daisy said meekly.

As they spoke, Prentice's car had backed after the Lanchester into the lane, and the van followed, going forward. Then the van backed up the lane and returned, facing towards the house now. It stopped and the driver jumped out. The doctor's car reappeared and the second man came to help lift Gooch into the rear of the van.

With considerable annoyance, Daisy saw the Lanchester's long bonnet nosing after the runabout. She debated asking Dryden-Jones to watch over the remains of Sir Harold and Mrs Gooch.

The van departed. The van man came to get the doctor's car. Handing Daisy a tartan rug from behind the seat, he said, 'Sure you'll be all right, ma'am?'

'Hurry back,' she begged.

He drove off. The Lanchester pulled up beside her.

'What's this, what's this?' demanded the orangutan, alias Struwwelpeter, alias Dryden-Jones. 'What were those fellows thinking, to leave you behind, Mrs Fletcher! Allow me to offer you a lift.'

'The men are needed at the house, and someone has to watch over the bodies.' Daisy indicated the two sheet-covered stretchers at the side of the drive. 'They couldn't fit everyone into the van.'

Dryden-Jones paled. 'Oh . . . er . . . yes . . . well.' Obviously he was not going to offer to take her place. Instead, he addressed his chauffeur, who, like a well-trained servant, had been pretending not to listen to their exchange: 'Hotchkiss, take Mrs Fletcher's place. I shall drive her to the house.'

Hotchkiss's training was not proof against this. He turned an alarmed face to his employer. 'Sir, do you think that's a good idea?'

'I know how to drive!' He started to get out. 'Nothing to it. Hop in, Mrs Fletcher. I'll take you to the Manor.'

As Daisy's path crossed Hotchkiss's, the chauffeur muttered to her, 'Better hang on tight, madam.'

She hung on. She needed to. With Dryden-Jones behind the steering wheel, the Lanchester started off like a startled rabbit and proceeded by leaps and bounds that would have done credit to a kangaroo. The big car shuddered and moaned.

Daisy was very glad she had not tried to drive, and more determined than ever to learn how. Properly.

Glancing back, she saw Wookleigh following at a cautious distance, his Bentley rolling smoothly along under his own control. She closed her eyes and tried to concentrate on what Gooch's being injured might mean to the investigation.

They reached the forecourt at last and came to a halt with a final convulsion. Daisy opened her eyes. They were stopped right across the bows of the van, which had been backed up to the front door.

'You can't stay there, old chap!' Wookleigh parked neatly beside the doctor's car. As the lawyer's small car pulled up beyond him, he strode over to the Lanchester and opened the rear door for Daisy. 'My dear lady, are you all right?'

'I think so.'

'Take my arm, do. Dryden-Jones, you'll have to move. The van can't get out.'

Dryden-Jones still hung on to the wheel with a rigid grip. Turning his head cautiously, as if afraid it might fall off, he said with the merest trace of his usual asperity, 'I shall go in only for a minute, just to make sure *my* county is providing the Chief Inspector with every facility.'

Wookleigh opened his mouth, but Daisy squeezed his arm and whispered, 'If it means he'll go quickly, leave it. The van driver can always move it if necessary.'

He looked down at her with approval and patted her hand. 'Quite right, my dear. He may have to in any case.'

Daisy was too well brought up to omit thanking Dryden-Jones for the lift. She just hoped he didn't think she was being sarcastic. He avoided meeting her eyes but climbed out of the car on wobbly legs. They all went into the house together.

They found Dr Prentice and his patient in the entrance hall. The doctor was once again kneeling beside the stretcher, looking very worried. Before Daisy could ask him if Gooch's condition had deteriorated, Babs came through from the passage. Behind her, a goggle-eyed maid peeked around the door.

Babs was breathing faster than normal, so she could only have arrived a few minutes earlier. After a glance of dismay at the gentlemen with Daisy, she disregarded them. 'Dr Prentice, I was ringing you up when I was told you'd just arrived, with Mr Gooch.'

'I was on my way here when I came across the accident. I need to get him to bed immediately so that I can make a proper examination.'

'Gwen's making up the cot in Father's dressing room for him. I hope that will do. Dilys, show them the way.'

The maid scurried to obey. As the stretcher men picked up their burden once again, Prentice said, 'I'll need hot water bottles, plenty of hot water, bandages and something suitable for splints.' Without waiting for a response, he followed his patient up the stairs.

'Daisy . . .'

'You go along, Babs,' said Daisy. 'I'll deal with things here. Sir Nigel, Mr Dryden-Jones, Mr . . . er-hm won't you sit down?'

'Lewin,' said the lawyer. 'Lewin, Lewin, Pent and Lewin. I really must insist—'

'All in good time, my dear fellow,' said Sir Nigel. 'Can't you see the household is all at sixes and sevens? Mrs Fletcher, you come and take a seat. You must be in need of rest after your . . . adventures.' He gave the Lord Lieutenant a scathing look.

'Just want a quick word with the Chief Inspector,' said Dryden-Jones feebly.

Daisy would have liked nothing better than to sit down, preferably with her legs up, but she said, 'I ought to see if I can find Jack Tyndall.'

'I'll do that,' the Chief Constable offered, 'if you'll point me in the right direction.'

'The last I saw of him, he was on the lowest terrace, dismantling the fireworks apparatus.'

'Not to worry, if he's there, I'll fetch him in a trice. I'll go out through the French doors, that will be quickest.'

As Sir Nigel's tall, narrow figure disappeared into the drawing room, Alec emerged from the passage, followed by Tom and Piper.

Dryden-Jones darted towards him with a cry, 'Chief Inspector, just the man I wanted to see.'

Not to be pipped at the post, the lawyer scurried after him. 'Chief Inspector? You are in charge of the case? I am as yet unaware of . . . er . . . precisely what has occurred, but—'

Dryden-Jones raised his voice. 'Since Gloucestershire is my county, I—'

'I consider it my duty, much as it goes against the grain—'

'I want to assure you—'

'I feel obliged to inform you,' Lewin persisted, rivalry provoking him into abandoning the discretion demanded of a lawyer, 'that Sir Harold disclosed to me last night that he intended to change his Last Will and Testament to disinherit his son.'

CHAPTER 15

Dryden-Jones broke the silence that followed the solicitor's revelation. Scarlet with embarrassment, he gabbled, 'Needn't tell you, shan't breathe a word, none of my business. Mum as the grave. Oh dear, not the best way to put it!' He pulled his gold hunter watch from his fob. 'Dash it, is that the time? Bit of a rush, don't you know. Anything my people can do for you, Chief Inspector ... Know you'll excuse me, Mrs Fletcher!'

Routed again, he bowed and fled, to Daisy's vast relief. '"Stand not upon the order of your going,"' she muttered to herself, '"but go at once." And don't come back.' She doubted he'd know how to start his car, but the van driver could move it when he came down.

Alec looked after him grimly. 'Let us hope he really can keep a still tongue in his head. Sir,' he said to Mr Lewin, 'while I appreciate the information, I can't but feel it would have been preferable to convey it privately. I take it you are Sir Harold's lawyer?'

Lewin was almost as red in the face as Struwwelpeter had been. 'I don't know what came over me,' he stuttered. 'I assure you, Chief Inspector, it is not my practice to ... er ... broadcast my clients' confidential affairs. Lewin's the name, of Lewin, Lewin, Pent and Lewin. I trust ... er ... dare I hope – that you will overlook my disgraceful error of judgement and not mention it to anyone? I feel it very deeply, indeed I do.' He took out a handkerchief, blotted his forehead and polished his glasses.

'You can count on my discretion, Mr Lewin, and that of my men. And my wife's.' Alec cast a minatory glance at Daisy, who had installed herself on the sofa by the fire. 'The Lord Lieutenant's I cannot speak for. We shall need to take a statement from you.'

'Oh no!'

'I'm afraid so. Detective Sergeant Tring will accompany you to the billiard room and you can tell him exactly what Sir Harold said to you. Thank you for coming forward, sir. Lawyers are rarely so accommodating to the needs of the police.'

With witnesses to his outburst, Lewin hadn't a leg to stand on. Looking very hangdog, he followed Tom through the door to the passage.

'That was a nasty dig, darling,' said Daisy as Alec sat down beside her, and Piper opposite. 'I suppose he deserved it, but I must say Mr Dryden-Jones is enough to make anyone forget himself. Thank heaven he's gone.'

'Yes, but Daisy, what's this about Gooch? All I know is a maid brought a message from Miss Tyndall saying he'd crashed his car. He was upset when he left us, but I didn't suppose him incapable of driving or I'd not have let him go!'

'He looked fearfully upset when he passed us – Babs and I were walking along the drive – but he'd have managed if it hadn't been for the rocket. It shot straight across in front of him. It would have been a miracle if he hadn't lost control.'

'Did you see who set off the rocket?'

'No, but—'

'We'll come back to that. Go on.'

'His car went into the ditch and hit the gatepost. He was unconscious and bleeding.' Daisy did her best not to picture the scene. 'I don't know what Babs and I would have done if the mortuary men hadn't turned out to be St John's Ambulance men as well.'

'Where did they take him?'

'Babs said to bring him here. Upstairs, in Sir Harold's dressing room.'

'Ernie.' Alec jerked his head towards the stairs.

'First floor, third door on the left,' Daisy directed as Piper hurried off. She moved closer to Alec and took his hand. 'It was the greatest of luck, darling, not only the ambulance men, but then Dr Prentice came along and took over.'

'Ah yes, I was expecting him. Good timing.'

'Except that Babs had already left to telephone for him when he arrived. Maybe I should have tried to catch up with her.'

'Certainly not! You didn't try to help the doctor, did you?'

'He made me sit in his car. And then the others kept turning up, Struwwelpeter, then—'

'Daisy! Struwwelpeter?'

'Don't you know that illustration of the children's rhyme? German, I think. The boy with hair like a bush and long, curly fingernails. Not that I've noticed anything wrong with the Lord Lieutenant's fingernails, but perhaps ingrowing hair would explain—'

'Daisy!' Alec reproved her again, but with a grin.

'Sir Nigel called him a stuffed orangutan.' She defended herself. 'Or at least, told him not to sit there like a stuffed orangutan. He was just sitting there in his great big car, with all the drama going on, and when Sir Nigel pulled up behind him, *he* hopped out to see if he could help.'

'Wookleigh's here, too?'

'Yes. He's gone to look for Jack. And then that little lawyer arrived and started fussing about how he had to get through because it was his duty to tell you— But I never guessed he was going to make quite such a shattering announcement.'

'One of the maids told Tom she overheard Sir Harold threatening to cut young Tyndall out of the will, yesterday afternoon. She assumed it was just another row. But if Sir Harold actually went so far as to speak to the lawyer, it doesn't look good for the boy.'

'Oh dear! I suppose you won't tell me whether Tom found out anything else.'

'If he had, I wouldn't, but he didn't. He got the impression the butler was "holding out on him", as the Americans say, but the old man is so senile, he may just be imagining he has a secret.' Alec looked up as heavy footsteps came down the stairs.

'The ambulance men,' Daisy told him. 'Mortuary men.'

He stood up and went over to them. 'In case no one else has got around to it, I want to thank you for your attentions to the accident victim. Did you see the crash?'

'That we did, sir. We wasn't too far behind the gentleman's car. A blooming great rocket come out of nowhere. Spitting coloured fire, weren't it, mate?'

'And making a noise fit to wake the dead. In a manner of speaking. Our van ain't the quietest and we could hear the bangs. Went right acrost the road in front of the poor gentleman.'

'I don't say as I wouldn't've druv off the road meself, and I can't say fairer'n that.'

'Did you see who fired the rocket?'

They looked at each other and both shook their heads regretfully.

'Nah, nor hide nor hair. In among the trees he must've bin, wouldn't you say, mate? Well, sir, we gotta-go pick up them corpuses of yourn, afore they gets up and walks away.'

'Great Scott, where are they?'

'Lying alongside of the drive, with t'other gentleman's shover on guard, and no knowing when he'll get tired of waiting.'

'Yes, you'd best be off. Thank you.' Alec returned to Daisy. 'All right, love, you didn't see who set off the rocket, *but . . .*'

'Babs may have seen.'

'If she saw her brother, she'll never tell us.'

'Jack! Why on earth should he fire a rocket at Gooch?'

'That I can't say,' Alec admitted, 'but Gooch knows something he's not telling.'

'About Jack?'

'It could be. Jack may have heard Sir Harold talking to Lewin about changing his will and realized he was serious. In that case, Jack's only hope was to kill his father before he did it. He was in a hurry. He couldn't wait for a chance to catch his father alone. Whatever Mrs Gooch's reason for going with Sir Harold to the study, it's quite likely that her husband kept an eye on her, and in so doing he'd have seen Jack following them.'

'And Jack noticed him watching?' Daisy said sceptically.

'Or he told Jack he'd seen him. There's still a whiff of blackmail about this whole affair.'

'I can't believe Jack would shoot Mrs Gooch, nor that Mr Gooch would blackmail his wife's murderer when he could denounce him. But suppose you're right, I still want to know, why on earth should Jack fire a rocket at Gooch's car? It's a very uncertain way to get rid of someone.'

'True. There's a chance, though, that he'd crash and be killed, and little or no risk in trying.'

'I call it pretty far-fetched. I bet Jack was with Miller the whole time. They were taking apart the firework scaffolding when I left.'

'Would Miller lie for Jack? For his own sake, or Gwen's?'

'Give him a false alibi? I doubt it. Not when it's a matter of murder, or attempted murder. In any case, it wasn't Jack Babs saw, if she saw anyone. She was sure it was Adelaide's boys.'

'That's what she claimed?'

'I'd be very surprised if she's wrong.'

'Because Jack says they stole some rockets.'

'And because when Gwen fetched me from the station, they threw squibs at the car in exactly the same place. Fortunately, Gwen has steady hands.'

'Fortunate indeed! If it can be proved the boys caused Gooch's accident, they're in serious trouble.'

'Don't worry, Babs is going to give them what for, and she seems to be the one person they're afraid of. They really are the most appalling children. To tell the truth, their mother's pretty appalling, too.'

'I'm not looking forward to interviewing her.'

'Let Tom do it,' Daisy suggested, tongue in cheek. 'She'd be so flabbergasted, she might even stop whining and showing off and give some sensible answers.'

'That's an idea! Here he comes. All in order, Sergeant?'

'Yes, sir.'

Tom's calm rumble contrasted with the agitated squeak of the solicitor. 'I assure you, Chief Inspector, I have given every assistance I feel able to justify consonant with my duty to my clients.'

'Of course, sir. I take it you'll be acting for the family should they be in need of legal advice?'

'Oh no, no, no indeed!' Lewin took off his spectacles and polished them vigorously. 'That is, you are referring to possible ... er ... criminal charges? Good gracious, no! Apart from the fact that I could, I fear, be called as a witness, my partners and I feel very strongly that ... er ... criminal matters are and should remain outside our province. I shall be happy, of course, to refer ... er ... anyone in need of such advice to a firm well versed in such issues. I shall consult my partners as to who might be suitable.'

'I see. As you're here, no doubt you'll be informing the Tyndalls of the provisions of the current will.'

'After the funeral is the customary time, though I believe Sir Harold made no secret of his ... er ... previous intentions. Oh dear, I suppose in the circumstances ... ?'

'We'll let you know when the funeral can be held.'

'Very good, very good. In the ... er ... circumstances, I believe I shall not linger to present my condolences. A note to Lady Tyndall will be more proper. Be so kind, Chief Inspector, as to express my regret that the family were all otherwise engaged when I called.'

'As you wish. No doubt the Tyndalls will be in touch, as will we if we require any further assistance from you.'

As soon as Lewin was out of earshot, Daisy said, '"The first thing we do, let's kill all the lawyers."'

Tom looked at her with eyebrows raised halfway up the shining dome of his head.

'Sorry, I'm feeling a bit Shakespearean this morning.'

'Shakespeare, eh?' Tom grinned, making his moustache twitch. 'Now that's a good bit. What they made us learn at school was a lot of twaddle about fairies.'

'"Hold, enough!"' said Alec. 'Tom, what did you get out of Lewin?'

'Sir Harold didn't tell him who was going to be his heir, just drew him aside when he arrived last evening and said he was going to disinherit "that damn disobedient puppy". Begging your pardon, Mrs Fletcher. Mr Lewin got the impression Sir Harold wasn't sure who to leave the estate to – it's not tied up in any way – but he can't pin down just what was said to give him that impression.'

'Did Sir Harold make a habit of threatening to change his will?'

'No, Chief. The boy was always "the apple of his father's eye", and Mr Lewin was astonished to hear he'd fallen from grace.'

'But Sir Harold was serious about it?'

'He actually made an appointment to go to the solicitors' offices this afternoon.'

'Sounds serious enough. Anything else?'

Tom quickly scanned his notes. 'That's about it, Chief. What's this about Mr Gooch?'

Alec explained in about a tenth as many words as Daisy

had employed to tell the story. While she admired his succinctness, he failed to convey the drama and horror of the event. Of course, he hadn't experienced it.

'It was beastly,' she said with a shudder. 'I don't know what Babs and I would have done if the men in the van hadn't turned up, and then the doctor. Although, to be perfectly honest, looking back, it was quite funny the way people kept arriving one after another, if it hadn't all been so dreadful. I do hope he'll be all right.'

Alec put his arm around her shoulders, hastily removed it as they heard footsteps on the stairs, then returned it to its comforting place when they saw Ernie Piper coming down.

'How is Mr Gooch?' Daisy asked eagerly.

'Pretty bad, Mrs Fletcher. Dr Prentice says he's badly concussed and several bones are broken. Well, the bones'll knit, but there's no telling what damage there is to his brain. He's still unconscious. I brought his wallet, Chief, and this.' Piper waved an envelope.

Alec once again removed his arm from Daisy's shoulders, leaving a chilly spot, as he took the wallet and opened it. 'Over a hundred pounds in notes. Book of cheques. And here's a receipted copy of a letter of credit from a bank in Australia, for a thousand pounds. They weren't doing themselves too shabbily! We'd better hang on to this for the moment. Here, make a list of the contents, Ernie. What's that you have there?'

'Addressed to Sir Harold Tyndall, Chief.' Piper handed over the envelope. 'Well, no address, just the name. It was in the inside pocket of his jacket.'

'Just to Sir Harold, not Lady Tyndall. So not a bread-and-butter letter written before the event.'

'They might not have realized thanks for hospitality ought to be addressed to the hostess,' Daisy pointed out.

'True. Tom, you have their passport? Let's have a look at their signatures . . . Yes, I thought so, it's her writing.'

'Back to the blackmail theory, Chief?' Tom suggested.

'Perhaps. An undelivered letter from a murdered woman to a murdered man. I suppose I'm justified in reading it.'

'Felt to me like it's got another envelope inside, Chief,' said Piper, opening and offering the penknife with which he kept sharp his endless supply of pencils.

Alec carefully slit the top of the envelope. 'Yes, there's another one inside. That's odd, it's addressed to "Jack". Just "Jack", no surname, no Mr or Esquire. Here's the covering letter.'

He unfolded the single sheet. The sprawling handwriting was easy to make out and Daisy read silently as he read aloud:

Dear Harry, I don't want to upset anybody you needn't wory I'm going to tell nobody else. But I thoght I better let you know I'm going to tell Jack. Its no good tryng to stop me. I'll do it weather you say yes or no but if you say yes you can give him this letter I writ for him so as it don't come like a shock when I tell him. Its my right. Yrs truly, Ellie Gooch (Mrs).

They gazed at each other with a wild surmise, silent (though not, thought Daisy, upon a peak in Darien. It wasn't only Shakespeare haunting her today). Dying of curiosity, she was about to ask Alec if he felt justified in opening the second envelope, when Jack came in from the drawing room, followed by Wookleigh and Miller.

'Mr Fletcher! Sir Nigel tells me Mr Gooch ran his car off the road, on our land. Is he badly hurt?'

'I'm afraid his injuries appear to be serious.'

'*I told* Father that turn into the lane was an accident waiting to happen. I'm going to take down the gateposts and straighten it out. I wouldn't have had this happen for anything! First Mrs Gooch, and now this! Where is he? Upstairs?'

'Dr Prentice is here,' Daisy said soothingly, 'and Gwen and Babs are doing what they can to help.' It was not the moment to tell him about the rocket.

'I'd only be in the way,' Jack said in frustration.

'Come and sit down, Mr Tyndall,' said Alec. 'Mr Gooch was carrying this, addressed to you.'

Still standing, Jack took the envelope and stared at it blankly. 'What on earth?'

'I'd like you to open it now, in my presence. I must warn you that anything you choose to say will be written down and may be produced in evidence. You are not obliged to say anything, and you are entitled to legal representation.'

Jack gave no sign of hearing the ominous words. With a frown, he ripped open the envelope, unfolded the letter and started to read. Utter astonishment was succeeded by shock as he turned the page. Ashen, he dropped into the nearest chair. He read on to the end, then folded the double sheet with automatic fingers. Leaning forward, he held it out to Alec without a word.

Alec took it. Jack slumped against the high back of the chair, his eyes closed, still deadly pale.

'Whisky?' Sir Nigel said in a loud whisper to Miller, who nodded and went off.

Alec unfolded the letter and started to read, silently this time. As before, Daisy read it with him.

My dearest boy,

You will be suprized to get this from me seeing we never met before last night but I'll explain. You are 21 and a man and you can deside for yourself. I waited all these yrs till you was old enogh to deside for yourself. This is hard to writ and I want you to be shure I'm not going to do anything to upset things. I won't never tell anyone else, I promise faithfuly. I come all the way from Australia to tell you and becaus I just wanted to see you and tell you and make shure your alright. Becaus my Jimmy is a good man and if theres anything you need he'll spring for it and won't never say nothing. Even if its a lot of money he's not short a penny, long as it don't take away from our boys you see you got three brothers. Half brothers I shuld say. You see, Jacky dear I'm youre real mother. Your dads youre real dad don't wory he wanted a boy so badly and him and me, well, you know about the birds and the bees your 21 like I said. And I couldn't a brung you up propper all on my one and he give me enugh money to start over in Australia and hear ladyship promised she be a propper mother to you from what I seen she kept her promis you been happy, so what could I do? But I cried and cried when they took you away and now I've come back to make shure your alright like I said and dont hold it agin me Jackie, I just want to see you and talk to you and for you to know I love you and that's all. And I won't tell no one else, like I said and me and Jimmy ll go back to Australia and leave

you be don't wory. But if you coud just come down to
the Three Ravens tomorrow just to talk a bit more, you
was so nice to me last night. O Jackie I love you dearly
tho I wasn't a good mother to you so please come.

Youre loving mother
Ellie Gooch

CHAPTER 16

Alec saw that Daisy was blotting her eyes with her fingertips. Dammit, he shouldn't have read the letter where she could see it. He gave her his spare handkerchief, the one he kept for weeping witnesses and suspects.

The letter, he passed to Tom Tring for him and Piper to read. Jack Tyndall had handed it over after receiving the warning. It was now an item of evidence. However, Sir Nigel Wookleigh had no right to see it, since – as Struwwelpeter correctly, if maddeningly, kept insisting – this was not his county. Fortunately, the Chief Constable realized this.

'Hmph,' he said, tugging on his whiskers, 'like to have a word with Lady Tyndall before I leave, assure her of any assistance I can properly offer. But this isn't the moment. Don't want to get in the way. Believe I'll take a turn on the terrace.'

'Thank you, sir,' said Alec with heartfelt appreciation. An interfering CC could be the very devil.

In the doorway to the drawing room, Wookleigh met Miller bearing a half-full glass and a soda siphon. 'Just the ticket,' he said approvingly, and went on.

Miller touched Jack's shoulder and, when he opened dazed eyes, put the glass into his hand. He took a gulp, spluttered, and mutely held out the glass for soda water. Alec watched the colour begin to return to his face. He couldn't possibly be acting. But the shattering surprise might have been the existence of the letter, not its contents. In that case, his handing it to the police rather than trying to conceal it could be considered a brilliant move.

While observing his chief suspect, Alec had not forgotten the third victim, who was still himself a suspect. 'Piper, you'd better go and sit with Gooch until I can organize a uniformed replacement.'

'Yes, sir.' Ernie Piper was bright enough and had worked with Alec long enough not to need his task spelled out for him: he was to catch any words Gooch might utter and to guard him from further harm. They had no proof the rocket had been a small boys' prank. The letter he had carried was enough to throw the Tyndall family into turmoil. He might have proof of its claims, or he might have further revelations equally unwelcome.

Tom, having folded the letter and consigned it to a capacious inner pocket, was watching Jack Tyndall equally closely. Alec had a job for him, too. But first he leant close to Daisy and asked in a low voice, 'Does Wookleigh know about the rocket?'

'No, I'm pretty sure not.'

So he couldn't have told Tyndall or Miller about it. Alec crooked his finger and Tom came over. 'Tom, see if Miller can give Tyndall an alibi for the past couple of hours.'

'I don't think Tom knows about the rocket, either,' Daisy whispered. 'He wasn't here.'

'Rocket, Chief?'

'A firework which probably caused Gooch's accident.'

'Ah.' No more than Piper did Tom need *t*s crossed or *i*s dotted.

Alec raised his voice. 'Mr Miller, if you wouldn't mind accompanying Sergeant Tring, he has a couple of questions for you.'

Miller gave young Tyndall a dubious look. 'Going to be all right, Jack?'

The boy nodded.

'All right.' He went with Tom into the drawing room.

Which left Daisy to take notes, as Alec didn't want Tyndall's attention drawn to the fact that his words were being written down. She was already taking out her journalist's notebook. Alec moved to a chair directly opposite Tyndall.

'She . . . I don't understand. Is it true? What she wrote?'

'That Mrs Gooch was your natural mother?'

'Yes. I don't understand! It can't be true?'

'That remains to be seen. You had no inkling?'

'How could I? I've always been Jack Tyndall of Edge Manor. Father, M-mother, three sisters. No one's ever called me a . . . bastard, at least not to my face. But if it's not true, why should she write it?'

'Good question.' Not one Alec intended to answer, though he could come up with a number of reasons. First, back to the blackmail theory, as Tom had said: an unfounded report of that nature could do almost as much damage as a true one. Second, Alec thought Mrs Gooch had been a bit young to have reached the climacteric, but perhaps she had suffered some other type of mental instability – possibly triggered by a baby lost in the past and a meeting with a charming young man of the right age, or by delusions of grandeur: 'My son the baronet.' Was it significant that the letter had been in her husband's possession? He wasn't at present available to be asked.

Jack was recovering his composure and beginning to think. 'Another thing I don't understand is why Gooch had the letter on him. Why didn't Mrs Gooch give it to me when she arrived? I talked to her, to both of them, for several minutes. Do you suppose he'd just found out what she'd written and took it away from her?'

'Did they behave as if that was the case?'

'No, not really. He was a bit glum. I assumed he wasn't frightfully comfortable hobnobbing with the nobs, so to speak. She was in high spirits, not at all as if he'd given her a wigging. Of course, if he'd taken the letter, she could have simply told me what she'd written. But why didn't she?'

'What would you have done if she had made such a claim to you immediately?'

'Oh Lord, I suppose I would have gone into a blue funk, as I did just now, only right in the middle of the party. You must think I'm a hopeless chump.'

'It must be a tremendous shock to find out suddenly that you're illegitimate.'

'Yes. But is it wishful thinking to say I absolutely can't believe it? I mean, surely one must have some inkling if one has been adopted. For twenty-one years I've been part of this family. I've never felt like an ugly duckling, a cuckoo in the nest. Not a soul has ever hinted that I don't belong. My sisters always teased me that I was Mother's pet and Father goes . . . used to go on and on about how I'd be the next baronet in a long line descending from father to son. I shan't be if it's true, shall I?'

'I believe not. The law does not recognize adoption.'

'Not that I care for such fuddy-duddy rubbish. It's not so important nowadays, is it, and anyway, I'm going to be an engineer. But the parents . . . No, it can't be true. I liked Mrs Gooch very much, but she couldn't possibly be my mother. Why should she have written such stuff?'

'Don't you have any ideas? What's your theory?'

'Well, I suppose you're wondering if it's something criminal.'

'That's my job.'

'I suppose it could conceivably have been a sort of threat in a roundabout way,' Jack said doubtfully, 'suggesting she would tell people I was her son if Father didn't pay her off. It could have been a terrific nuisance. But why write all that about Mr Gooch having plenty of money? Besides, she wasn't at all that sort of person, I'd swear to it. I say, Mr Fletcher, do you think *he* actually wrote it?'

Daisy looked up, startled. Alec had to admit, 'I hadn't considered that possibility.' Seeing Tom Tring reappear in the drawing room doorway, he added, 'Unfortunately, he can't be questioned.'

'No, and even if he did write the letter, I feel dreadful about his accident. And I didn't know. I wasn't there to help!'

'Where were you when it happened? Say for the last couple of hours?'

'Miller and I were taking apart the fireworks apparatus.'

Tom nodded, confirming that Miller had told the same story.

'Down on the lowest terrace?' Much too far for a quick

dash up to the far end of the drive to set off a rocket, and he couldn't have known exactly when Gooch was going to leave.

'Yes. It was just complicated enough to keep my mind off . . . things. I can't believe this, any of it. It hasn't really sunk in yet, you know. I mean, Father dead, Mrs Gooch dead, let alone that she could be my mother!'

'Jack, dearest!'

'Mother!' Looking up at the stairs, Jack jumped up. 'Jupiter!' he groaned. 'Does she have to know?'

'I'm afraid it can't be helped.'

Jack went towards the stairs, saying, 'Mother, should you have come down? You're not well.'

'I'm never quite well, dearest, but I'm not an invalid.' Though she took Jack's arm down the last few steps, Lady Tyndall didn't appear to lean on it. Wraithlike in a charcoal grey costume that emphasized her frailty and the dark circles below her eyes, she glided across the floor in a way evocative of the Victorian ballrooms she must have adorned in her youth. No modern young woman accustomed to tennis, golf and the tango could match that ethereal grace.

Alec rose to meet her, and Daisy started to stand, but Lady Tyndall said warmly, 'No, don't get up, my dear. I'm so sorry such dreadful things have happened while you've been staying with us. I don't remember much about last night, but the girls tell me you were a veritable tower of strength. I hope you haven't suffered for your exertions.'

'Not at all, Lady Tyndall, not that I did very much. Mostly ordered everyone else about.'

'You were a great help.' She turned to Alec. 'Mr Fletcher, I'm afraid I wasn't much help to you last night.'

'It wasn't to be expected, ma'am. But as you seem to be

somewhat recovered, I do have a number of questions to ask you.'

'Of course.' She sat down beside Daisy.

'Mr Tyndall, will you go with Sergeant Tring, please. Tell him again all you can recall about your dealings with the Gooches.'

Jack hesitated, looking at his mother.

'You'd be surprised, sir,' said Tom, his manner fatherly, 'how much more you remember second time around.'

'Daisy will stay with me, Jack, if Mr Fletcher has no objection. She will be a support without *hovering*, as my children tend to.'

'Certainly,' said Alec.

Still reluctant, glancing back, Jack followed Tom through the door to the passage.

'You won't mind if I take notes, Lady Tyndall?' Daisy asked. 'It's a journalist's habit, and it helps Alec keep things straight.'

A spasm of indefinable emotion crossed Lady Tyndall's face. Journalism might be a barely acceptable occupation for an aristocratic young lady, but helping the police question witnesses was not. Alec was glad Daisy was turning to a fresh page in her notebook and didn't notice. Pencil poised, she looked expectantly at Alec.

'I hope you'll forgive me if I repeat myself, ma'am,' he said. 'I haven't got my notes from last night with me. I believe you said neither you nor – to your knowledge – Sir Harold had invited Mr and Mrs Gooch?'

'How could we have? We had never heard of the Gooches. The children didn't mention them. Indeed, neither Barbara nor Gwen could have done so without admitting to having visited the public house, which in my day no respectable unmarried lady would have dreamt of doing. Nor would Harold or I have dreamt of inviting people who happened to be staying at the local inn, not without a proper letter of introduction. My son invited them, an act of impulsive kindness and very like him.'

'Did that annoy you?'

'Frankly, I thought it a little bit thoughtless of him. They really didn't fit in with our other guests. But he's an adult and it was a family affair. He had a right to issue his own invitations. I'm afraid Harold was quite annoyed.' Lady Tyndall hesitated, visibly steeling herself. 'Is it true . . . The girls tell me Harold didn't kill himself after shooting the woman, that someone else shot them both?'

'Such appears to be the case.'

She gave a little sigh, perhaps of relief. Her husband was still dead, but at least he wasn't guilty of both murder and *felo-de-se*. 'It must have been a burglar. Harold often had money in the study, for servants' wages and tradesmen's bills and so on, and he paid them up there. Anyone could have known. And everyone knew we'd all be out on the terrace watching the fireworks, with all the doors unlocked. They wouldn't have expected to find him there.'

'Nor to find Mrs Gooch. Suppose it was a burglar. That still leaves the question of why she was there with your husband, in the middle of his party. Have you any ideas on the subject, Lady Tyndall?'

'None at all. If it hadn't been Bonfire Night, she might have said something that captured his interest. He was subject to sudden enthusiasms, like having Daisy write about our Guy Fawkes celebration for an American magazine. I quite thought he'd be appalled when Gwen broached the possibility, but he was very keen, wasn't he, Daisy?'

'Very,' Daisy agreed with commendable brevity.

'Did you see Sir Harold talking to Mrs Gooch before the fireworks?' Alec asked Lady Tyndall. 'Or to Mr Gooch, come to that.'

'Only to say "How do you do" when they arrived. Our guests were spread out through this hall and the drawing room, and I was moving about, trying to have a few words with each of them.'

'Did *you* speak to either of the Gooches?'

'No, I'm afraid I missed quite a few people. I find entertaining quite exhausting these days.' She looked quite exhausted now.

Just a couple more questions, Alec decided, then he'd cut it short. He could always come back to her later. 'But you went out with the rest to watch the fireworks?'

'Oh yes, Harold would have been most disappointed if I'd missed his show.'

'Did you see him or speak to him on the terrace?'

'No, I can't say I did. I spoke to various people, of course, whomever I found myself beside. I doubt I can remember exactly. So many people, all muffled up against the cold, and the light was very variable.'

'Did you—' Alec swung round as the front door opened to admit a young woman in a fur-trimmed coat, Cuban-heeled boots in the latest style and rather too much makeup for a morning in the country.

'Mother! Oh, hello, Daisy.' She eyed Alec with disfavour. 'Mother, what's going on? I've been waiting and waiting for someone to come and tell me. I telephoned, but Jennings refused to put me through or call anyone to the phone or tell me what's happened. He said the house is all at sixes and sevens, and the line had to be kept clear for police business anyway. Are you Daisy's policeman?'

Having risen at her approach, Alec bowed.

Her mother frowned at her. 'This is Detective Chief Inspector Fletcher, Adelaide. Mr Fletcher, my daughter Mrs Yarborough. Mrs Stephen Yarborough.'

'Well, I do think it's too bad of you to tie up the telephone lines and not come and tell me all about it.' She seated herself with languid, practised grace. 'Is it true my father's dead?'

Her bluntness made Lady Tyndall gasp.

'Yes,' said Alec with equal bluntness, interested to observe Mrs Yarborough's reaction.

She withdrew a wispy embroidered handkerchief from her coat pocket, applied it to her eyes and burst into noisy and not entirely convincing sobs.

'For pity's sake, Adelaide,' said her mother sharply, 'try for a little self-control.'

The handkerchief was lowered just far enough to allow a resentful glance. Eye makeup unsmudged, Alec noted.

'I can't help but feel it more than the rest of you,' Mrs Yarborough wailed. 'Father was never angry with me the way he was—'

'Not since you moved out at least!' Babs came down the stairs. 'You just walked out whenever it looked as if a row was about to start. Addie, how can you carry on so? Hasn't Mother enough to cope with without your melodramatics?'

'Barbara, squabbling doesn't help.'

'No, sorry, Mother. However,' she added grimly, 'I have an extremely serious matter to discuss with Addie. Let's get out of Mr Fletcher's way. Come along to the drawing room, Addie. Daisy, why don't you come, too? You saw everything.'

'You all pick on me,' Adelaide whined, but she followed Babs.

Daisy looked at Alec. He nodded, so Daisy went with them. He wouldn't trust her to report impartially on Gwen, but she had no particular ties to the elder sisters. He lost his note-taker, but on the other hand he didn't want to distress Lady Tyndall with unnecessary witnesses to her reaction to the news of Mrs Gooch's letter. True or not, it was bound to upset her.

Babs strode towards the drawing room. Adelaide, pouting, tittupped after her. Daisy brought up the rear, feeling like a sheepdog herding a recalcitrant ewe.

She wasn't sure what Alec wanted her to do, other than keep her eyes and ears open. Obviously he didn't want Babs and Addie to find out yet about Mrs Gooch's extraordinary assertion, so she'd better try to keep them away from the hall until he was finished with Lady Tyndall.

That shouldn't be difficult. The usually impassive Babs was clearly spoiling for a fight, to judge by her stormy face as she turned to confront Adelaide. The two sisters glared at each other. They made an odd pair, Addie in her furs and silk stockings, Babs in well-worn work boots and breeches.

Daisy sat down. She was the only witness to both the rocket attack on Gooch and the squib attack on the Triumph, with the subsequent capture of the culprits. However frightening it had been at the time, she intended to tell her story with dispassionate calm.

She saw Sir Nigel and Miller pacing out on the terrace, deep in conversation. She hoped they would not come in too soon, forcing Babs and Addie to assume their company faces before Reggie's and Adrian's misdeeds had been thoroughly exposed.

Addie put her word in first. 'It's not fair! I don't even know what happened to Father.'

'That's because you skived off with the guests instead of sticking it out with the family.'

'Mother Yarborough made me go. She said we had to take the children home and we'd only be in the way.'

'She was quite right.'

'Then stop ragging me. What is it? Why are the police still here?'

'Because, sister dear, Father was murdered,' Babs said bluntly. 'And so was Mrs Gooch.'

'Mrs Gooch? Who's— Murdered!' squealed Adelaide, dropping without her usual careful grace onto a sofa. 'I don't believe it!'

'Believe what you want. That's what the police say. But that's not what I want to talk to you about.'

Given her ignorance of the day's events, Addie's protest was quite reasonable: 'Father murdered and you want to talk about something else?'

'Another murder. Or it will be if *Mr* Gooch dies. And your boys are responsible.'

'You're always trying to blame Reggie and Adrian for everything!' Beneath her makeup, Addie's face was blotchy with anger. 'But murder – that's going too far, Babs. How can you say such a dreadful thing about your own nephews?'

Babs turned to Daisy. 'Tell her.'

'When Gwen fetched me from the station, the boys threw squibs at the car as we passed the trees by the gatekeeper's cottage. Gwen caught them in the act. Then, today, Babs and I saw a rocket come out of those same trees as Mr Gooch drove past. It startled him and he went off the road. He's badly hurt.' Despite her determination to be matter-of-fact, Daisy's voice wobbled a bit. 'We couldn't leave him to go chasing after the boys.'

'You saw them?'

'Not this time, but it was exactly the same as—'

'I'm sure it wasn't Reggie and Adrian. It must have been some louts from the village.'

'Bosh!' Babs exclaimed. 'The village lads are not louts. They work hard for a living. If they had any spare cash for fireworks, they wouldn't waste them up here in broad daylight. Let alone shooting at motor-cars, as Reggie and Adrian are known to have done. You're doing about as bad a job of raising those two as is conceivable.'

'It's not my fault,' Addie said sulkily. 'You're an old maid, you don't understand.'

'If I were lucky enough to have borne Frank's children,' Babs retorted, her tone icy, heartbreak in her face, 'I'd be bringing them up so that he'd be proud of them.' Unexpectedly, her voice softened. 'Addie, can't you see what a disservice you're doing them? If they're not taught to behave, they'll spend their lives running from one disaster to the next. Do you want to see them end up in Borstal?'

'Of course not. They're only mischievous little boys, not criminals.'

'If Gooch dies ... If Father were alive, this couldn't be kept from him, you know. He'd send them to the most disciplinarian school in the country. In fact, I'm sure that's what Jack will do.'

'Jack! It's none of Jack's business!'

'Father was their trustee. I'm not absolutely certain, but I imagine that's one thing Jack will have to take on as his heir.'

'Poor Jack,' said Daisy involuntarily. 'Sorry, none of my business.' Supposing Jack were really Mrs Gooch's son, perhaps he'd be able to escape responsibility for those two horrors. She felt she ought to mention the letter to Babs, if not to Addie, but Alec would undoubtedly be furious.

The temptation was removed by the arrival of Wookleigh and Miller, coming in through the French doors from the terrace.

Alec decided he needed to get down to brass tacks before anyone else walked in on his interview with Lady Tyndall. The entrance hall was the reverse of an ideal place to question a witness, but he didn't want to exhaust her by moving elsewhere.

Watching her daughters depart with Daisy, she said, 'I'm afraid I can guess what Barbara has to say to Adelaide. Will my grandsons face legal sanctions for causing Mr Gooch's accident?'

'Unlikely. Neither Miss Tyndall nor Daisy actually saw them. Even if I could spare men to search, any traces of their presence in that spinney could be from their previous exploits. The ground has been hard with frost for days.'

'Jack will deal with them. He's grown up these last few months. That's what Harold refused to recognize. He never saw the boys' mischief, either. They behaved in his presence, and I'm afraid we all held our tongues to avert yet another tantrum. Poor Mr Gooch has suffered horribly for our cowardice.' Her pity and regret seemed quite sincere, despite the possibility that Gooch had killed both her husband and his own wife. 'He must stay here until he's quite well. We'll hire nurses and pay Dr Prentice's fees, of course.'

'Gooch appears to be well able to pay his own way. We found his wallet in his pocket. We also found a letter to Sir Harold, and another to your son.'

Again, that indefinable expression – dismay? distaste? – flitted across her face, as when Daisy had offered to take notes. Searching pockets and reading private letters – the unacceptable side of police work was intruding on her kindly efforts to treat Alec as the acceptable husband of her daughter's school friend. She said nothing.

Alec could think of no way to soften what he had to tell her. 'The letters appear to have been written by Mrs Gooch. She claims to be Mr Tyndall's – Jack's – natural mother.'

Lady Tyndall's face went completely blank. Then, with an obvious effort, but gently, without anger, she said, 'Why on earth should she do such a thing? The poor woman must have been delusional. Jack is my son.'

CHAPTER 17

'Chilly,' observed Wookleigh. 'Bit of a breeze come up. Morning, Mrs Yarborough. Don't let us disturb you, ladies,' he continued apologetically. 'It's time I was getting along.'

'Won't you stay for lunch, Sir Nigel?' asked Babs, her invitation extended with more propriety than enthusiasm.

'That's kind of you, Miss Tyndall, but you won't want an unexpected guest on a day like this. I just stopped in for a word with Fletcher, but he's obviously up to his ears in his investigation. Mrs Fletcher, please tell him to telephone if there's anything I or my force can do to help. And not a word to your revered mama, eh? Miller, my dear chap, it's been enlightening talking to you.' He shook hands with the engineer. 'I might take you up on your offer one of these days. Good day to you all.'

He bowed, and Babs escorted him towards the door to the entrance hall. Daisy wondered whether she ought to suggest he leave by the French doors so as not to disturb Alec. Indecisive, she drifted after the pair. After exchanging a frigid 'Good morning,' Adelaide and Miller followed.

At the door, Babs turned back. 'I suppose you'd better lunch here, Addie,' she said.

Daisy continued into the hall behind the chief constable. As Babs, Adelaide and Miller followed her, Alec glanced up, his dark brows lowering in annoyance at the interruption. Lady Tyndall summoned up a faint smile for Sir Nigel, who went to her to present his mingled apologies and condolences.

A voice from the stairs drew everyone's attention. 'He needs full-time care, of course,' said the doctor to Gwen as they reached the bottom. 'I'll send day and night nurses.'

Lady Tyndall stood up, steadying herself with a hand on the back of a chair. 'Yes, Dr Prentice, please do,' she said firmly. 'The best possible.'

He came over. 'And you, Lady Tyndall, are not to sit up with him. Take care of yourself, or we'll have you laid up, too.' He turned to Alec. 'Chief Inspector? I must speak to you. You'll want a report of my findings last night.'

'Yes—'

'I'm first,' Addie declared.

'Dr Prentice must be anxious to return to his patients. Detective Sergeant Tring will take your statement, Mrs Yarborough.'

'A sergeant!' Addie was outraged.

'Adelaide,' her mother said sharply, 'you forget yourself. Kindly remember why Mr Fletcher is here. You are to comply with his requirements without a fuss.'

'Bravo, Mother,' said Babs in an undertone.

A modest cough from the direction of the door to the passage turned every head that way. PC Blount blushed and saluted. 'I come as soon as I could, sir,' he said to Alec.

Even more like Piccadilly Circus than the far end of the drive, thought Daisy. Who would turn up next?

Alec looked a fraction of a degree less harassed. 'Thank

you, Constable. Go upstairs and relieve DC Piper, please. He'll explain.'

'I'll show you the way, Blount,' Gwen offered. 'I must have accommodations prepared for the nurses. Then I'll sit with him until they arrive.'

'Who would that be, miss?' Blount enquired, mystified, as he tramped after her to the stairs. 'Nurses?'

'I must get back to work,' said Babs, 'if you can spare me, Mr Fletcher.'

'For the moment, yes, as long as you're not going to be too far from the house. Let me know, please, if you intend to go as far as the village, or farther.'

'Right-oh.' She went out with Sir Nigel.

'I should like a little fresh air before luncheon,' said Lady Tyndall. 'Daisy, would you care to walk with me? We might see if there are any flowers to be cut for the table.'

Daisy had already set out for one morning walk that day, only for it to end in catastrophe. She reminded herself that she had actually walked only one way, though the trip back to the house in Struwwelpeter's car had been anything but restful. Besides, her kind hostess ought to have someone with her, and all her daughters were otherwise occupied. If Lady Tyndall should happen to want to talk about Mrs Gooch's letter, so much the better.

'Do let's,' she said. 'It's jolly cold outside, though. You'd better wrap up well.'

She was still wearing her outdoor clothes. Lady Tyndall went to the cloakroom and emerged bundled up in hat, gloves, scarf and a long dark grey woollen cape trimmed with green.

'Gosh, that looks warm,' said Daisy.

'It is, and fairly waterproof, too, though it gets rather heavy when it's wet. It's Tyrolean. *Lodenmantel*, they call it. I've had it over twenty years, well before the Germans and Austrians became our enemies, but I didn't wear it during the war.'

'It looks good for another twenty.'

They went out through the drawing room, leaving Miller looking rather lost, Adelaide sulking on a sofa, and Alec and the doctor in close confab at a discreet distance from both.

From the north end of the terrace, a stone-paved path led into a shrubbery of evergreens, ilex, yew and laurustinus.

'Rather gloomy at this time of year.' Lady Tyndall apologized.

'The holly and yew berries brighten it up a bit, and it's sheltered from the breeze.'

'It's pleasantly shady in the summer. I love to walk here on hot days.' She continued to utter polite nothings, but her mind, unsurprisingly, seemed elsewhere. Why had she invited Daisy to go with her unless she really wanted to talk about the calamities afflicting her family? Perhaps she simply didn't know how to begin.

Daisy, bursting with questions, tried in vain to think of a tactful way to broach the subject of Jack's parentage.

A side path took them to a well-concealed potting shed, its weathered wooden walls and lichened slate roof blending into the bushes.

'I'll just fetch a trug and secateurs.' Lady Tyndall lifted the latch and went in. Daisy stood in the doorway.

The shed contained the usual clutter of garden implements – clay pots, watering cans, bottles of turps and linseed oil, balls of twine, old sacks, a stepladder, bamboo plant stakes, a scythe hanging from a high hook, and a still higher shelf with rusty tins and dusty jars of poisons equally fatal to insects and humans.

'I simply can't persuade Biddle to keep it tidy. Of course, the poor man has far too much to do these days with just a boy to help. But my flower things belong in this corner – yes, here they are.'

She tucked the secateurs into one of the *Lodenmantel*'s capacious pockets. Daisy took the shallow reed basket and followed Lady Tyndall past the shed. The shrubbery opened out into a sheltered vegetable garden with several beds dedicated to cutting flowers for the house. Not much was in bloom at this season, but they managed to fill the trug with Michaelmas daisies, calendulas and greenery.

'That will do for now. The Chinese lanterns are ready to cut for drying, but they can wait.' She turned towards the path, saying in a detached tone, 'Isn't it odd. Everything is . . . falling apart, yet one carries on doing the little, everyday things, as if they still mattered. Did your husband tell you about the letter from that woman?'

'Gosh no, Alec wouldn't tell me something like that. But I happened to be there when Jack opened it, and I know what she wrote.'

'It's nonsense. Jack doesn't believe it, does he? He mustn't! He's my son, the best son any mother could ask for.'

'He said he absolutely couldn't believe it.'

'Thank heaven! He must have been hurt and bewildered, though. I thought he seemed distressed when I came downstairs. I should have stayed with him.'

'He was very anxious that you should not be distressed. He hoped Alec wouldn't have to tell you about the letter, but it's part of the investigation. He couldn't keep it from you.'

'Part of the investigation?' Lady Tyndall looked shocked. 'Oh, surely not.'

Daisy decided it was inadvisable to point out that Mrs Gooch's claim must somehow explain her meeting with Sir Harold. 'Well, let me put it this way: Alec has to treat it as if it's part of the investigation. That's his job.'

'I suppose so. But does he believe what it says? Your husband?'

'He wouldn't tell me if he'd made up his mind, but I'd be surprised if he's not keeping an open mind about it. That's also part of his job.'

'Oh dear, just when one thinks things can't possibly get any worse, some new horror raises its head. Is it true that my grandsons caused Mr Gooch's accident?'

'I'm afraid it seems very likely.'

Lady Tyndall fell silent. They entered the house by a back door and thence into a small whitewashed scullery with a stone sink. Daisy set the trug on the slate draining board. Lady Tyndall opened a cupboard and surveyed the several shelves of vases. She selected a tall one, green porcelain, for the Michaelmas daisies, and reached for a step stool.

'Let me help,' Daisy offered.

'That's all right, dear, I always do the flowers myself.' She stepped up on the stool and took down a pair of smaller vases from a higher shelf. 'I find it soothing, and I have a great deal to think about.'

Daisy accepted this gentle dismissal. 'I'll leave you in peace, then.'

At the door, she glanced back. The big vase was in the sink, filling with water, while Lady Tyndall stripped and snipped the stems of the Michaelmas daisies. Though she seemed completely intent on her task, the slump of her thin shoulders looked less like weariness than utter defeat.

What must it be like to have doubt cast on the legitimacy of one's beloved son? Mrs Gooch's letter had made a strong impression on Daisy, but after due consideration, she couldn't believe it was true.

Things had changed since the days of the Warming-Pan Plot, when people believed the Old Pretender, as a baby, had been smuggled into the Queen's bed to provide James II with an heir. Even the King hadn't been able to suppress the rumours.

Sir Harold couldn't possibly have introduced his love child into Edge Manor with only his wife's knowledge. The notion was preposterous. For a start, why would Lady Tyndall have agreed to the deception? But supposing he had persuaded her, too many people would have had to be in the secret: doctor, midwife, monthly nurse, vicar, registrar, lady's maid and other servants – and what the servants knew, the village knew.

If Sir Harold had actually pulled it off, though, the arrival of the Gooches had set off an explosion greater than anything Babs's boys had so far accomplished. Like a Catherine wheel throwing off glittering sparks, Daisy's brain whirled with multiplying motives.

At the luciferous centre, one fact stood out: Jack had by far the most to lose from a revelation of his illegitimacy.

But it couldn't be true!

'Prognosis?' Alec asked.

'I believe he'll live,' Dr Prentice told him, 'but severe head injuries are the very devil to predict. He may have permanent brain damage. He may not be able to speak.'

'Or write?'

'Or write. But he may recover fully, soon, or in time.'

'Poor chap! All right, what about your examination of the murder victims?'

Prentice's brief oral report confirmed Tom's, Alec's, and the police surgeon's conclusions. Tucking the written report into his pocket, Alec said, 'Thank you, Doctor, that's admirably clear. If you should ever want a position as police surgeon, I'd be happy to recommend you. You realize, I'm sure, this is as confidential as your relations with your patients.'

'Of course.'

'And what I have to ask you now is equally confidential. Am I right in assuming you were not in practice in this area twenty-one years ago?'

'Nor anywhere,' Prentice agreed with a touch of amusement. 'I would guess we are much of an age, you and I.'

'I don't suppose you can put me in touch with your predecessor?'

'Unless you believe in table turning, no. I bought the practice on Dr Gunnicott's death. But my attic is full of his records. Apparently he never discarded anything. I haven't found time to go through any but the most recent of those applicable to patients I took over, and I hate to throw them out wholesale.'

'Good! I'll send DC Piper to go through them.'

'Just a minute, Chief Inspector. It was you who brought up the subject of patient confidentiality.'

Alec grinned. 'Oh well, it's always worth a try, to save time. You live in Gloucestershire?'

'In Chipping Campden, just up the road.'

'Then Dryden-Jones will no doubt be delighted to make himself useful in obtaining a warrant.'

'Send your man with a warrant and he may ransack my attic to his heart's content.'

They shook hands cordially, and Prentice went to the telephone cubby under the stairs to ring up a nursing agency.

While they were talking, Piper had come down from Gooch's room. Alec quickly brought him up-to-date, then sent him after the doctor. As soon as the line was free, he was to go to the telephone in the butler's pantry to start the process of applying for a search warrant, and then to get in touch with the county officers in charge of questioning all last night's guests.

Adelaide Yarborough and Martin Miller were both still hanging about in the hall, not speaking to each other. She sat flipping through a copy of *Vogue*; he stood staring out of a window. When Piper left, they converged on Alec.

The engineer reached him first. 'I don't think I'm doing a lot of good staying—'

'Mr Fletcher,' Mrs Yarborough interrupted impatiently, 'how much longer do you expect me to wait? I do have more important things to do with my time, you know.'

Miller stared at her with undisguised astonishment.

Alec raised his eyebrows. 'Indeed? More important than helping us discover who killed your father?'

'I can't honestly see that it matters who did it. That stupid Australian, I expect. The fact is, Father's gone, so there's no chance now of Reggie inheriting more than a paltry amount. I don't see how Babs expects me to send them away to a good school when I've got hardly anything to live on as it is. Jack will have to pay the fees.'

Alec wondered who would be the residuary legatee if Jack were convicted of his father's murder (and his mother's?) . He ought to have asked the solicitor. Whoever, he or she would undoubtedly have to deal with the young malefactors. If Prentice was mistaken and Gooch died, the police would be drawn into the matter, though Alec doubted there was a provable case against the boys.

Mrs Yarborough started to fidget under Alec's icy gaze. 'How much longer?' she repeated.

'I'll be with you in a moment, to escort you to Sergeant Tring.'

'There's no one else here. I haven't anything to tell you, but I don't see why you can't interview me yourself.'

'I have more important things to do with my time.' A police officer ought not to resort to frivolous sarcasm, however true, but Mrs Yarborough didn't seem to recognize the echo of her own words. She was cross but not offended. Turning to Miller, however, Alec surprised a quickly hidden grin. He ignored it, beckoning the engineer aside. 'I think you're wrong,' he said. 'You may be at a loose end just now, but I think your presence will be a comfort and support to more than one of the family.'

Miller gave him a probing look. 'Does this mean I'm no longer under suspicion?'

'I wouldn't go quite so far as that. But new information has come to light which changes the entire tenor of this enquiry. I can't justify telling you about it, but if young Tyndall chooses to confide in you, I have no objection.'

'Does this mysterious information tend to implicate him?'

'Not exactly. I can only say that his position is precarious.'

'I shan't advise him to confess,' Miller said bluntly.

Maybe not, though Alec suspected the engineer was a

conventional, law-abiding soul. If Jack confided anything suggesting guilt, whatever advice Miller gave, the relationship between the two was bound to change. Alec might learn a lot simply by observing them.

'I shouldn't dream of asking you to do so,' he said. 'My hope is that your common sense will prevent his doing anything foolish. You'll stay?'

'For the present.'

'Good. Mrs Yarborough, come with me, please.'

In the passage, they found the ancient butler perched on a stool outside the door to his pantry.

'Young whippersnapper,' he muttered resentfully, 'has to use my telephone, says he, in private, says he. What's a man to do when a whippersnapper of a policeman can turf him unceremonious out of the place that's his by right?'

'Oh, do stop fussing, Jennings,' snapped Mrs Yarborough. 'It's not as if he's going to pinch the silver. Nor as if you were doing anything useful in there, or have for a hundred years.'

Dignity injured, the butler drew himself up as straight as his bent back allowed. 'I do my best, Miss Adelaide, and it's not for you to criticize if others are satisfied.'

Alec forestalled Mrs Yarborough's retort. 'Mr Jennings, I'm Chief Inspector Fletcher. I'm sorry my man has disturbed you, but I'm afraid it's unavoidable.' He kept his tone more incisive than apologetic. 'I'd like a few words with you, in a couple of minutes.'

'I'll be here,' Jennings said morosely.

In general, Tom Tring got along almost as well with butlers as with female servants, but the old man might respond better to authority than chumminess. If he really had a secret to tell, maybe Alec could extract it from him.

Mrs Yarborough proceeded towards the billiard room, her stiff back expressive of her outrage that the Chief Inspector chose to question the butler rather than herself.

As she and Alec entered the room, Tom Tring and Jack Tyndall looked around and rose from their seats at the gun table. Light gleamed on Tom's shining dome as he gave Alec a barely perceptible shake of the head: Jack had revealed nothing new, or at least nothing useful.

Jack jumped up. 'Mr Fletcher, where's my mother?'

'She went out to get some fresh air. And to pick some flowers, I gathered.'

'To pick flowers?' Jack was stunned. 'You told her everything?'

'Just a moment, Mr Tyndall, please. Mrs Yarborough, Detective Sergeant Tring has a few questions for you. Mrs Yarborough was Miss Adelaide Tyndall, Sergeant.'

'Do sit down, madam,' offered Tom in his best fatherly manner. 'I'm sure this won't take long.'

Alec took Jack through the other door into the dining room, where the table was already laid for luncheon. Fortunately no one was there. 'Lady Tyndall knows about the letter and its contents,' he said, 'though she hasn't actually read it. She denied Mrs Gooch's claim, as no doubt she will tell you.'

'I knew it couldn't be true! But Mother must have been upset, all the same.'

'She was distressed, more on your account than her own. We were interrupted before we could discuss it, but I believe she wanted time to reflect before speaking to you about it.' Alec suppressed the fact that her ladyship had invited Daisy to go with her.

'Ought I to go after her?'

'Best let her decide when she's ready.'

'Yes, of course.' Jack paused, then continued with dread in his voice. 'I say, sir, you don't think she's denying it to protect me?'

'From what?'

'From the knowledge that I'm illegitimate? From suspicion of having killed my ... my natural mother to protect the secret?'

'I have no idea. Do you feel in need of protection?'

'From the knowledge, no. If it's true, it has to be faced. But obviously it must look awfully fishy to the police. To you.'

'It's not a possibility we can ignore. Did you shoot her?'

'No! Nor my father.'

'Then I shouldn't worry. We generally get the right person in the end. We'll get there faster if you tell us everything, without reservation.'

'I have, everything I can remember and more than I ever thought I could remember. Sergeant Tring's pretty good, isn't he? Looking at him, you wouldn't think he's so sharp. But obviously you can't take my word for it. I can't believe this is happening! I suppose my sisters will have to know. Is it cowardly not to want to tell them myself?'

'Not at all.'

'But I have to talk to *some*one.'

'How about Mr Miller? He has a good head on his shoulders, and an outsider's perspective. And I'd say he's far less interested in your birth than your engineering ability.'

As Alec had rather expected, Jack clung to the thought of Miller as a point of sanity in a world gone insane. Watching the lad go off in search of his friend, some of the resilience of youth restored to his bearing, Alec chided himself for feeling so much sympathy for his chief suspect. Was Jack Tyndall an innocent caught up in a nightmare, or a patricide, a matricide and a superb actor?

Daisy said he had kept his engineering studies secret from his family for a couple of years, leading his father to believe he was indulging in the frivolities expected of aristocratic undergrads at Oxford and Cambridge. That must have taken some acting ability. The heir to Edge Manor remained at the top of Alec's list.

CHAPTER 18

With the help of a chance-met maid, Daisy found her way from the flower room to the main hall. As she entered, she saw Jack and Miller leaving through the door to the drawing room. Going to finish off dismantling the fireworks apparatus, she thought. How long ago the Guy Fawkes celebration seemed!

She nearly called out to them, but stopped herself just in time. She didn't know whether Miller had heard about Mrs Gooch's letter; she couldn't pretend she didn't know about it; and anyway, she wasn't at all sure what to say to Jack next time they met. Not that she cared who his mother was. It wasn't his fault if his father had had an affair with a young woman from Evesham, twenty-one years ago.

Nearer twenty-two. *Someone* must know whether Lady Tyndall had been pregnant or not.

As though in response to the thought, the baby turned head over heels inside her. 'It's all right,' she said soothingly, patting her bulge. 'It's nearly lunchtime. I expect you're as ravenous as I am. Somehow we missed elevenses.'

Still a bit chilled from her tramp around the gardens with Lady Tyndall, Daisy subsided into a chair by the fire. She stretched out hands and feet towards the flickering flames, then quickly assumed a more ladylike posture when Adelaide came in from the passage.

'Oh, Daisy.' Addie didn't sound pleased to see her but came to sit down. 'I do think your husband is the pink limit, foisting me off on that sergeant while he talked to Jennings.'

'I'm sure he had a good reason.'

'I can't imagine what Jennings could tell him. He never does a stroke of work, hardly ever leaves his pantry. He should have been pensioned off twenty years ago.'

'He's worked here that long?'

'As long as I can remember.'

'How far back can you remember?'

'When I was five or six, I suppose. I remember the first time I joined in lessons with Babs. We had a perfectly foul German governess. I wasn't a bit surprised when we went to war with Germany.'

'So you don't remember Gwen being born.'

'Of course not. If I remembered that far back, it would be her suddenly appearing out of nowhere. Children weren't allowed to know about pregnancies.'

'True,' Daisy agreed with an inward sigh. She should have realized it was no use expecting Jack's sisters to know anything about his birth. After all, she hadn't told her eleven-year-old stepdaughter she was pregnant. Belinda had found out for herself.

'I suppose you want to talk about pregnancy and childbirth and all that,' said Adelaide. She didn't utter the words but her tone said, *What a crashing bore!*

'No, actually, I'd much rather talk about food. Are you staying to lunch?'

'I suppose I might as well.'

'The butler may not be up to much, but the cook is jolly good. Has she been here long?'

'Several years. The previous cook was a man and he got called up. From what I've heard of army food, cooking it must have come as a nasty shock to him after Edge Manor. Father offered to take him back when he was demobbed, but he found a job in a London restaurant. Servants are so disloyal nowadays.'

Once started on this theme, Addie was easily kept going. By the time the gong rang for lunch, Daisy had learnt that Jennings was the only member of the manor's staff who had worked here at the time of Jack's birth.

Whether the doddering old man had any recollection of the circumstances was another matter.

'Tom, you have my deepest sympathy,' Alec declared, entering the billiard room.

'That's nice, Chief. What for?'

'For having had to question the butler.'

'Ah.' Tom grinned. 'Selective deafness.'

'Selective senility! As you said, he thinks he has a secret. It may be entirely in his imagination, or he may have forgotten what it is. In any case, I would hesitate to rely on anything he says, if he ever says anything. He's a perverse old curmudgeon and who knows what goes on in his head.'

'Who knows what goes on in any of their heads. Young Mr Tyndall, f'r instance. Horrified by what's happened; helpful as you please; don't care about the tide, nor the money, much; shocked and incredulous over the letter; worried about its effect on his ma, and the rest of the family if rumour gets about. Nice lad, butter wouldn't melt in his mouth, but he's got means, opportunity and the best motive I've seen in a long while. Motives, if the letter's true.'

Alec asked the question that was topmost in his mind: 'You think he's a good actor?'

'Ah!' Tom ruminated. 'Seems to me, if you've got a father with a short fuse like that, unless you're a saint or you actually enjoy brangling, you'd grow up spending a lot of effort keeping things from him.'

'Yes, they all seem to have gone to great lengths to cover up the Yarborough boys' misdeeds, just for the sake of peace and quiet. I imagine that's fairly typical.'

'Hardened deceivers, the lot of them, you reckon?'

'That's putting it rather strongly. You didn't get anything useful out of Tyndall.'

'Not a thing. He remembered a few more details of this and that, but nothing to help us. As for that Mrs Yarborough, a more self-centred creature I hope I never meet. Just about all she can remember of last night is how many compliments she got on her frock, how her brother wrongfully accused her sons of stealing rockets, and how she was forced to help act as hostess though she's no longer a member of this household.'

'For which they must all breathe frequent sighs of relief. All right, let me see your notes on the interviews with her, Tyndall and the servants. Here's mine on the second half of Lady Tyndall's. I can tell you what was said before, but Daisy has the verbatim notes, in her indecipherable shorthand. She'll type them up after lunch.'

As if the mention of lunch had summoned them, two maids

came in with trays. Miss Gwendolyn had invited Alec to join the family in the dining room, but he had far too much to discuss with his men. Besides, sitting down to eat with a group of suspects was always uncomfortable, though he'd had to do it more than once. Usually because Daisy was a guest of the suspects, come to think of it.

'Ah, hot soup,' said Tom, rubbing his hands together. In spite of the fire Gwen had had made up for them, the room was chilly. 'And very welcome, too.'

The girls both beamed, and one of them giggled. 'There's cold meat for after, Mr Tring. Miss Gwen said you wouldn't want us popping in and out, disturbing you. And apple charlotte.'

The other nudged her. 'For three.'

'DC Piper will be joining us,' Alec said, and thanked them.

He and Tom had finished their thick vegetable soup and embarked on cold beef and ham and hot jacket potatoes when Ernie finally arrived.

'Food!' he said with alacrity, taking a seat. 'Report first,' said Tom.

'Have a heart, Sarge! The soup'll be stone-cold.'

'Soup first,' Alec decreed, 'unless there's something urgent.'

'I'd've told you right off, Chief, if there was.' The soup rapidly disappeared. As he served himself a lavish helping of sliced meat and a couple of potatoes, Ernie said, 'Nothing interesting from any of the guests they've talked to, which is most of the list. Half of 'em can't remember who they talked to, and none of 'em noticed the time, nor noticed Sir Harold or anyone else entering the house.'

'Pretty much as I expected. What about the search warrant?'

'The Lord Lieutenant's going to get one for us. He offered to bring it over himself, but I think I managed to persuade him to send a motorcycle officer.'

'Good for you, laddie!' Tom said approvingly.

'Yes, we can do without Mr Dryden-Jones. All right, eat up: we've a busy afternoon ahead.'

Luncheon in the dining room was one of the most dismal meals Daisy had ever attended. Not that there was anything wrong with the food, but the nervous tension was palpable.

Everyone was there. Gwen had deputed the housekeeper to take her place at Gooch's side while she ate, and Babs eschewed her usual bread and cheese with the farm workers in favour of family solidarity. As far as Daisy could tell, she and Gwen, like Adelaide, didn't know about Mrs Gooch's letter. Neither the letter nor the murders were discussed, and a brief enquiry from Lady Tyndall to Gwen was the only mention of Gooch's accident.

He was still deeply unconscious.

Everyone was too well brought up to talk about tragedy and trepidation at table, with servants bobbing in and out. But no one was able to forget for long enough to carry on a conversation about anything else – no one but Addie. She had seen an evening dress she fancied in *Vogue* and she went on and on about it, and the handbag, shoes, gloves, and jewellery to go with it, in the most excruciating detail. Daisy alternated between wanting to wring her neck and being grateful that she saved everyone else from having to think of things to say.

After lunch, as they left the room, Lady Tyndall held Daisy

back. 'My dear, I have a favour to ask. But you must promise to tell me if you don't feel up to it.'

'Right-oh. What can I do for you?'

'You know about this . . . this wretched letter. The girls will have to hear about it. That is, not Adelaide perhaps, but Gwen and Barbara must.'

'Did Alec tell you not to mention it?'

'No.'

'He won't tell them unless he absolutely has to.'

'He might consider it necessary, and it's not fair to let them learn about it from the police. Yet I don't think I can bear to explain it to them. It's a lot to ask, but would you mind very much . . . ? I don't want to impose, but it can't be as painful a subject for you, not being one of the family . . .'

'Willingly,' said Daisy. 'I'd better go and catch Babs before she goes back to work.'

What luck, she thought, hurrying after the others. With Lady Tyndall practically begging her to talk to Gwen and Babs about the letter, Alec could hardly cavil when she did so. Well, he could and doubtless would object, but at least she had a defence, for once.

Her quarry was just going out of the front door.

'Babs!' she called. 'I'll walk a little way with you, if you don't mind waiting a moment while I fetch my coat. It's down here.'

'Shouldn't you put your feet up for a while? You had quite an energetic morning.'

'It's no good lying down right after a meal, believe me. In fact, *quite* the wrong thing to do. The pressure—'

'Spare me the details, please! I can cope with cows and sheep, but if you'd heard how Addie carried on . . . !'

Daisy laughed. 'Right-oh. I'll just come a little way, so I won't hold you up.'

She fetched her coat and hat from the cloakroom and they set out.

'I'll spare you the details,' Daisy said, 'but really on the whole I'm very well. I gather your mother had a hard time with her pregnancies.'

'Yes. At the time, we didn't know why she was sometimes such an invalid, of course.'

'You must have been ten when Jack was born, though. It's hard to keep anything from a child that age. Didn't you find out what was going on?'

'I dare say I might have if she'd been here. Father took her to a sanatarium abroad. Switzerland, I think. Don't the Swiss rather go in for that sort of thing? Rest cures and such?'

'I believe so,' said Daisy, trying to hide her shock. What better cover for a secret adoption? How on earth was she going to tell Babs about the letter?

Babs gave her an odd look, but she was distracted at that moment, as Adelaide sailed by in her chauffeur-driven Humber, giving Babs and Daisy a regal nod as she passed. Babs uttered a wordless growl.

'I would hate,' she muttered, 'to have gone through a difficult pregnancy and have nothing to show for it but Adelaide.'

'You should sympathize with Addie, even if her pregnancies were easy, for having gone through two with nothing to show for them but Reggie and Adrian.'

'They're still young. Jack and I and a decent school will soon straighten them out. As long as Gooch doesn't die!'

'It'd be almost worse if his brain is permanently damaged.'

'They won't be able to try him for murder if he can't defend himself, will they?'

'I shouldn't think so. Even if they were pretty sure he did it, which they're not.' Daisy ordered herself to stop procrastinating. 'He had a letter in his pocket. Your mother asked me to tell you about it.'

'What?' Babs stopped and turned to face Daisy. 'Why on earth . . . ?'

'It's rather upsetting, and I don't think she felt up to talking about it.'

'A letter in *Gooch*'s pocket that *Mother* doesn't want to talk to *me* about?'

'Or Gwen. Jack already knows. It was addressed to him. Actually, there were two letters. I'm explaining this very badly.'

'Start again at the beginning. Pretend you're writing an article and your readers expect to understand what you've written,' Babs suggested sardonically. 'Gooch had a letter – two letters – in his pocket?'

'An envelope, sealed, with your father's name on it.' Under Babs's somewhat fierce regard, Daisy's busy morning caught up with her and she began to feel rather weak at the knees. 'Oh dear, is there somewhere we could sit down while I tell you?'

'There's a stile a few yards farther on. You're not going to faint, are you?'

'Heavens no!'

They reached the stile, flat stones projecting out of the banked wall on the uphill side of the drive. Daisy perched precariously on one of the steps.

Babs stood in front of her and resumed in gender tones, 'Gooch had two letters in his pocket in an envelope addressed to Father?'

'Yes. In the circumstances, Alec opened it and read the note to Sir Harold.'

'In the circumstances, I can see that he had to.'

'I ought not to have read it over his shoulder, though,' Daisy admitted guiltily. 'I'm afraid curiosity is my besetting sin.'

'"'Satiable curtiosity", like the Elephant's Child?'

'Exactly!'

'Well, your nose seems to have survived intact. What did it say?'

'That she – it was written by Mrs Gooch – she felt she ought to warn your father first but, whether he approved or not, she was going to tell Jack the facts.'

'For pity's sake, Daisy, what facts?'

'That came later.' Daisy explained about the inner envelope, how Alec had given it to Jack and he, after reading it, had handed it back. 'So of course he read it. Oh Babs, it was heartbreaking! Mrs Gooch said she'd come all the way from Australia to see him. She wasn't going to upset his life, but she wanted to make sure he was happy, and when he was so friendly to her at the pub she simply had to tell him the truth. She said she and Sir Harold had an affair and she's Jack's mother.'

'Good Lord,' said Babs blankly, 'can it possibly be true? Or was it some sort of attempt at blackmail?'

'It could have been.'

'But it would fit, wouldn't it, with Father dragging Mother off abroad and coming back months later with baby Jack? Father was so desperate for a son! And I'll tell you what, it would explain why Gooch shot both of them. It must have been just plain old jealousy!'

CHAPTER 19

As Daisy entered the billiard room, Alec, Tom and Ernie looked up from the papers spread out on the gun table.

'Sorry, darling, I must have drowsed off. I didn't mean to. But here are the notes I took for you, all typed and legible. And also a report of what Babs told me.' She couldn't keep a touch of triumph from her voice.

'Daisy, you haven't been asking questions—'

'Gosh no. Well, not exactly. You see, Lady Tyndall asked me to tell Gwen and Babs about Mrs Gooch's letter. I couldn't very well refuse, could I? By the time I reached Gwen, Mr Miller had told her already, at Jack's request. He really is quite a nice man. I think he'll do for her.'

'What did Miss Tyndall say?' Alec demanded with precarious patience. 'Cut the cackle and get to the horses.'

'We were talking about' – Daisy blushed, a Victorian affection she despised, and avoided looking at Tom and Piper, but continued stoutly – 'about pregnancy, and about how children aren't told a baby is expected until it arrives. You know, they're given that myth about storks bringing them. And I said Babs was ten or eleven when Jack was born, so surely she'd had some idea. Belinda knew without ever being told, remember, darling?'

'I remember.' Alec was now interested, Tom's moustache was twitching in the way that meant it hid a grin, and Piper was frankly admiring.

'Babs said perhaps she would have found out, if it hadn't been that Sir Harold— you see, Lady Tyndall had difficult pregnancies with the girls and never quite recovered her health, so when he took her abroad to a sanatarium, everyone assumed it was for her general health. But when she came home, she brought Jack with her.'

'Great Scott! How long was she away?'

'I don't know. I didn't like to ask questions,' Daisy said virtuously.

Tom's grin was open. 'Of course, it don't prove anything, but it would explain how they fiddled it without anyone finding out. He takes his wife and his mistress – begging your pardon, Mrs Fletcher – abroad, makes sure the girl's well cared for till the baby's born, gives her enough money to start a new life in Australia, and comes home with a brand-new son and heir.'

'A bit chancy, Sarge,' Piper observed. 'What if she'd had a girl?'

'Nothing lost. She could take the baby with her to Australia, or he could arrange for it to be adopted on the Continent. No, the fly in the ointment, as I see it, is how does he persuade his missus – her ladyship, that is – to go along with the hoax? To bring up the boy as her own?'

'She was accustomed to trying to please him,' said Alec, frowning, 'to avert his fits of bad temper. But she certainly gives the impression of being very fond of the lad.'

'I'm sure she is,' said Daisy decidedly. 'She may not have liked it at first, but I bet she forgets most of the time that he's not her own. I sometimes do with Belinda, and I've only known her a couple of years, since she was nine. Lady Tyndall's had Jack since he was a little tiny baby, for twenty-one years. I'm sure she loves him as much as her daughters, or even more.'

'More?' Tom asked, eyebrows crawling up his limitless forehead.

'Because he's the youngest, and one boy among three girls. Just because he's a boy. My brother was always my parents' favourite, though he wasn't nearly as well behaved as my sister.'

'I've known it to happen,' Tom admitted, 'though not with what you might call a cuckoo in the nest.'

'But cuckoos push the other babies out of the nest, don't they? Jack got on very well with his sisters. Except Addie perhaps, though I don't know about when they were children. But he was especially close to Gwen, who's nearest to him in age. What's more, as far as I can gather, he never gave Sir Harold and Lady Tyndall any trouble, until he decided he wanted to be an engineer.'

'Which a lot of parents would give their eyeteeth to see their sons aiming for. A very respectable profession.'

'But one which Sir Harold strongly objected to,' said Alec. 'Don't let's lose sight of that in the middle of this panegyric. I wonder whether he was angry enough to throw the boy's illegitimacy in his face in the course of that row yesterday afternoon, which you so unfortunately missed, Daisy.'

'Good gracious, I never thought I'd hear you say such a thing, darling! But no, I'm sure he didn't. It could hardly have failed to upset Jack dreadfully, and he was in very good spirits at the beginning of the evening, when he showed me the guy he'd made for the bonfire.'

'I reckon him inviting the Gooches to the party was the last straw,' Piper ventured. 'Sir Harold would've been put out just because they were the wrong sort of people, but when he reckernized Mrs Gooch he'd fly off the handle. That'd be when he told Mr Tyndall.'

'Oh no, not in the middle of his party. Not a chance.'

'Then maybe *she* told him. Mrs Gooch.'

'She'd written the letter to Sir Harold, remember. She intended to give him a chance to warn Jack.'

'She might've been too excited to wait.'

This, Daisy could not deny. 'Then why go up to the study with Sir Harold?' she queried doubtfully. 'I suppose she might have felt she owed him an explanation.'

'There's still the possibility of blackmail,' Tom reminded them.

'I still think Babs's explanation is more likely.'

'And what is Miss Tyndall's explanation?' asked Alec, who had been jotting down notes while listening to the other three argue their various theories.

'Well, naturally she'd rather Gooch was the villain than one of the family. She thinks he shot them both in a fit of jealousy. It makes sense, doesn't it? Not only jealous of the past relationship between Sir Harold and his wife, which for all we know he had only just found out about, but jealous of her love for Jack, for his own sons' sake.'

'Ah,' said Tom broodingly, 'that'd be nice and straightforward at least.'

'Yes,' Alec agreed, 'not one of your wilder speculations, Daisy. Though there's still the oddity of his finding the gun, in the dark, in a house he'd never before visited. But until we know whether Mrs Gooch's letter told the truth, we're theorizing ahead of our facts. Did Miss Tyndall come up with the tale of Lady Tyndall's sojourn abroad before or after you told her about the letter?'

Daisy thought back. 'Before.'

'And you're as sure as you can be that she didn't already know about the letter's claim?'

'I think not, but I wouldn't swear to it. She was quite calm when I told her, and she saw at once the connection with her mother's absence. But why should she make it up?'

'The memory's a funny thing, Mrs Fletcher,' said Tom. 'If Miss Tyndall knew about the letter, after twenty years she could easily mix up some other trip Lady Tyndall took to the Continent and honestly believe it happened just before her brother appeared on the scene.'

'But I'm pretty sure she didn't know, so it's probably a genuine memory, so Mrs Gooch was probably telling the truth.'

Alec shook his head. 'It doesn't follow. Lady Tyndall could very well have given birth abroad.'

'Oh dear.' Daisy sighed. 'I'm reasoning in circles again.'

''Fraid so, love. Unfortunately, what Miss Tyndall's story does mean, if true, is that the local doctor didn't attend the birth, so we won't get proof one way or t'other from his records.'

'You still want me to look, Chief?' asked Piper.

'Yes, of course. If we're lucky – if Jack Tyndall is lucky – you'll find a record of his coming into the world right here at Edge Manor. Then we can start wondering why Mrs Gooch made up such a convincing tale, and what the connection is with her death and Sir Harold's. Daisy, let me just look through these notes of yours, and then we won't keep you any longer.'

'I can tell when I'm not wanted. Oh, before I forget, Gwen asked about getting Mr Gooch's luggage from the Three Ravens.'

'Tom's going to take care of that.'

'I expect Mr Miller would give you a lift, Mr Tring. He offered to go. and fetch the stuff when Gwen mentioned it, but I said it mustn't be touched before the police have seen it.'

'Quite right, Mrs Fletcher. I won't trouble Mr Miller for a lift down, as young Piper's going to drop me off on his way to the doctor's, but d'you think he'd be offended if I telephoned when I'm ready to come away?'

'I shouldn't think so,' said Daisy. 'He seems to want to be useful, in the spirit of knight errantry.'

'Good. I won't have to hire a car to bring it all back.'

'Farm cart more like, Sarge,' Piper said wistfully, as if regretful that he'd miss the spectacle of Tom Tring perched on top of the Gooches' possessions in the back of a hay cart.

Alec looked up from Daisy's notes. 'Knight errantry? And you said something about Miller being all right for Gwen. I gathered earlier that you didn't believe those two were serious about each other.'

'Are you going to start suspecting them again, darling? I don't think they were frightfully serious before last night. Coping with a crisis is liable to show people in their best or worst light', and they've both come through with flying colours. I'll go and tell Mr Miller to expect a telephone call from the Ravens, shall I?'

'If you'd be so kind, Mrs Fletcher,' said Tom.

Reluctantly, Daisy left. It wasn't that she would ever choose to be mixed up in a murder investigation, but once inadvertently involved, she felt being shut out of discussions was really rather unfair.

As the door closed behind her, Alec said, 'We mustn't forget the others just because young Tyndall and Gooch have such obvious motives.'

'Miller and Miss Gwendolyn,' said Tom. 'Mrs Fletcher is right, of course, that you can learn a lot about a person by watching how they behave in a crisis. But there's two ways of looking at it. It's all very well saying Miller makes a good living and don't care about her couple of thousand quid, but there's been murder done for a lot less. Sir Harold disapproves of Miller. Sir Harold dies. All of a sudden, Miller and Miss Gwendolyn are all lovey-dovey.'

'We may have to go into Miller's financial position,' Alec agreed. 'Unsound investments or gambling catch even practical chaps like engineers. For all we know, he's desperate for that couple of thousand. You'd better ask him a few questions on the way back from the village.'

'Right, Chief.'

'And what about Miss Gwendolyn?' Ernie put in eagerly. 'Could be her last chance to get married afore she's too old to have children, and her father's spiking her guns.'

'Pity he didn't spike his own,' Tom observed. 'But you're right, laddie. It needn't be thwarted love, just fear of ending up an old maid.'

Alec was glad Daisy wasn't present to hear her friend depicted as a desperate husband-hunter. 'They could even be in it together, I suppose,' he said, 'though the actual shooting was a one-man job. What about Miss Tyndall?'

'Ah, now,' said Tom, 'barring Gooch with his Wild West experience, Miss Tyndall's the only one of the lot I'd reckon has the nerve for it.'

'All the Tyndalls learnt to shoot in the war, Sarge.'

'Shooting at a target's very different from shooting at a person, young feller-me-lad. On the other hand, her motive's pretty thin. As long as Sir Harold was alive, there was always the chance he might relent and leave the place to her.'

'Good point, Tom.'

'She's the only one we know went into the house during the fireworks,' Ernie argued, 'not counting the victims. She told Mrs Fletcher she was going to find sparklers for the kiddies.'

'Which she did.'

'Good excuse if she was seen going in. 'Sides, she didn't hand 'em out till after the show, and she talked to Mrs Fletcher at the beginning. Isn't that right, Chief?'

'That's what she said, but she'd hardly have mentioned it if she'd felt in need of an alibi. She could have counted on Daisy not being sure at what point in the proceedings she spoke to whom. No, Miss Tyndall stays on the list but near—' A knock on the door interrupted him. 'Near the bottom. Come in!'

In came a constable in motorcycling gear, bringing the search warrant they were waiting for. Tom and Ernie went off with him, Ernie requesting directions to Chipping Campden. Ernie had become a good driver, which often came in handy, but Alec was always slightly nervous about letting him drive his precious Austin Seven.

To take his mind off it, he decided to go and see how Gooch was doing, make sure Blount was keeping an eye –

and more important, an ear – on him, and have a word with
Gwen. While reviewing the notes, he had realized he hadn't
yet asked her about anything but meeting the Gooches at the
pub. Gooch's accident and the subsequent revelation of the
letters in his pocket had disrupted the intended course of the
investigation.

Daisy had delivered Tom's message to Miller, who was still
with Gwen in the sickroom. Time to put her feet up for half
an hour, she decided as she closed the door behind her. Then
Alec came up the steps from the landing. She went to meet
him.

'Darling, Mr Miller says he'll be happy to fetch Tom when
he rings.'

'It'll be a while.'

'I take it Tom will search all the poor man's possessions
before he packs them up. What's he looking for? Blackmail
letters?'

'Anything anomalous. He'll talk to the landlord and the
inn servants, too. Someone may have heard something.'

'The Gooches quarrelling, you mean? They seemed like the
least quarrelsome of couples. I wish you'd seen them
together. I can't believe he shot her.'

'If he didn't, then almost certainly your friend, or one of
her family, or her boyfriend did.'

'I suppose so,' Daisy admitted, troubled. 'It's a trifle
far-fetched that someone else Mrs Gooch knew in her youth
happened to be at the party and happened also to have a
grudge against Sir Harold.'

'Far-fetched but not impossible. The Gloucestershire

police are checking her background. After twenty years, I'm afraid it's far-fetched, though not impossible, that they'll find something useful. Cheer up, love, you know we're not going to arrest any of the Tyndalls or Miller or Gooch without proof.'

'I know. It's just that everyone else suffers, too, whether the rest of the family or Gooch's children in Australia.'

'You wouldn't rather a murderer went unpunished!'

'No,' she agreed, but doubtfully. After all, no punishment would bring back the dead, and the arrest of any of the suspects would cause immense heartache to the innocent. 'Though if it weren't that he might decide to kill someone else next . . .'

'That being the case, how would you feel about taking the constable's place at Gooch's side for a while? I shamelessly shanghaied Blount, but it's just dawned on me that he must have his own duties, his rounds to make.'

'I can't nurse Gooch!'

'Of course not. Just in case he wakes and says something, or even speaks without regaining consciousness, which sometimes happens. Gwen will stay till the nurses arrive.'

'If Gwen has to be there anyway . . . No, I suppose you can't trust her not to invent a confession to keep her family out of the picture.'

'Sorry.'

'That's all right.' She sighed. 'I know it's necessary.'

Alec knocked on the door of the late baronet's dressing room and opened it. PC Blount was sitting by the bed, notebook and pencil on the small table at his elbow. Gwen and Miller stood by the window, deep in low-voiced conversation.

Blount sprang to his feet and saluted as Alec entered. 'He ha'n't stirred, sir, nor yet made a sound.'

'Thank you, Constable, you've done me a great favour by taking over here. You must be behind on your usual rounds. If your superiors give you grief, send them to me, and I'll refer them to the Chief Constable if necessary.'

The Constable looked awed and gratified. 'Don't 'spect that'll be needed, sir,' he said with regret. 'I'll just tell the Sergeant I were giving Scotland Yard a hand.' Grinning, he saluted again.

Accompanying him to the door, Alec said, 'There's something more you can do for me while you're out and about.' He closed the door behind them, and strain as she might, Daisy couldn't hear anything more than a brief murmur of voices before he came back in.

'Are you taking the bobby's place, Chief Inspector?' Miller asked.

'No, Daisy will for the present. I appreciate your offer to fetch DS Tring from the Ravens.'

'I hope all the Gooches' bags will fit in my little bus. Their Vauxhall was much bigger.'

Daisy could tell Alec was pondering the addition of his mountainous sergeant to a mountain of luggage. Tom could always walk up— But no, that would leave Miller in sole possession of what might be valuable evidence.

'If not,' he said, 'Tring can have the landlord store the less important stuff, or hire a cart to bring it up. I'm going to ask you to await his telephone call downstairs, if you please. I have a few questions for Miss Gwen.'

Miller frowned. 'I can just as well wait here. The servants will let me know when he rings.'

'It's all right, Martin. Daisy will be here if I need protection. Which I don't anticipate,' she added hastily as his frown deepened and Daisy opened her mouth to protest.

He smiled ruefully. 'No, of course not. I beg your pardon. I've never had anything to do with the police before, barring a summons or two for speeding. I promise I won't speed with your sergeant aboard, Mr Fletcher.'

'What with Tom and all the Gooches' belongings and that narrow lane and the hill,' said Daisy, 'I doubt you could speed if you tried.'

CHAPTER 20

As Miller left, Daisy sat down wearily on the chair the constable had vacated, and for the first time she gave the patient a proper look. Gooch's head was practically mummified, only his closed eyes, one ear, nostrils, and mouth visible. One arm was splinted, and a frame holding up the eiderdown suggested one or more broken legs. He was breathing strongly, though, and the pulse in his neck beat visibly.

'He's a bit of a mess, isn't he.'

'It's awful,' said Gwen, 'but it could have been worse. Dr Prentice says the arm and leg are clean breaks. His neck and spine seem to have escaped intact, and his rib cage is just bruised. His face was cut by broken glass, not too badly, though. It's the head injury that's worrisome.'

'No way to predict the outcome,' Alec said.

'None. He'll likely survive, but in what condition ... Reggie and Adrian are lucky we all have other things on our minds at present. When this is all cleared up, they aren't going to know what hit them. Daisy, if you're going to be on duty for a while, you ought to have a more comfortable chair.'

'Mind reader!'

Gwen rang for a maid, and soon Daisy was ensconced in an easy chair, with her feet on a foot-stool and a rug over her legs.

'Don't fall asleep,' Alec warned with a grin.

'I shan't let her,' Gwen promised. 'Now, what did you want to ask me?'

'Rather more than a few questions, I'm afraid. Last night, we only talked about your meeting with the Gooches at the Three Ravens. Before we revisit that in the light of what's happened since—'

'It *can't* be true about Jack!'

'We'll come to that later. This morning, events overtook us and I haven't had a chance to talk to you about your movements and observations last night. Let's start with the arrival of the Gooches.'

Despite her reassurance to Miller, Gwen was plainly nervous, her hands clenched together in her lap. Busy elsewhere, she had not noticed the Gooches' entrance. 'You can't hear Jennings announcing people unless you're standing right beside him,' she explained. When she did catch sight of the Australians, she made a point of welcoming them. Later, she had seen Jack talking to them for a short time, but none of the rest of the family.

Shepherding guests, Gwen had been one of the last out to the terrace. As she tried to recall whom she had spoken to, Daisy felt her eyelids growing heavier. She struggled to stay awake – and realized she had failed only when she was roused by a maid ushering in a couple of uniformed nurses.

Alec and Gwen rose to greet the newcomers, leaving Daisy uncertain as to whether they had observed her dereliction of duty. She glanced at Gooch. He didn't appear to have stirred so much as a finger. If he'd been quietly muttering to himself while she slept, it was too late to worry about it now. She was sorry, though, that she'd missed what Gwen had been saying.

The nurses had received instructions about their patient from Dr Prentice via their agency, but no one had mentioned that the police were involved. The younger, with a bush of frizzy dark hair attempting to escape her cap, was inclined to be indignant. 'Well, I never! I must say, it's not a very nice position to find yourself in, being mixed up in a murder case. If you ask me, they ought to've told us and let us choose if we wanted the job.'

'Now we're here, there's no sense making a fuss,' said the other. Middle-aged, she was lean but strong-looking, the severe lines of her face offset by a gleam of excitement in her eyes. She listened eagerly as Alec explained that he must be called at the slightest sign of their patient rousing, and anything he said must be written down at once. 'We always do that in any case when there's been a motor-car smash-up,' she said. 'You'd be surprised what they say sometimes. Not a bit like what the other driver's said. Quite funny it is sometimes.'

'Well,' observed the younger nurse, 'murderer or no, one thing's for sure: he's not going to be attacking us when he wakes up, not in the state he's in.' Resigned, she went off to rest in the bedroom already shown her by the maid.

The older shooed Gwen, Alec and Daisy out of the sickroom. They left her straightening the already-neat bed-covers into rigid perfection.

Standing in the passage, Alec said, 'We're nearly done. Let's adjourn to the schoolroom.'

'Please come, Daisy,' Gwen begged.

No mention was made of Daisy's lapse, so she assumed hopefully that they hadn't noticed. Alec should have asked her to take notes if he expected her to stay awake.

They went upstairs and sat down at the table. Apparently, while Daisy slept, the others had finished with the fireworks show and moved on to Jack's quarrel with Adelaide.

'I was pretty upset,' said Gwen. 'Jack had every right to be furious, but to burst into the dining room when guests were still helping themselves at the buffet . . . Daisy can tell you, they left in a hurry.'

'Not I,' said Daisy. 'I was starving.'

'As usual,' Alec interjected *sotto voce*.

'And Mr Gooch and Mr Miller nobly stood by me in spite of being a bit embarrassed. It was an awkward moment, I must say.'

'Mother was awfully upset. She was already tired, and that made her quite ill.'

'Just a minute— Gooch was with you in the dining room during the row, Daisy? No one else has mentioned his presence.'

'Yes. You apologized to him, Gwen, remember?'

'I only remember Martin.'

'Gooch was there,' Daisy said positively. 'Martin – Mr Miller – and I tried to find some plain food for him. He said . . . Oh, what was the word he used? He said that in Australia they don't muck about with their tucker. We found some cold meat for him, but then he decided he wasn't really hungry and went off to the drawing room to look for Mrs Gooch.'

'You say he seemed embarrassed by the family argument, and he'd lost his appetite. How else would you describe him?'

'He was rather fidgety, but no more so than earlier.

Inattentive when Mr Miller talked about rocket propulsion, though he'd asked about it, I think. He really wasn't at all comfortable with coming to the Manor.' Daisy suddenly realized what Alec was driving at. 'He was concerned that Mrs Gooch might be wondering where he was, and that she might not have anything to eat. Honestly, darling, he didn't behave at all like a man who's just shot his wife, or anyone else.'

'Miss Gwen, would you agree?'

Gwen bit her lip. 'I can't say I really noticed. What with the squabble and Mother taking ill, I wasn't paying attention. Does this mean it wasn't Gooch? That one of us did it?'

'I wouldn't go so far. If he had been in a state of extreme agitation, it might have been more helpful.'

'He was absolutely shattered when he heard Mrs Gooch had been shot,' Daisy said. 'If you'd seen his face ... I don't believe the best actor in the world could turn that colour. I'm sorry, Gwen, but when I think back to that moment, I simply can't believe he did it.'

Daisy felt as if she was betraying Gwen. She knew Alec would take her words the more seriously because she was not protecting a friend – he always complained about her shielding people she liked when she found herself mixed up in his cases. Not that he'd cross Gooch off his list of suspects on her say-so, but he'd probably move him down a notch or two.

Which left Jack very much in the centre of the picture, especially if he really was Mrs Gooch's son.

Gwen buried her face in her hands, making Daisy feel even worse. 'Sorry,' she said again, inadequately.

'No, you have to say what you saw.'

'It's not what Daisy saw,' Alec pointed out, 'it's her opinion of what she saw. You were there. What's your opinion?'

After a long hesitation, Gwen shook her head. 'No, I can't say. It's not that I've forgotten, it's that I was too distraught myself to notice, as I said before. Believe me, I wish I could tell you I thought he was acting, but it wouldn't be true. All I could think about was having to tell him she had had an accident. I was too cowardly to say she was dead, let alone that Father had shot her. That was what we thought had happened.'

'Because that's what your brother told you?'

'Of course. Didn't it look that way, at a quick glance? Martin and Dr Prentice went up there and didn't say anything to contradict that impression. Oh, and Sir Nigel, and he's a policeman.'

'A courtesy policeman. No, I don't imagine Jack lingered at the scene to analyse the evidence. How long was he gone?'

Gwen looked questioningly at Daisy, who said, 'Just—'

'No, I want your opinion, not Daisy's. I presume none of you were checking the time.'

'Just a couple of minutes, if that. He must have run up the stairs. He was still livid about the stolen rockets and he wanted to tell Father what those wretched boys had done. Father would have made them give them up, and then Mr Gooch wouldn't . . .' Her voice trailed away as the futility of this line of wishful thinking struck her.

'He was *still* livid,' Alec repeated. 'Let's go back to the beginning of the quarrel with Mrs Yarborough. You said Jack came in when most of your guests had helped themselves at the buffet and moved into the drawing room or on to the hall. Would you please describe his arrival?'

'He came dashing in, positively fuming, and immediately accused Addie of letting Reggie and Adrian run riot. He was quite sure they had pinched the rockets. I can't recall his exact words, I'm afraid.'

'No matter. What next?'

'Babs came in – she'd been herding the children upstairs – and took Jack's part. Then Mother arrived, some busybody having told her about the row, and Addie appealed to her, and she said she was afraid Jack was probably quite right. I think it must be worse having thoroughly badly behaved grandchildren than children, don't you? You have little or no control over their upbringing, and you want to love them and perhaps you just can't. Anyway, Addie decided to look for Father. She thought he'd support her.'

'Had she any justification for such a hope?'

'Well, he'd never ragged on the boys, but only because he'd never seen their bad side. They were afraid of him, and none of us ever told tales. It must seem odd to an outsider, when he – if anyone – was quite capable of correcting them, but when one is accustomed to not telling a person anything that might upset him, the habit is difficult to break. Jack had reached that point, though. He went tearing after Addie, saying he'd tell Father himself.'

Daisy contradicted her. 'No. Now I come to think of it, he went striding off and Addie ran after him. If it makes any difference.'

Alec gave her a look. 'Where did they go to search?' he asked Gwen.

'To the drawing room and hall, of course, where everyone had gone to eat. But he wasn't there, so they came back— No, Jack came back without Addie. She was probably relieved not to find Father. I said maybe he'd popped into the gun room to show off the antiques. Jack glanced in but he wasn't there, so I said he'd better check upstairs. How I wish I hadn't!'

'I'm afraid it wouldn't have changed anything,' Alec said sympathetically, 'and from my point of view, it's lucky he was found while the doctor and the Chief Constable were here.'

And even Struwwelpeter, Daisy thought, since it was he who had advised his CC to beg for Alec's help.

'I suppose it was,' conceded Gwen. 'We'd have had to send for Dr Prentice anyway.'

'Go on.'

'Jack came back, white as a sheet, and said Father had shot Mrs Gooch and himself.' Gwen was herself nearly as white as a sheet. Daisy took her hand. 'That was bad enough, heaven knows, but at least it was over, finished with, apart from the scandal. This – not knowing what happened or who . . . it's an endless nightmare!'

Daisy simply couldn't think of anything comforting to say. The Tyndalls' nightmare could end only with an arrest, and then a different sort of nightmare would begin. Unless she was wrong about Gooch. Was it possible he had committed a double murder and then come to fill his plate looking mildly worried and fussing about his food?

Set him against Jack, bursting into the room in a state of high agitation, and there was no contest for the more likely murderer.

Alec continued asking questions. His gentle tone suggested to Daisy that he had moved Gwen, with or without Miller as her conspirator, to the bottom of his list. He came at last to Mrs Gooch's letters.

'Martin came to Father's dressing room and told me. Jack asked him to. Jack told him the letter was very affecting, but I think it was positively wicked.'

Alec's raised eyebrows encouraged her to elaborate.

'I can understand, if it's true, that she might want to see her child and make sure he's well and happy, but to push herself in, to disrupt everyone's lives, that was wicked! Just look what it led to.'

'Do you think she was telling the truth?'

'I haven't the faintest idea. At first I thought it was utter rubbish. It's difficult to imagine one's father having a . . . a mistress. But if he did, that's exactly how he might have acted, riding roughshod over Mother for the sake of having a male heir. It doesn't really matter Jack's my brother no matter what.'

'Do you remember Lady Tyndall being away from home at about the time he was born?'

'No. I was six. I remember being told I had a baby brother and being excited and happy. I wasn't going to be the youngest any longer, and I suppose I thought of him as a sort of living doll at first. I remember dressing him up, playing mother. Babs and Addie weren't particularly interested and Mother was often ill. He was a nice little boy, and a nice schoolboy, and a nice young man. Nothing, *nothing*, will make me believe he shot Father and Mrs Gooch!' Gwen concluded, fiercely vehement.

'Most understandable,' said Alec gravely. 'That's all for now. Thank you for your cooperation.'

'Gwen, do go and lie down for a bit. You've had an exhausting day.'

Gwen smiled with an effort. 'I may do just that. But first

I'll just pop down and make sure Mother is all right and the nurse has everything she needs.'

'Would you mind asking Lady Tyndall when it will be convenient for me to see her?'

'Must you? I suppose you must. All right.'

She left, and Alec turned to Daisy. 'What else have you not told me?' he asked resignedly.

'Darling, last night you were in a rush to find out what had happened and to see everyone, and today I've hardly had a chance to talk to you at all, except about Babs and Lady Tyndall's trip abroad. Else besides what?'

'Besides Gooch being with you in the dining room. I'd better hear your version of what went on last night, from the Gooches' arrival at the party. Try to stick to the essential points, love.'

'I'll try,' Daisy promised. 'First, I happened to be watching when the Gooches arrived. I wasn't close enough to hear what was said, but as the Gooches continued into the hall, I saw Sir Harold and Lady Tyndall turn and look after them with horrified expressions.'

'Both Tyndalls?'

'Both. I thought—'

'Just the facts, Daisy.'

'Yes, but you mustn't jump to the conclusion that they recognized Mrs Gooch. It might just have been the prospect of Gooch's Australian accent mingling with the august company.'

'I'll take that into account.'

'You must, honestly. Martin Miller has hardly any accent, but it's enough to make them eye him askance. He was very helpful, incidentally. I wanted to go down and see the merrymaking at the bonfire in the meadow, where the villagers gathered, and he drove me down. We went just after the Gooches got here, and got back to the house as people started to move out to the terrace, so I didn't see anything that happened indoors in between.'

'Pity. I'd give a good deal to know what Sir Harold said to Mrs Gooch and vice versa, or at least in what spirit it was said.'

'Sorry, can't help. I can tell you, though, that she didn't go outside with her husband. I did. I had an idea for an article . . . but you don't want to hear about that, and it's dead as the dodo now anyway.'

'How long did you talk to him?'

'Just a couple of minutes. As soon as the fireworks started, everyone moved forward and I lost him. Let's see, who was next? Babs, I think. She collared the Yarborough boys as they were about to disappear down the steps. Obviously her prohibition didn't have a lasting effect. Later I had a word with Addie's mama-in-law, and lastly Jack, for just a moment before *he* disappeared down the steps. That was just as the final grand spectacle started.'

'I don't suppose you noticed what direction he came from.'

'Not a hope. It was dark, darling, except for the weird light of the fireworks, and people kept moving around. I didn't see anyone heading for the house until after the grand finale. I would have told you right away.'

'Yes, of course.' Alec sighed. 'Go on. If Jack did the shooting, it must have been before you saw him?'

'I should think so. No time afterwards, not if the fireworks covered the sound of the shots, which they must have, mustn't they?'

'That's our assumption. How did he behave?'

'I didn't notice anything out of the ordinary. At least, he looked as normal as one can with a blue face. The missing rockets – or rather, the ones that didn't go missing – showered down green and blue sparks to represent rain, to make the tree—'

'Great Scott, Daisy!'

'Sorry. What was I . . . Oh yes, Jack sounded normal. But he said only a few words before he noticed something wrong with the rockets and got upset and went down.'

'So the missing rockets could have been a very convenient excuse to cover the real reason for his being in a state of nerves.'

'I suppose so,' Daisy admitted reluctantly.

'I gather you were one of the last to return to the house.'

'I'd seen the supper buffet earlier and knew they weren't going to run out of food, so I stayed to watch the bonfire blaze up. I sort of assumed at the time, without really thinking about it, that Gooch and Miller hung back because they weren't entirely comfortable with the company. But Gooch was probably hoping to see his wife as she went in, and Miller may have been waiting till Gwen finished helping Babs hand out sparklers to the children. Anyway, we all went in together and we were at the end of the line. By then, I was—'

'Ravenous.'

'I was going to say "famished",' Daisy said with dignity. 'And my toes were getting frostbitten. I know you don't want to hear about my toes, but every little bit helps me remember exactly what happened. You're always saying any detail may prove significant.'

'It may. I don't want to rush you. It's just that I can't recall
an investigation when I've had so many interviews cut short
in the middle, and I was hoping we might get through the
whole story before we're interrupted. But you're right. Tell it
your own way, love.'

As if on cue, there came a knock on the door.

'Come in!' called Alec, exasperated.

A maid peeked nervously around the door. 'Telephone, sir,
if you please, sir.'

'Who is it?'

'Mr Jennings didn't say, sir, just that it's for you, sir.'

Alec slammed his hand down on the table. The maid
jumped. 'See what I mean?' he snarled, eyebrows meeting
above his nose. 'I must say I never before appreciated what a
difference a good butler makes to a household like this.'

'I'll write down everything I can remember,' Daisy said
diplomatically as he strode to the door. 'I hope it's someone
ringing with information you desperately need.'

But she'd venture a bet on its being Struwwelpeter, eager
to reassert his claim to 'his' county.

Less averse to being disturbed than Alec, Daisy took her
writing things down to the drawing room. Not that she was
positively courting interruptions, she assured herself, or she
would have stationed herself in the front hall, with its
acknowledged resemblance to Piccadilly Circus. She just
didn't want to appear to be avoiding the family in their time
of trouble.

The drawing room was deserted. With nothing to distract
her, Daisy soon wrote down all she could recall up to the

point where Jack returned from the study to report the shooting. She was wondering whether she need go any further, when Miller wandered in. His disconsolate face brightened at the sight of her.

'Mrs Fletcher! I was hoping I might come across you. But you're busy . . .'

'I'm just about finished. Do sit down. What can I do for you?'

He took a packet of cigarettes from his pocket, half offered it to Daisy, then drew back. 'No, you don't, do you? Half the girls seem to smoke these days.' To her relief, he returned the packet to his pocket without lighting up. 'Do you mind if I ask your advice?'

'Not at all. I can't promise to be able to give you any. At least, I can't promise it'd be *good* advice.'

'Of course not. But you know how people like the Tyndalls think. What's good form and what's bad form and that sort of thing. It's sometimes a bit mystifying to an ordinary bloke like me.'

'I know what you mean,' Daisy agreed. 'I'll try to help.'

'The thing is, I wonder if I ought to buzz off after all, after I've fetched the sergeant from the village. The only subject on Jack's mind is who he really is. He's not going to be making decisions about his future till that's sorted out. I can't even help him by being there for him to talk to. He went riding. I've never been on a horse in my life. He's my host, and for all I know he's wishing me away but too polite to tell me.'

'Yes, I see your difficulty.'

'I'd stay for Gwen, only I've hardly seen her since that wretched Australian crashed his motor. She's too busy nursing him to—'

'Not any longer. A couple of professional nurses turned up. Didn't you know? I made Gwen go and lie down. She's exhausted. But wasn't the last you saw of her when Jack asked you to explain about Mrs Gooch's letter? It seems to me they both need you here, even if they're rather leaving you to your own devices at the moment. I shouldn't cut and run if I were you.'

'But what about Lady Tyndall? She wasn't too happy with me coming here in the first place. I wouldn't be surprised if she blames me for everything that's happened.'

'For shooting Sir Harold and Mrs Gooch?' Daisy asked, astonished. 'Why on earth should she think you did it?'

'Oh, not that, exactly,' Miller said gloomily. 'But it was for my sake Jack wanted to go down to the Ravens. If we hadn't gone, he'd not have met the Gooches and invited them to the house.'

'You might as well blame me for suggesting inviting them to our table. Alec's half inclined to think it's all my fault.'

'Is he really? I'm sorry I told him about that.'

'Not seriously. I'd have had to tell him myself, so don't worry about it. But to get back to your original concern, I doubt if Lady Tyndall has the slightest idea that your preference for beer led to the visit to the pub. And I don't see how your presence could possibly be as disturbing to her as ours – mine and Scotland Yard's – not to mention Gooch's. Who knows, she may even be glad you're here because you're someone else outside the family for Alec to suspect.'

Miller smiled wryly. 'I hadn't thought of that.'

'Anyway, you see, it's as much my fault as yours, but if you ask me, the Gooches would have found some other way to meet Jack.'

'Perhaps not one that would lead to murder.'

'Perhaps not,' Daisy had to acknowledge. 'The fireworks were perfect cover for the shooting. I wouldn't be so sure, though. That letter was pretty incendiary.'

'Do you think it's true? That Jack is not Lady Tyndall's son?'

Daisy hesitated. 'The letter is awfully convincing.'

'If they made a practice of writing blackmailing letters, I suppose they'd have got pretty good at it.'

'The trouble is, it doesn't matter so much whether it's true or not. It's whether Mrs Gooch told the story to Jack and either convinced him, or he thought her claim might convince other people.'

'Eh?' After a moment's confusion, Miller sorted it out. 'Oh, I see what you mean. So you believe Jack killed them?'

'I don't believe anything,' Daisy said crossly. 'I'm waiting for Alec to find out. Isn't it time for tea yet?'

Alec took the telephone call in the study, which had been cleaned since the removal of the bodies. Bloodstains were still visible – they would never completely disappear; the desk and carpet would doubtless be replaced as soon as the family had leisure for such niceties – and a slight sickly smell hung in the air, overlaid with acrid whiffs of carbolic disinfectant. But it was preferable to either battling the butler for the use of his pantry or forgoing privacy in the hall.

He picked up the telephone apparatus and sat down in the desk chair, pushed back a bit from the damp desk. Unhooking the receiver, he said, 'Hello? DCI Fletcher speaking.'

'Dryden-Jones here, Chief Inspector.' The voice was pompous, with an undertone of complaint.

For a moment, Alec couldn't think who the hell Dryden-Jones was. Ah, Daisy's Struwwelpeter, alas, alias Sir Nigel's stuffed orangutan, not to mention Lord Lieutenant of Gloucestershire. 'What can I do for you, sir?'

'Perhaps I didn't make it clear, Chief Inspector, that I expect to be kept up-to-date with your progress in the enquiry into this horrible crime in *my* county.'

Though his position gave him absolutely no right to such information, he had been helpful over the search warrant, and there was no sense in antagonizing him. 'Sorry, sir. The usual enquiries are proceeding.' Useful phrase, that. 'But this is a very early stage in the investigation. With the able assistance of the Gloucestershire police force, we have interviewed every guest at the party. Unfortunately, none of them appears to have observed anything helpful. I'm very grateful for your assistance in obtaining a warrant—'

'Yes, yes, man, and what came of it? That's what I want to know.'

'Nothing as yet. My detective constable is serving it as we speak. I shall, of course, be in touch with your chief constable as soon as I have anything to report, and he will no doubt keep you up-to-date. I'm expecting a vital telephone call, sir, so if you don't mind . . .'

'Of course, of course, I'll clear the line. Keep up the good work, Chief Inspector.'

'I shall, sir, never fear.' Alec breathed a sigh of relief as he hung up. The man was a pest, but easily routed. Whether he'd take the hint and apply to Herriott for information in future remained to be seen.

Leaning back, Alec surveyed the room. The sun was sinking beyond the western window, burnishing a few streaks of cloud. Jack had said the electric lights were on when he came upstairs. Those heavy curtains would have made them unnoticeable from the terrace. Sir Harold had been sitting here, apparently about to write something for the woman seated opposite him, when someone came in.

Through the door to the passage or that to the stairs? Probably the stairs, having picked up the pistol on the way.

Gun in hand, or concealed in a pocket? Very likely concealed, as the baronet had only half-risen by the time the murderer had advanced several paces into the room. Surely he'd have jumped to his feet and dropped the pen had he seen the weapon immediately. Mrs Gooch didn't appear to have made any attempt to stand up.

Did any of these assumptions offer a hint as to who had interrupted their tête-à-tête? Was there any point in building speculation upon speculation? He was constantly warning Daisy against wild theorizing.

What he really wanted was a spot of shut-eye. They had worked long hours on the Birmingham job and he hadn't slept much last night. He longed to lay his head down on his arms and let himself drift. The state of the desk and the memory of its recent occupant prevented such indulgence, but his eyelids started to droop.

Brring-brring. Brring-brring.

Groaning, he reached for the telephone.

'Is that you?' said a creaky voice before Alec could speak. 'Are you still there?'

Who the . . . ? The butler, of course. 'Fletcher here,' he growled.

'I'm not one to complain,' creaked Jennings, 'but all these here telephone callers ringing up night and day is not what I'm accustomed to.'

'I dare say you're not accustomed to murder, either. You're going to have to put up with it. Do you have someone on the line to speak to me? Put him through.'

Click, ping, click-click. 'Hello, Fletcher? Wookleigh speaking. I know you're busy, my dear fellow, and I won't keep you. Just wanted to make sure my chaps are cooperating with your chaps all down the line.'

'They've been very helpful, sir. They've managed to get in touch with everyone on the guest list—'

'Including me,' said the Chief Constable dryly.

'That proves how thorough they were. Unfortunately, no one saw any more of what was going on than you did. The local constable, Blount, is carrying on a few enquiries for me in his district. A good man.'

'I'll remember that. All right, I won't trouble you any longer. Carry on, Fletcher, and let me know if there's anything else we can do to help.'

'Thank you, sir.' If only all CCs were like Sir Nigel!

Alec had hardly stuck the receiver back in its hook when the bell rang again.

'Chief Inspector?' enquired a harassed voice he didn't recognize. 'This is Herriott. I've just had the Lord Lieutenant on the line demanding the latest news of your little murder. He says you told him to ask me.'

'I'm sorry, sir. What I told him was that I'd be reporting to you in due time and I was sure you'd be in touch with him.'

'Oh. Right-oh. Anything to report?'

'No, sir. Enquiries are proceeding, et cetera.'

The Gloucestershire CC produced a gruff guffaw. 'Like that, is it? Well, I hope you'll get a move on. I've asked Superintendent Crane to have you come here when you've bagged your man. Nasty business, this Customs raid. They blew up an unfortunate watchman with the vault and have got away with a load of bullion. The Yard is sending me a detective inspector, but I want you. How long do you reckon?'

Alec swallowed an unprintable retort. So much for his leisurely drive home with Daisy. He was going to demand a week off after this, and they would go away without leaving an address. 'I can't say, sir. We've pretty much narrowed it down to two, but one is unconscious after a motor smash-up and we're still investigating the other's motive. There's very little in the way of hard evidence. It may be one of those cases where we have a moral certainty but can't prosecute.'

'Well, reach your moral certainty quickly, and in the meantime, I'll fend off Dryden-Jones.'

'Thank you, sir,' said Alec.

CHAPTER 21

Wide-awake now, Alec glanced at his watch. Just five minutes before he was due to see Lady Tyndall – on the way to the study, he had met Gwen in the passage as she came out of her mother's room.

He ran down the stairs to the billiard room and quickly looked through the notes of his previous meetings with her ladyship. They had covered remarkably little ground. Questioning the widow of a murder victim was always a touchy business.

Alec reached the sitting room door at the same time as a maid bearing a tea tray. He wasn't sure whether to be glad or sorry. Sometimes the ritual of serving tea relaxed the person to be interviewed; sometimes fussing over teacups was an irritating distraction.

He knocked and held the door open for the girl. As he followed her into the room, his attention flew to the window opposite. The sun was a red ball on the horizon, and thickening bands of cloud flamed in a display that outdid any fireworks show he had ever seen.

'"What is man, that thou art mindful of him?"' murmured

Lady Tyndall. She was seated in a chair by the window, angled to look out. She motioned him to another, set opposite at an equivalent angle, as the maid laid out the tea things on a small table between them.

Man is – Alec thought but didn't say – as far as we know, the only creature able to appreciate a sunset, and it is a crime to kill him.

He would have preferred to face her directly, but failing that he turned his chair slightly towards her before he sat down. She looked much less fragile than last night, but he couldn't tell how much the change was due to the healthy glow imparted by the pink light of the evening sky. She was, at least, more composed.

'I hope you like Lapsang Souchong, Mr Fletcher,' she said, holding the teapot poised over a flowery, gold-rimmed porcelain cup. 'It is my favourite at this time of day. But Bella can bring something else if you prefer.'

'Lapsang Souchong will do very well, thank you, Lady Tyndall.'

'Milk? Lemon? Sugar? Please help yourself to sandwiches and cake. Thank you, Bella, that will be all.'

'A little milk, no sugar, thanks.' As he had feared, teatime was already interfering with the interview. Though a cuppa was welcome, he had no intention of encumbering himself with mouthfuls of food.

'Oh dear, it's rather strong. Shall I add a little hot water?' She lifted the silver hot-water jug.

'No, thank you, that's perfect. Lady Tyndall, I'm sorry to have to take you back to last night, but it can't be helped. You told me you were dismayed that your son invited the Gooches but accepted his right to do so. Your husband was less accommodating. Did he tax your son with his opinion?'

'I believe not.' Her voice was constrained. 'I was occupied with our other guests and didn't watch them, but even Harold would not start a row at a party, and Jack certainly showed no sign of being disturbed. Not until . . . afterwards.'

'After the fireworks.'

'The . . . ? Oh, yes, the missing rockets. I'd almost forgotten. That fuss was almost too much for me, on top of the strain of entertaining a large number of people.'

'You must have been tempted to stay in the warm house when everyone went outside.'

'Oh, I couldn't do that.' Her smile was sudden, charming. 'But I confess I made up my mind not to mingle with the throng, making polite conversation. Everyone would presume I was talking to someone else.'

'You were at leisure, then, to watch the rest. Did you see Sir Harold or Mrs Gooch or anyone else go inside?'

'No,' she answered quickly – too quickly. 'I was watching the fireworks. I knew Harold would ask me about them later. You must understand that he spent months planning the show. He was very secretive, like a child with a new toy he doesn't want to share. That's why the display had to be constructed at the last minute, so that no one could guess the details. And afterwards, he always wanted everyone to say how wonderful it was. It combined his two passions: family tradition and gunpowder explosions.'

The vigour of her words was belied by a fading tone, like a gramophone in need of winding. Alec sipped his tea, letting the ensuing pause lengthen.

Experience suggested she had worked out in advance

exactly what to say. She was protecting someone, and she had no conceivable reason to protect Gooch, or Miller. She had seen one of her family, one of her children, enter the house.

In silence, Alec considered the four. Adelaide: no hint of a motive had come to light. Barbara: the greed for land was a powerful force, but would she have killed for the chance not to own but to manage the estate for her brother? Gwen: call it love, lust, or simply a biological urge to reproduce, it was a drive as powerful as greed, and Sir Harold had tried to thwart her last chance in a world where women her age vastly outnumbered the surviving men; she might kill her father, but the woman she'd first met just the previous day?

There remained Jack, with his overwhelming reasons for wanting both the baronet and Mrs Gooch out of his way. Whichever way one looked at it, Jack Tyndall was in the centre of the picture. His motive was still greater if he really was the woman's son, but if such was the case, why would Lady Tyndall deny it? Why should she lie to the police to protect the young man her husband had forced her to pass off as her own?

'May I pour you another cup?' Few could resist filling a silence that stretched so long and Lady Tyndall eventually succumbed, though not with the helpful gush of words Alec had hoped for.

'Yes, please.'

'I'm afraid it's steeped rather too long.' After emptying the dregs from his cup into the matching slop basin, she poured simultaneous streams of tea and hot water through the silver strainer. Her hands were as steady as if she were entertaining a close friend, not a police detective in a murder enquiry. But now that the sunset glow was fading, her face showed the strain – parchment-pale, with a pinched look about the mouth.

'It's getting dark. Shall I turn on a light?' Alec suggested. He wanted to be able to see her expression, so, not waiting for her response, he reached up to switch on the standard lamp behind his chair.

It had scarcely clicked on when her personal maid came in, her status made plain by the lack of cap and apron. She ignored Alec. 'Now, my lady, you'll be getting chilled there by the window. Come over to the fire, do. I'll poke it up nice and draw the curtains and move the tray for you. Why, you haven't eaten a thing. You must keep your strength up, my lady, indeed you must.'

Bustling about, she suited action to words and resettled Lady Tyndall by the fireplace with a shawl over her knees and a plate with a slice of cherry cake before her.

'Thank you, Mendicott, but I'm not hungry, I'm afraid.'

Rejoining her, Alec made up his mind: tomorrow, if not this evening, he was going to start questioning people at Constable Blount's station house in the village to avoid the constant interruptions at Edge Manor.

As soon as the maid closed the door behind her, he said, 'I understand Mr Tyndall was born abroad.'

The morsel of cake she was listlessly breaking from the slice crumbled. 'Oh, how clumsy of rne.' She pushed the plate away and wiped her fingers on her napkin with a nervous motion. 'Yes, Jack was born in Switzerland. Bearing children didn't agree with me, you see. I was quite ill when Gwen was born. So when we were expecting another, it was thought advisable that I should try a different climate and complete rest. Harold was . . . was very good. He stayed with me most of the time, though he'd rather have been at home. We brought Jack home when he was six weeks old. His birth was registered here, of course. There's no question of his not being British.'

As before, she ran out of steam, or, more likely, out of the speech she had prepared. Alec told himself it didn't necessarily mean she was attempting to mislead him. An elderly lady of her class, unused to dealing with the police, might well think it a good idea to arrange her thoughts beforehand, especially after breaking down the previous evening. The stiff-upper-lip ethos tended to be even stronger among the 'county' families than the aristocracy.

Though, in Alec's opinion, anyone might be forgiven for hysterics when informed her husband had shot and killed a woman, a virtual stranger, and himself.

The second blow, the claim that her son was not her own, she was taking with more outward calm, whether because it was not true or because she had been half-expecting it for twenty-one years. With luck, Ernie Piper would discover the truth among the late doctor's papers. Alec saw no point in putting the question to Lady Tyndall again at present.

Again the silence lengthened. This time, it was shattered by a knock on the door, followed by the irruption into the sitting room of Mrs Yarborough.

'Mother! I've brought your grandsons to comfort you.'

Lady Tyndall closed her eyes and appeared to utter a silent prayer. Alec regarded with interest the two boys who had almost certainly committed an assault on a motorist, causing grievous bodily harm, which would certainly have landed them in prison had they been older.

Butter wouldn't melt in their mouths. They were scrubbed

to a glow, hair slicked down, ties neatly knotted, shirts tucked into their shorts, jacket pockets flat instead of bulging with the bits and bobs boys customarily collect. Even their socks were pulled up to the knee and their shoes shone.

'Good afternoon, Grandmama,' they chorused. 'We're very sorry about Grandpapa.' But as they spoke, they stared at Alec.

'Mummy, is that the Scotland Yard 'tec?' the elder whispered.

'Yes, darling. It's rude to point, remember.' Mrs Yarborough gave Alec a hostile look, the first notice she had taken of him since entering.

The younger boy immediately burst into tears. 'We didn't mean to—'

The elder kicked him on the ankle. 'Shut up, Adrian!' he hissed.

A young and nervous maid came in with a tray. 'Mrs Yarborough said to bring tea, my lady.'

'That's quite all right, Dilys. Mr Fletcher, you've met my daughter Mrs Yarborough, I believe. These two are my grandsons, Reginald and Adrian.'

Prompted by a nudge from their mother, the boys muttered, 'How do you do' before making for the tray, which the maid set on the table by the window.

'I don't want milk. I want tea with lots of sugar,' Reginald demanded, while Adrian picked the cherries out of a hunk of cake and dropped them on his brother's plate, then stuffed the cake into his mouth.

Alec made his excuses and departed. Tomorrow the police station, he promised himself.

* * *

Daisy and Miller were watching the sunset when Gwen, looking slightly less worn out after her lie-down, joined them in the drawing room.

'Tea is on its way,' she said. 'I'm sorry you two have been left to your own devices.'

'In the circs,' said Daisy, 'we hardly expect to be entertained. Did you enquire after Mr Gooch on your way down? How is he?'

'Beginning to be restless. The nurse says it's a hopeful sign that he's not still lying like a log. I'm so thankful!'

'"Thankful"?' Babs enquired sardonically, coming in, breeched and booted. 'What is there to be thankful for?'

'Mr Gooch seems to be on the mend.'

'I suppose that's a good thing. One less murder, and maybe the fear of death will induce him to confess to the other two. Where's tea? I could eat a horse!'

'Not mine.' Jack appeared in jodhpurs and riding boots. 'I say, Mrs Fletcher, do you object to a slight equine effluvium? Just say the word and I'll go and change.'

'Not for my sake.' Daisy was pleased, though surprised, to see him so much more composed.

He was closely followed by a couple of maids with the tea things. Gwen poured. Jack brought Daisy her tea and a generous selection from the array of sandwiches, biscuits, and cakes.

As he returned to get his own tea, Babs asked him where he'd been riding.

'Over the Edge.'

'The Edge of the World.'

Gwen laughed. 'That's what we used to call it,' she told Miller. 'Up the hill and over the Edge of the World.'

She and Babs and Jack started reminiscing about long-ago rides. Miller came over to Daisy, looking rather down in the mouth.

'You see,' he said, 'we're tuned to different wavelengths.'

'"Wavelengths"?' she asked cautiously. 'Isn't that something to do with the wireless?'

'That's right, among other things. Sorry. I meant, half the time I have no idea what they're talking about.'

'But presumably Jack knows all about wavelengths, which I don't. And I always preferred a bicycle to a horse. I liked riding ponies, when I was little, but horses are so *big*.'

'I like bicycling.' Miller cheered up.

'Well, Gwen and I used to go biking together when she came to stay at Fairacres. And you have a motor-car, and she drives. And I am absolutely determined to learn to drive,' Daisy added.

Jack heard her. 'Don't let a relative teach you,' he advised. 'I taught Gwen, and believe me, it's a recipe for murder.' He turned bright red as a horrified silence fell. 'You know what I mean! Mrs Fletcher, would you like another cup of tea?'

'Yes, please, and I wouldn't say no to another macaroon. They're so frightfully moreish.'

He fetched her cup. While it was being refilled, a maid came in and told Miller the sergeant had rung up from the Three Ravens. Miller went off to fetch him, and Jack brought Daisy her tea. He set a plate of macaroons dangerously close. Daisy swore to herself that she'd only eat one, or at most two. One each for herself and the baby. Almonds and egg whites must be good for both of them, weren't they?

'I'm awfully sorry,' Jack said in a low voice, sitting down

next to her, 'for what I said about teaching Gwen to drive. Of all the asinine remarks!'

'Exactly the sort of thing that does slip out at just the wrong moment,' she said lightly. 'It's bound to; that's what's on your mind.'

'I've been doing my best not to think about it. But I did come to one conclusion while I was out: it doesn't really matter whether Mrs Gooch's letter is true or not. I never had any great desire to be Sir John, and when I'm working as an engineer, no one will care a hoot. It might be better not to use the title, even if it turns out I'm entitled to it. I wouldn't want the other fellows to think I expect to trade on it.'

'That's just how I feel! Except,' Daisy confessed, 'I'm afraid I did rather trade on the Honourable at first, when I started writing, just to get the first commission.'

'It's harder for girls,' Jack said generously. 'Look at the trouble Babs has had being taken seriously. No one would have thought twice if I'd taken over the estate, however little I know about farming. She'll do a far better job than I ever could. She and Gwen will still be my sisters, whatever the truth of the matter.'

'I should hope so!'

'I'm not so sure about Addie. She may decide to disown me, which would be no great loss, except that I'd like to have a hand in straightening out my nephews. But Mother will always be Mother, even if she isn't really.' He paused. 'You know, if Mrs Gooch really is . . . was my mother, I'm glad I liked her. And I'm very sorry she's dead, but I didn't really know her, after all. Mother is Mother.'

'Have you told her so? I can't help feeling she must be wondering how you feel about it all.'

'Ye-es. Yes, I know I ought. It's . . . Somehow it's easier to talk to you about it than to the family.'

'That's often the way. But—'

'I know, I must talk to Mother. I wonder if she'll tell me whether it's true or not.'

'I shouldn't ask, if I were you.'

'I expect the police will find out soon enough. They're just waiting for that to arrest me, aren't they? No, sorry, pretend I didn't say that. I didn't shoot them, but even I can see I'm by far the best prospect.'

'If you ask me, Gooch is quite as likely,' said Daisy. 'Jealousy is—'

'Daisy!' Alec came in from the front hall, looking irritable.

'Hello, darling. Have you had tea?'

'Do sit down,' Gwen said. 'I'll ring for some fresh.'

'Thank you, but I've already had mine. Daisy, there's a minor point or two I hope you can clear up for me. We'll go to the billiard room.'

'Right-oh.' Daisy hurriedly swallowed the last bite of her macaroon – oh dear, had she really eaten half a plateful? – and washed it down with the last of her tea.

Meanwhile, she racked her brain over what she might have done to annoy him. Her conscience was clear, apart from eating more macaroons than twins or even triplets could justify. Well, fairly clear. Perhaps she should not have encouraged Jack to go and talk to Lady Tyndall about Mrs Gooch's letter, but Alec didn't know about that, and anyway, it was a perfectly natural thing for Jack to do.

CHAPTER 22

Daisy held her tongue until the door closed behind her and Alec. Then she asked, 'Why so snippy, darling?'

'Snippy? Was I? Sorry, it's nothing to do with you. It's just that every time I start interviewing anyone in this house, there's an interruption. Mrs Yarborough and her young criminals-in-training just arrived in Lady Tyndall's sitting room.'

'That's enough to drive anyone away. Jack was just telling me he has plans to reform the boys, if you don't arrest him. Are you about to?'

'Not without some proof, or a confession, but it doesn't look good for him, even before I know the truth about his parentage.'

'I can't believe it. He's such a nice boy. What about Gooch?'

'Gooch is still a possibility, but there's one major flaw in any theory of him as murderer. Which relates to what I wanted to ask you. Think back to when Jack was looking for his father after the fireworks.'

'Right-oh. Do you want me to run through it again from the beginning of the quarrel?'

'That might be the best way. No, on second thoughts, jump to when he came back from searching in the drawing room and hall.'

'Gosh, it's hard to remember. Only last night, but so much has happened since.'

'Try.'

'Let's see. Did Adelaide come back with him? No, I think not. He came back just as Gooch went out, and he told us he couldn't find Sir Harold. Then Gwen said Sir Harold had been talking to someone about the antique pistols earlier, so he might be in here, showing them off. Jack went over and looked in and said no one was there.'

'Slow down. Jack went over to the door between here and the dining room, correct?'

'Yes.'

'Was it open or closed?'

Daisy shut her eyes and tried to picture the scene. 'Closed. It was closed. He – or maybe someone else, but I think it was Jack – actually said something like, 'Why would he have closed the door?'

'But Jack opened it.'

'Yes,' she said, puzzled.

'And?'

'He said, "It's dark", or something similar. "No light", that's it. "No light. No one's there." And Gwen said, "Maybe he went up to the study?" Jack was ready to stop looking, but Gwen felt their father ought to take his share of entertaining the guests, especially as her mother was quite exhausted. He gave in and went—'

'In the dark?'

'No, of course not. He switched on the light.' Opening her

eyes, she asked, 'Is that what you wanted? I distinctly remember the click of the switch and light coming on beyond the doorway. What's so significant about it?'

Alec sighed. 'Not much, as it was off. Had it been on, it might have explained how Gooch found the pistol. Jack would be unlikely to turn on the light, since he had a torch and knew his way about. Besides, he'd have been concerned about a stray gleam escaping through the curtains. He knew the house was supposed to be dark.'

'But Gooch could have turned the light on and then turned it off again.'

'Exactly. So we're no further forward. Supposing a premeditated murder by Gooch, who probably knew his wife intended a meeting with Sir Harold, he could have brought a weapon but decided, when he saw the Tyndalls' guns, to use one of them.'

'If they'd been locked up, or hadn't been loaded, he couldn't have done it. He'd have had to use his own and you'd know it was he.'

'If we're lucky, Tom may have found whatever he originally meant to use. Again, not proof but indicative.'

'If it wasn't premeditated,' Daisy mused, 'then perhaps he followed them in, noticed the guns in passing, followed them up, and overheard something which made him come down again and get a gun.'

'Which applies equally to Jack. We've been wondering whether Mrs Gooch could have told him before the fireworks that she was his mother, but there's no indication that he was under any degree of strain at that point.'

'So why, in that case, would he have followed them?'

'Good question,' Alec admitted.

'If he saw them go in together, what would he have thought?'

'I have absolutely no idea.'

'Probably that she had asked for the loan of a woolly scarf or hat or something like that. They had stacks available. Maybe she realized when she stepped outside that her own hat wasn't going to keep her ears warm. Maybe—'

'Daisy, now you're entering the realm of pure speculation. In any case, Jack denies absolutely having seen them. But your point is valid. Offhand, I can't think of any reason why Jack should follow them.'

'And he had duties to attend to outside. Whereas it wouldn't be at all surprising if Gooch, who was thoroughly uncomfortable with the whole situation, went after them.'

'True enough. I'll bear it in mind. What were you and Jack discussing when I so rudely interrupted?'

'When you so rudely interrupted, he was telling me he expected you to arrest him any minute, though he hadn't done it. He'd been expounding on his feelings about Mrs Gooch's letter.'

'To *you*? Great Scott, Daisy—'

'Don't say it! I swear I didn't invite his confidences. I think he needed to put it in words, and he said it was easier to talk to me than to his family.'

'Would you object to passing on what he told you?'

'Not at all. It tends to do away with his motive for murder, so I don't suppose you'll believe it, but you might as well hear it.' She explained how Jack had come to terms with the possibility of his illegitimacy. 'Though I can't believe he won't be pleased if it turns out to be untrue,' she added.

'That would be unnatural,' Alec agreed. 'I hope Ernie has found proof one way or the other.'

A few minutes later, Tom Tring came in. He carried a black calf-covered case, about fifteen inches by a foot, and four inches deep, with a monogram on the lid.

'Her jewellery,' Daisy guessed.

'That's right, Mrs Fletcher.' Tom set it on the table and fumbled with the tiny key. 'I'm no expert, Chief, but if half of this is what it looks like, the Gooches had no need to be resorting to blackmail.' He lifted the lid to reveal little cushions of black velvet.

Daisy lifted the cushions and gasped at the gleam and glitter within. 'Heavens above!' She folded out the two side pieces. 'I'm no expert, either, alas, but it looks good to me. Look at the lustre of those pearls. They must be real, and worth a fortune on their own.'

'I wouldn't care to bet against them,' said Alec. 'Was the case in a safe place, Tom?'

'Down in the inn's cellar, in a stout cupboard the landlord keeps his spirits locked up in, on account of a tramp breaking in a few years back and smashing what he didn't drink. I gave him a receipt.'

'Fair enough. It'll all have to be checked against the list, but I'm prepared to believe it's the real thing, honestly come by.'

'"The list"?' Daisy queried.

'Stolen property, Mrs Fletcher. By the stamp in the passport, they haven't been in the country long enough to have set up a theft this big, but they could've bought the lot off a fence for a fraction of the actual value.'

'It's funny, she didn't strike me as the kind of woman to enjoy wearing a lot of jewellery. I didn't see her at the party, but at the Ravens she just had a brooch, besides her wedding ring. It's not here.'

'Gold and opal? She was wearing it,' said Alec.

'It must have been a favourite. A souvenir from the gold fields perhaps. I bet Mr Gooch just liked to buy her good stuff. He must have loved her a lot.'

'The more reason to be jealous,' Tom pointed out, 'if he reckoned she was taking up again with her old lover. By the by, Chief, PC Blount came by the Ravens to report. He'd talked to some of the local people and two or three remembered Lady Tyndall going abroad for her health and coming back with the baby boy.'

'Yes, she's confirmed herself that Jack was born abroad. I must bring you up-to-date on what little she told me. Daisy . . .' He stopped on the point of dismissing her as Piper came in with a sheaf of papers. 'What have you got there, Ernie?'

'Blimey, Chief, the old doctor wrote everything down and never threw anything out. I'm surprised the attic floor hasn't collapsed. I found the Tyndalls' records in the end, and I brought her ladyship's.' He laid the papers in front of Alec with the triumphant air of a dog presenting a ball to its master. 'Seems like after Miss Gwendolyn was born, Dr Gunnicott was pretty sure Lady Tyndall couldn't have any more children, and if she could, she shouldn't.'

'"Pretty sure"! That's a fat lot of use,' grumbled Tom.

'He did say it'd prob'ly kill her, Sarge. Sorry, Mrs Fletcher, I didn't ought to be talking about it in front of you.'

'That's all right, Mr Piper. You wouldn't believe the horror stories women who've had children think suitable for the ears of one about to have a go for the first time. It does look as if Jack isn't her son, doesn't it?'

'Medicine is not an exact science,' said Alec.

'There's a bit more, Chief. I found all the records of the three daughters' births. Dr Gunnicott attended the lot, along with a midwife, and her ladyship had a hard time of it every time. But there's nothing for the son, though Gunnicott was still the family's doctor. Not even a note that she was in the family way again, no referral to a Harley Street specialist, like you might expect, considering.'

'Any mention of advising her to go abroad for her health?'

'That,' said Ernie portentously, 'was Sir Harold's idea. The doc wrote down that he advised against it 'cause the stress of the journey was likely to do more harm than a rest cure in the most sal-salyew—'

'Salubrious, laddie.' Tom's vast vocabulary, as extensive as his girth but rarely displayed, always came as a bit of a surprise.

Ernie was catching up but had some way to go, though he had the advantage of being able to write down practically anything in shorthand, whether he understood it or not. 'Cor, ta, Sarge. How d'you guess?'

'Guess! It'll be a sorry day when I don't know what's in your mind before you do, my boy.'

'The most salubrious climate,' Alec said, 'or something of the sort. Sir Harold went against the doctor's advice, then. That lends a good deal of credibility to Mrs Gooch's story.'

'If Lady Tyndall hadn't survived the journey,' Daisy said indignantly, 'no doubt he would have come home with the baby and told everyone she died in childbirth.'

'Quite likely. He seems to have had no scruples where securing the succession was concerned. We'll never know how serious he was about changing his will. You knew him, Daisy—'

'Slightly.'

'Is it possible he spoke in a temper and would have changed his mind by the morning?'

'Darling, I didn't know him anywhere near well enough to predict. I expect he said things when he was in a passion that he wouldn't have said in calmer moments, but whether he had the strength of mind to recant when he came to his senses, I haven't the foggiest. The family are the ones to ask ... No, of course they'll say yes, and you won't be able to believe them. The servants? Neighbours? The lawyer?'

'Lewin said Sir Harold had never before threatened to change his will, remember. He made an appointment for today, and the lawyer was certainly under the impression that he intended to do it.'

'And Babs said she was sure he wouldn't. We're going round in circles.'

'My fault,' Alec acknowledged. 'I shouldn't start speculating about things we'll never know.'

'It must be contagious,' said Daisy.

Unfortunately, Alec was reminded that she shouldn't be there, which he was apt to forget in the heat of discussion. At least he remembered that she hadn't butted in uninvited, that he had requested her help. As she left, he was telling Tom and Piper what she had said about the light in the billiard room.

In the passage, she met a maid.

'Oh, madam! Nurse sent me to fetch the 'tective gentleman. Mr Gooch is come to his senses an' he can say a few words, but he's in dreadful pain an' she's going to give him a 'jection the doctor left to make him sleep, so please to come quick.'

'Chief Inspector Fletcher is in the billiard room.' If she

hurried, she could get there before him. She'd just say she was enquiring after Gooch. No, better not. Alec was sure to guess the maid had told her the news.

She considered going to see Lady Tyndall. But meeting her was going to be a bit awkward, given the near certainty that she had lied about Jack's birth. Dinnertime, with others present, would be more comfortable.

A glance into the drawing room showed only Miller and Gwen, talking quietly by the fire. They didn't notice her. She went up to her room and started to work on her article, but she couldn't concentrate. Inevitably, her mind turned to the Tyndalls' affairs. The sins of the fathers are visited upon the children, she reflected. As a threat from God, she had always thought it most unfair, but there was no denying it did seem to happen all too often.

Alec entered the sickroom with misgivings. An interview with a sick or injured man was always difficult. Besides his own natural reluctance to disturb the patient, perhaps to set back his recovery, he was sure to be cut short by the intervention of a nurse or doctor.

Following Alec, Ernie Piper gently closed the door and whipped out his notebook and one of his perpetual supply of well-sharpened pencils.

The nurse stood at the foot of the bed, watchful. Alec sat down at the bedside, leaned forward. Gooch stared at him with a blurry, out-of-focus gaze.

'You're the copper.' His voice was soft, slow and slurred. 'It's true, ain't it? Ellie's dead?'

'I'm afraid so, sir.'

'I keep hoping it's a nightmare, hoping I'll wake up. I told her we shouldn't come. I told her it was asking for trouble. She wanted to see her boy, just to see him. Ought to've put me foot down, but I never could say no to Ellie.' Tears oozed from under his lids and trickled down, dampening the bandages. 'Then we met him, a nice lad, friendly as you please, and nothing would do for her but to tell him she was his mum.'

'You knew that before you came here?'

'She told me before we got married. Fair dinkum she was, my Ellie. But it was me said she ought to talk to his old man first, just to warn him what she was going to do. If I hadn't ...' His voice faded, and the nurse made a motion towards Alec, but then Gooch started again, fainter, but determined to tell the story. 'It was all his doing, the bastard. Made his lady take the boy for her own. Ellie wouldn't give him up – the baby – till she heard her ladyship's own promise to be a good mother to him. Which she was, by all accounts. *Him*, though. Crook, he was, too right, and he killed my Ellie!'

'We think not, sir, and—'

'He killed her!' In his fury, Gooch raised his bandaged head, then sank back with a moan. Eyes closed, he mumbled, 'Let me go home to my boys ...'

'That's enough now, Chief Inspector,' said the nurse adamantly, picking up a hypodermic needle and a vial of colourless liquid.

Alec and Piper left.

'Seems to me, Chief, he wasn't in any state to make stuff up.'

'You're right. I think he honestly believes Sir Harold shot

his wife. That still leaves the possibility of Gooch himself having shot Sir Harold in revenge – if it is a possibility.' Alec sighed. 'We'd better go over our notes on the scene in the study and make sure that theory won't wash. If we still can't make it work, Jack Tyndall looks like our man.'

CHAPTER 23

If Edge Manor had worn an air of gloom on Thursday, on Friday the atmosphere was thick with doom. No matter what Daisy said about 'helping the police with their enquiries', she was unable to convince the Tyndalls that Jack had not been arrested.

Immediately after breakfast, the detectives from Scotland Yard had taken him off to the village police station. Martin Miller, having adjured him not to say anything without a lawyer present, had then taken it upon himself to ring up Mr Lewin to request the name of a local solicitor who handled criminal matters.

Lady Tyndall was deathly pale but would not go to bed, even at the behest of Dr Prentice, who came to see Gooch (and pronounced him out of danger). Babs muttered about a thaw and rain coming and jobs that needed doing. She went off to the farm but came back half an hour later to mope about in the hall with the rest. Adelaide turned up, without her sons, to complain that the whole family was bound to be ostracized. Babs and Gwen turned on her, and she flounced away again in a miff.

Daisy found the situation extremely uncomfortable. She decided to leave after lunch by train, without waiting for Alec. But Gwen, when asked for a lift to the station, begged her to stay.

By mid-morning, Daisy was in desperate need of a breath of fresh air. The cloud banks of last night's sunset had solidified to a thick grey pall, but no rain yet fell. She fetched her coat and slipped out. No one appeared to notice her going.

The wind that brought the clouds had subsided to a breeze, warm in comparison to the past few days' frosts. She stood for a few minutes on the terrace, gazing down at the meadow and the village. The last of the autumn leaves had been torn from the skeletal trees, revealing the roofs of houses and shops.

Daisy didn't know which was the police house, but she picked out the inn. There in the cosy tap-room of the Three Ravens, the machinery of tragedy, created more than twenty years ago, had been set in motion. The meadow where children had danced around the bonfire was empty but for a bull, pastured there to keep unwanted visitors at bay. The only sign of the celebration was a black circle in the middle. The fireworks apparatus was gone from the lowest terrace, the chattering crowds from the top terrace. Would the Tyndalls ever again celebrate the Gunpowder Plot with their friends and neighbours?

In a melancholy mood, Daisy walked along the terrace and into the shrubbery, murkier than ever beneath the overcast sky.

'Daisy!'

She swung round. Lady Tyndall, enveloped in her Loden cloak, came towards her with snort, quick steps. The cloak was done up to the chin and her hands were buried in the pockets, but she had forgotten her hat. She looked cold, with an inner chill nothing could ever warm.

'Daisy, I'm sorry, I expect you wanted to get away from ... from us all.' She paused, but Daisy was far too well brought up to agree. 'I have to talk to you.'

'Right-oh.' Daisy gave her an expectant look but walked on slowly.

Lady Tyndall kept pace. 'You must tell your husband that Jack didn't shoot his father and that woman!'

'I'm afraid Alec can't accept my unsupported assertion any more than anyone else's,' Daisy said with all the patience she could muster. 'He has to have evidence.'

'But he had no reason to! He didn't know she was— she claimed to be his mother. He wasn't there, so he didn't hear Harold say he didn't care what she told his 'damned underbred, misbegotten son.' And even if he had ...' Her voice trailed away as she met Daisy's eyes.

And Daisy knew who had shot Sir Harold and Lady Gooch, and she saw Lady Tyndall realize that she knew.

'"He wasn't there." Outside the study, you mean?'

'Yes.'

'You were.'

'Yes. I saw them go off together. I followed. Harold didn't close the study door properly, and I heard every word. They were conspiring to drive my boy away from me!' The words came out as a cry of anguish. 'I went down and took a gun from the cabinet. Harold insisted I learn to shoot, during the war. I hoped ... but I can't let Jack be blamed. I've written—'

An explosion made both their heads turn. It came from the direction of the potting shed and was followed by shrill screams.

'Reggie and Adrian!' Lady Tyndall started running through the bushes towards the shed.

Daisy was not supposed to run, but she followed at a fast walk. Approaching the wooden building, she heard more explosions, and a rocket smashed through the small cob-webbed window, scattering shards of glass and glowing balls of silver, blue and green fire. Behind the broken panes, flames flickered.

Lady Tyndall flung open the door and plunged into the shed.

She emerged, coughing, with a limp grandson in her arms, just as Daisy arrived. 'Get him away from here!'

As Daisy took the child from her, she rushed into the shed again. Staggering under the boy's weight, Daisy carried him a few paces away and laid him down. His hair was frizzled on one side and his face, hands and clothes were smudged with soot, but he was breathing, thank heaven. After a moment, his body convulsed with a racking series of coughs, the sound vying with the continuing explosions and the crackle of the fire.

Daisy hurried back towards the shed. Now flames shot from the window and the collapsing roof. A final flurry of bangs announced the demise of the last rocket.

Through thick smoke, Lady Tyndall tottered out with the second boy. Her face was black, her eyes red and staring. She sank to her knees, her burden slipping to the ground. It was the elder brother; too heavy for Daisy to lift. She grabbed him under the arms and dragged him over to the other boy, then turned to help Lady Tyndall.

The elderly woman had somehow risen to her feet. She seemed to be struggling to take an object from her pocket. As

Daisy started forward, she saw Lady Tyndall whirl around and dart back into the burning building.

The shed was engulfed in a roaring inferno, clouds of smoke billowing into the sky. And then came one final *crack*.

Her legs suddenly weak, Daisy sat down on the ground, watching aghast.

'Mrs Fletcher!' Constable Blount came pounding towards her, the gardener, Biddle, close at his heels. 'What's happened?'

Only then did Daisy realize that all along she had been shouting, screaming for help. She pointed at the boys. 'Stolen rockets,' she gasped hoarsely, and surrendered to tears.

CHAPTER 24

'I told them she was confused by the flames and smoke,' Daisy said sombrely. 'They were too busy getting Reggie breathing to ask questions. There wasn't the slightest chance of saving her, even if she hadn't shot herself.'

'You're quite certain of that?' said Alec. 'That she shot herself, I mean.'

'Oh yes. I saw her take the gun from her pocket. You'll find it when the embers cool.'

They were sitting with Tom, Piper, Sir Nigel Wookleigh and an unusually silent Dryden-Jones in the billiard room. Piper had his notebook and pencils at the ready, but at Daisy's insistence, he was not taking notes.

They all looked at the gun cabinet. Two Webley & Scott automatics were missing.

'She went back in deliberately?'

'Yes. She knew exactly what she was doing. I'm sure she brought the pistol because she intended to commit suicide. The fire gave her a chance both to heroically save the children and to make her death appear an accident.'

'And you say you found a confession in her bedroom?' Sir Nigel put in. 'No, no, I don't want to read it.'

'You realize, sir, that in a case like this, we can't accept a confession, or even suicide, as proof of guilt. However, Lady Tyndall mentioned details only the murderer could have known. Besides, our interview with Mr Tyndall was leading us in the same direction. I did, in fact, send PC Blount up to the house to request that her ladyship come down to the police station.'

'Don't say the boy implicated his mother!' the Lord Lieutenant burst out.

'Great Scott no, sir! Far from it. I'm afraid I can't let you see the report, but—'

'Why not, dash it?' Dryden-Jones muttered, but in a subdued tone. 'My county, after all.'

'I'll have to send it to your chief constable. If he chooses to show it to you . . .'

'No, no. But what about my coroner? King's Coroner, don't you know, and I'm His Majesty's representative in the county. The inquest is already scheduled for tomorrow.'

'Daisy?' said Alec, and sat back with his arms crossed.

She shot him an indignant look. She had hoped he would explain her proposal and persuade the Chief Constable and Lord Lieutenant to go along with it. But it was unorthodox, and he was an officer of the law, and no doubt the less he had to do with it, the better.

'The . . . the person responsible for the tragedy is dead.' She simply could not bring herself to call Lady Tyndall a murderess. 'The Tyndalls are in for a horrible time, whatever happens next.'

'Murder is frowned upon in the best families,' Dryden-Jones commented, apparently without facetious intent.

'So is suicide,' Daisy pointed out. 'But rescuing one's

grandchildren from a burning building and dying in the process ... Well, I simply can't see why the world has to know she killed herself after shooting the others. She really was extraordinarily brave. A gun is a much quicker way to die than fire. I was terrified. And quite apart from having the nerve, I don't know how she had the strength to do it.'

'It's not uncommon,' said Alec, 'for people in similar situations to tap reserves they can't normally draw on.'

'So, if people think Sir Harold shot Mrs Gooch and then himself, her heroism may counteract the scandal to some extent.'

Dryden-Jones nodded. 'See what you mean, Mrs Fletcher.'

'It's a point,' Sir Nigel agreed, then asked gruffly, 'Does young Tyndall intend to make a clean breast of the matter of his birth? To the Heralds' College, that is.'

'Yes, he has no interest in trying to keep a title that isn't legitimately his, though Mr Gooch wouldn't dream of making public his wife's youthful peccadillo. Jack will try to keep her name out of it.'

'There will be scandal there, too, all the same. Well, what do you think, Dryden-Jones? It's a shocking thing to mislead an official of the Crown, but the way Mrs Fletcher would have us put the case would somewhat mitigate the Tyndalls' situation without going too far astray.'

'Yes, yes, that's all very well, and I'm sure we all want to avoid as much scandal as possible. The newspapers seem to get worse every year. But you really can't expect me to go and pitch a tale to the Coroner!'

'Your county, my dear fellow,' said Sir Nigel maliciously.

The Lord Lieutenant's face purpled, and Alec hastily intervened.

'There's no question of that, sir. In homicide cases where

the Met has been called in by a county force and completes the investigation before the inquest, it is quite in order for us to leave the local force to deal with the Coroner. I shall report to Mr Herriott—'

'Herriott? Herriott? The Gloucestershire CC? Could have sworn the man's name was Hazlitt.'

'To the Chief Constable,' Alec amended patiently, 'that the murder weapon was found close to Sir Harold's right hand, as indeed it was. He's unlikely to demand a detailed report, as he's already requested my help with another case. He won't want me and my men wasting time writing up a case that's already solved. He or one of his chaps will relay the information to the Coroner. I'd be very surprised if the jury didn't bring a verdict of murder-suicide by the late baronet.'

'Bit hard on the poor chap,' Dryden-Jones protested.

Sir Nigel disagreed. 'Since the whole disaster was brought about by his actions, I shan't weep for him.'

'As for Lady Tyndall's death,' Alec continued, 'that will be a separate inquest. In view of my wife's . . . er . . . condition, I trust the Coroner will be satisfied with her written testimony.'

'Which will state, with perfect truth, that I witnessed Lady Tyndall rescue her grandsons from a burning building but unfortunately she didn't survive her injuries. PC Blount and the gardener won't contradict that.'

'By Jove, Mrs Fletcher, you've got it all worked out!' said Sir Nigel with ironic admiration. 'Tell me, Chief Inspector: I suppose there are a few cases when you have to do without your wife's assistance. How on earth do you manage?'

Piper snickered. Tom's moustache twitched and his eyes twinkled.

Alec grinned. 'Less *interestingly*, sir,' he said.

* * *

'Gwen, you will keep in touch, won't you?' said Daisy as they drove through dank drizzle to the station.

'If you're sure you want to associate with such a disreputable family.' Gwen's smile was feeble. Her nose and eyes were red. Her mother, however guilty, was truly mourned, as her father was not.

'Don't be an ass. I want to hear how things work out for all of you, even your nephews. Horrors that they are, I'm glad they weren't seriously hurt.'

'Yes, superficial burns and smoke inhalation. They deserve every pang. And Dr Prentice is pretty sure Mr Gooch will recover fully. We have much to be thankful for. Not least that you were there. Daisy, I don't know how we'd have coped without you. And Alec, too, instead of some beastly flat-footed bobby with no manners and no sensitivity.'

'Speaking of sensitivity, are you quite sure you're all willing for my article to be published?'

'Oh yes, Jack and Babs don't mind. You did say you won't put in anything about . . . what's been happening.'

'Of course not. It's not that sort of magazine. My editor would have forty fits. But it is possible you'll get the odd American tourist turning up to see the show.'

'That's a whole year away. We'll worry about it then. We haven't even begun to think about whether we'll continue to put on a Bonfire Night celebration.'

'It would be a pity to stop, after four hundred years.'

'At present,' said Gwen wryly, 'my respect for the demands of tradition is not high.'

* * *

'Great Scott, another dozen Christmas cards!' said Alec, regarding the pile of envelopes beside Daisy's plate as he sat down to his eggs and bacon.

'Between the two of us, we know a lot of people. Better cards than letters which have to be answered. Oh dear, here's one from Sir Nigel Wookleigh. I didn't send him one.'

'Still time. Are you really feeling up to meeting the school train at Liverpool Street, love?'

'Gosh, yes. I wouldn't fail Belinda for anything. It'll be lovely to have her at home over Christmas. I've really missed her.'

'Yes, sometimes I wish she hadn't chosen to go to boarding school. You're to take a taxi both ways, no nonsense about hopping on a bus. Do you have enough money?'

'I think so,' Daisy said absently, opening another envelope. 'Oh, darling, here's a letter from Gwen. Gwen *Miller*! She's married him.'

'The aeronautical engineer?'

'Yes. Let's see. She's written pages.' Skimming through the letter, she relayed the salient bits to Alec as he ate. 'A quiet registry office wedding. Jack's joined Miller's firm and they're all sharing a house in Coventry, but they usually go to Edge Manor at the weekends and will spend Christmas there. Lucky it's so near. Babs is running the place and ... Poor Babs, Addie and her boys have moved in!'

'Miss Tyndall will cope, I feel sure.'

'Reggie and Adrian will be going away to a proper prep school in January, one with a reputation for firm discipline. And Mr Gooch has sailed for home, in a wheelchair, but he's expected to be on his feet by the time he gets to Perth.' She sighed. 'Poor Mr Gooch, he really got the worst of it, and through no fault of his own.'

'That's the way it generally is with murder. The innocent suffer most. If people thought about that first, maybe there would be fewer murders committed.'

'And you'd be out of a job, darling.'

'Or work shorter hours.' He finished his coffee, stood up, pushed in his chair, and came round the table to kiss her. 'Give Bel my love, and I promise to do my very best to get home on time.'

'That'll be the day,' said Daisy.